POLITICS

Adam Thirlwell was born in 1978. His first novel, *Politics*, was translated into thirty languages. In 2003, he was chosen as one of Granta's Best British Novelists under forty. *Miss Herbert*, a book about novels, was published in 2007 and won a Somerset Maugham Award. He lives in London.

ADAM THIRLWELL

Politics

VINTAGE BOOKS
London

Published by Vintage 2006

4 6 8 10 9 7 5

An extract from this novel has previously appeared in *Areté*

First published in Great Britain in 2003 by
Jonathan Cape

Vintage
Random House, 20 Vauxhall Bridge Road,
London SW1V 2SA

www.vintage-books.co.uk

Addresses for companies within The Random House Group Limited
can be found at: www.randomhouse.co.uk/offices.htm

The Random House Group Limited Reg. No. 954009

A CIP catalogue record for this book
is available from the British Library

ISBN 9780099459026

The Random House Group Limited supports The Forest
Stewardship Council (FSC), the leading international forest
certification organisation. All our titles that are printed on
Greenpeace approved FSC certified paper carry the FSC logo.
Our paper procurement policy can be found at:
www.rbooks.co.uk/environment

Mixed Sources
Product group from well-managed
forests and other controlled sources
www.fsc.org Cert no. TT-COC-2139
© 1996 Forest Stewardship Council
FSC

Printed and bound in Great Britain by
CPI Bookmarque, Croydon, CR0 4TD

To
June Goldman

1921–1998

I

1 The prologue
2 The principals

II

3 They fall in love
4 Romance
5 Intrigue
6 They fall in love
7 They fall out of love
8 Romance
9 Intrigue
10 They fall out of love

III

11 The finale

I

I

The prologue

I

AS MOSHE TRIED, gently, to tighten the pink fluffy handcuffs surrounding his girlfriend's wrists, he noticed a tiny frown.

I think you are going to like Moshe. His girlfriend's name was Nana. I think you will like her too.

'Pussy!' he said. 'What's wrong?'

He was crouching by her neck. She was lying on her stomach. Her arms were stretched, like a diver, above her head.

This is what was wrong. Nana's hands were too slender for the handcuffs. That was why she was frowning. There was a logistical problem. And Nana was a girl who cared about logistics. She took her sex seriously. But it was difficult to take sex seriously when, if she wriggled, her hands nearly slipped out. It was not, she explained, ideal. Wriggling was the charm of it.

As Nana glanced up, she saw Moshe's dejected face. 'Kitten!' she said. 'What's wrong?'

3

Unfussed, Nana explained that she would just have to act it out. She would have to stay still and mockstruggle. She was sweet to him. It was true, she said wistfully, talking into the duvet, that there had been another plan. She knew she was meant to be trapped, defenceless, while Moshe the tyrant gleefully mimed the loss of both sets of keys to the handcuffs, the real ones and the spares. But the fun was improvisation.

I like this couple. They are a do-it-yourself couple, and I like that.

Nana had imagined it. She had sketched out a synopsis. Nana would be tied up and then sodomised, ruthlessly. She wanted her powerful man to prove his potency. And – because they were a couple who tried to be mutual – Moshe had responded by suggesting a little trip to *Sh!*, Hoxton's sex boutique with a door policy.

A door policy? Yes yes. Men without women were banned.

Nervously, in *Sh!*, Moshe and Nana browsed for four minutes. *Sh!* smelled of incense. Moshe decided they should leave. Then he reconsidered. If they left, thought Moshe, then it might look like they were not comfortable with sex toys. It would look like they were afraid of sex.

I am not sure why Moshe was so worried by this. It was true. Moshe was afraid. He was afraid of sex toys. He was particularly afraid of a twelve-inch dildo, with an extra veined prong for the anus. But he did not want to look scared. He wanted to look indifferent.

They bought a petite and smooth leopardskin-print dildo, for him or her, that was now peeping from beneath the bed in its cardboard packet. They bought some rope. Gesturing towards bondage, they bought a black leather bra for Nana. It was three sizes too small. It was like a leather training bra. It flattened her breasts. Doing her best at the role of the submissive, Nana had the breasts of a thirteen-year-old. As for Moshe, his domain was control. So Moshe was the purchaser and practitioner of pink fluffy handcuffs – or at least he would have been if the catches, the teeth, the locks, whatever, were not too loose for Nana's delicate frame.

They were too loose. She had to act it out.

Abandoning the handcuffs, Moshe scooped up the length of thin pink bondage rope. He wrapped it in a figure of eight round her quasi-handcuffed hands, then knotted the rope on to the bed frame. He arranged her wrists in a floppy fluorescent cross.

In a painful way Nana was comfortable. Which was perfect, she thought. It was just the right feeling. She wanted to make pain a pleasure.

Then Moshe spread her buttocks apart.

Nana's first reaction was embarrassment. This was quickly followed, however, by glee. Moshe was snuffling in her crack. It had an allure. Doggedly Moshe licked, he lapped at Nana's arsehole. He dabbed his tongue into the darker puckered pock.

Maybe I should be more specific here. Nana was a blonde. She was an all-over blonde. I do not want 'darker' to imply dark. No, Nana had a very pale arsehole. It was an albino arsehole.

Moshe began to enjoy himself, elongating her pink arsehole as he stretched her buttocks with his hands. It was – Nana thought, self-conscious, being used – a new sensation. This, she thought, was Rimming. It was not quite a turn-on but rimming was interesting. It gave her a new shiver.

5

And Nana said, 'Talk to me.' More precisely, in homage to pornography, she drawled, 'Tor tme.'

2

There are many attitudes to talk during sex. There are many varieties of talk during sex. Some individuals like to shout out commands. They will say, 'Suck my cock.' Commands can get quite paradoxical. For instance, sometimes a boy will say, 'Ask if you can suck me' – which is a command for a request. Or a girl or a boy will say, 'Tell me to suck your cock' – which is a command for a command. This almost turns the command into a request. Other people want their partner to do the talking. They want to hear guttural and lavish obscenities. This is especially exciting when a person suspects that his or her partner is repressed. On the other hand, there are people for whom talk is just reassuring. In fact, sometimes they do not even need talk to get the re-assurance they want. Noise is quite enough. For these people, noise during sex is a version of talk. The other extreme, I suppose, involves some degree of reality shift or role play. A lot of people like to be someone else during sex. A lot of people like to imagine that someone else is someone else during sex.

And Nana, today, was a fantasist. She wanted a narra-tive. She wanted a role play.

Normally, however, Nana disdained all talk during sex. Even a whisper annoyed her. But just now, in a flat in the scuzzier part of Finsbury, slightly distracted by the leather gear of the woman on the dildo packet, and the black wire from the Habitat bedside lamp, Nana was pro talking. A fantasy, she thought, would be a treat for Moshe. It would make the evening flow.

She was being solicitous. She was thinking about being calm. But Nana's request did not make Moshe calmer. If anything, it made him more nervous. Moshe was *a bundle of nerves.*

Why is it never enough simply being dirty? That was what Moshe was thinking. But he did not get downcast, not yet. He mused. He planned a plot. He thought to himself, and he was right, that Nana wanted a performance. She wanted a detailed fantasy. She wanted imagination.

Moshe imagined an anti-Semitic fantasy. I know that this might come as a surprise, but that was the fantasy Moshe came up with.

In between his laps and licks Moshe taunted his suburban girl, the only daughter of a rich goy man, with tales concerning the riches of Moshe's Jewish ancestry. This was the triumph of the underdog. Or rather, Nana might have thought he was the underdog but Moshe had power and breeding. Moshe's father was on board the SS *Shalom* on its maiden voyage in 1964. The *Shalom* was the pride of Israel – a model of razzmatazz, down to the padded modernism of each cabin's Eames leather chair. It even had its own private synagogue.

Her lover had powerful provenance. Moshe's great-grandfather, for instance, was an East End hero. He was a prizefighter. He had taken the name of Yussel the Muscle. While Nana was just Papa's princess. Unlike Moshe, she was cosseted, unmetropolitan. She lived in the suburbs. She lived, said Moshe with disgust, in Edgware.

And it was true. This was not a fantasy. She was

suburban. Nana had grown up in Edgware with her father. Edgware is in the suburbs of North London.

At this point in his narrative, Moshe decided that a disciplinary gesture was appropriate. He had run out of material. So he spanked her, lightly. Nana moaned and twisted her neck up, then settled it down. He spanked her again, harder, except because Moshe was excitable his hand sort of slipped and fell and he spanked her dappily, on the fleshy meeting place of buttock and upper thigh.

His clumsiness annoyed him. He suddenly felt vulnerable, kneeling there between Nana's legs, his right arm aloft. He did not feel tyrannic. He did not feel Sultanic. He only felt like Moshe.

In the flat upstairs, a toddler fell over. It crashed and cried. This made Moshe even more self-conscious.

Poor Moshe. He was a nervous sadist, a shy sodomite. He had not had the practice. That was his worry. Another worry was how much practice Nana had ever had. The two worries were inextricable.

Out of character, Moshe hit Nana. He hit her very hard. Nana made an uninterpretable noise.

3

Then, on his knees, Moshe readied himself. He dabbed two fingers into her cunt while his thumb pushed at her arsehole. His fingers formed the configuration more commonly used to grip a bowling ball. Then he wetted his penis and pushed it where he hoped her arsehole was, angling his penis down with his right hand.

Nana asked him to stop. She said it hurt too much.

That was Moshe's cue to persevere.

Every shiksa likes being fucked by a Jewboy, replied Moshe, hamming it up.

What noble perseverance! A little unsure, Moshe was still continuing with his fantasy. And I think this perseverance is admirable, I really do. Some people might be sneering. Some people might be commenting that, when it comes to sex, only skill is important – but I think that's wrong. Persevering is also noble. Moshe was being noble.

Balancing on his left hand, the other girlishly guiding the head of his penis while a thin first finger located her arsehole, he tried to push it in. But this arrangement presented a conundrum. His left arm, unable, wobbling, wasn't strong enough. And it was, after all, thought Moshe, quite difficult – fucking the arse of a motionless girl. He toyed with saying, 'Sex doll! Can you lift yourself up a little?' But Nana could not help. He knew that. He knew she could not raise her docile expectant arsehole. The thrill was not to be seen to be thrilled.

It made him pause. Nana, her face squashed, noted the pause. If she squinted she could read the Dunlopillo lettering on the mattress's label, faint beneath the sheet.

But there are moments of inspiration and this was one of them.

Moshe reached and stretched and grabbed at some hand cream – Ren Tahitian Vanilla Hand and Body Milk – by the bed. He flicked it open with his thumb and first finger and then, exhausted, just wiped it straight on to the head of his cock, the glans, the fraenum, his complete erection. Then he left the tube above Nana's blonde and feathered hair. It stayed there throughout.

The cream made his cock glowy stingy. He pushed at her

9

again and felt an odd warm tightness so he stopped there. *Waves of relief washed over Moshe.* He allowed himself a smug moment. And who would not? Let us not get hypocritical here. He was fucking his little girl's arse. He waited inside her, feeling himself drift slippy, slowly, further in.

This was *the highpoint* of Moshe's evening.

He moved his penis back a bit, back a bit, before embarking further, and it slipped out and down and past. And panicking, dismayed, ashamed, he tried to shove it quickly, back to its unnatural home, but only finished up in Nana's surprised vagina.

Optimistically, for a moment he fucked Nana anyway. He persuaded himself that sex from behind was almost the same as sodomy. He twisted. He dipped. He angled.

But no.

This was not anal sex. Moshe knew that. This was the opposite of anal sex. It was straight heterosexual vaginal intercourse.

He relaxed on top of Nana and mused on Israel.

Now, this should have been *the lowpoint* of Moshe's evening. But it was not. It got worse. He lay there, quiet, and started to think. As he thought, he became mildly hysterical. Yes, free to do anything he liked, Moshe became hysterical.

This, thought Moshe, must be the most nervous sex scene. It must be the most nervous scene in the history of sex. He wondered in a general way about the other couples, the worldwide satiated couples. In every other bedroom, girls and boys, in twos and threes and – who knows? – fours, were crying out in ecstasy. They were prancing, thought solid and motionless Moshe. They were ecstatic. He was sure of it.

4

I am going to expand a little on Moshe's problem. It is a universal problem. It is the universal insecurity that one is not universal.

In his book called *Love*, the famous French novelist Stendhal explains his theory of why we like reading. It is this. 'Just as a man has almost no physiological self-knowledge except by studying comparative anatomy, so vanity and various other causes of illusion prevent us from having a clear picture of our own passions except by studying the weaknesses of others. If this essay of mine happens to serve any useful purpose, it will be in training the mind to make this sort of comparison.'

Let me explain. Just as you don't know what your own stomach looks like, you don't know what your own feelings look like either. You don't know what your stomach looks like because of your skin. You don't know what your feelings look like because of vanity and other causes of illusion. To get over the problem of skin, we have anatomy textbooks. To get over the problem of vanity and other causes of illusion, we have novels.

Compare this to Moshe's magnified worry as he lay on Nana's back. He was worried that everyone else had better sex than he did. He was suffering from pique. Now, the cure for pique is to compare yourself honestly and calmly to other people. When you do this, then you realise that everyone, at some point, is equally clumsy. Only a select few succeed at anal sex, every time. You recover a sense of proportion.

Moshe needed a novel. (He needed this novel.) Moshe was suffering from the absence of the novel. This novel, for example, is one huge act of miniaturisation. Everything is the right size. If Moshe had read this novel, then I think he would have been happy.

It is a universal problem. Compare this to you. Perhaps, for instance, your first reaction to Moshe's little worry just now was to dismiss it. You thought that he seemed unrealistically weak. You simply could not imagine a boy who was neurotic about sex like Moshe. Maybe you even thought that the writing was also obscene. Well, that's what you might have thought at first. Your vanity and other causes of illusion might have made you think that. But actually, I do not think you are really upset. My idea is that you are like this too. Maybe, just maybe, you are not. But I reckon that, at some point in your life, something almost identical to this has happened to you.

Of course it has! This book is meant to be reassuring. This book is universal. It is a comparative study. The last thing I want is for this to be just me.

Because it is universal, there should be no local difficulties in this book. For instance, perhaps Moshe's name is difficult. It is a very Jewish name. That is because it was the one concession Moshe's father made to his Jewish family, after marrying a non-Jewish woman. Perhaps you do not know how this name should be pronounced. Possibly, you have not had a Jewish upbringing. Well, I will tell you. Moshe is pronounced 'Moisha'. That is how you pronounce it. You see? I don't want this to be private at all.

5

As for Nana, she was feeling a little uncomfortable. Her wrists had chafed on the metal handcuffs while she pretended to be trapped. Also, one of Moshe's ragged fingernails had scratched her.

She said to him, 'Le mgo.'

Moshe leaned forward, untwisted the loose pink rope, then rolled over on to his back and watched his penis sadden, shorten, stop. Nana stroked her wrists. As she stroked, she noticed a meek silence. So she twisted on to her back to check on Moshe. She was worried he was sad. She was worried he might be mournful. But the way not to be mournful is to talk, she reasoned, reasonably.

Oh Nana, if only things were so simple. If only, just for now, Moshe possessed the necessary calm. But he did not. Instead, Moshe was theatrical. He was theatrical at heart.

Nana's boyfriend was two emotions. Neither was useful. As outlined above, their common element was hysteria. Moshe was scared and ashamed. He felt ashamed because he had failed her. He had not been a believable fantasy. He was not realistic. And because he thought he had failed her, he also believed she was angry. She must be. And this scared him, because he thought that, due to her anger, she might be sarcastic, or frustrated. This made him particularly scared because if Nana was truly frustrated then he would feel even more ashamed.

On balance, then, he was more ashamed than scared.

But Nana, not sarcastic, not frustrated, was all solicitude. She was friendly and undismayed. 'Are you okay?' said Nana.

She is all solicitude! The girl is worried! worried Moshe.

His reaction, however, was simple. He improvised a persona of calm success. Everything, he decided, had gone well. Moshe was an assured seducer. First an astonishing sexual procedure had taken place and now, as they lay there, fulfilled, he decided to woo her all over again, telling her the secrets of his damaged unconscious. It was what people had sex for – the afterwards, the quiet intimacy, the talk.

This was a night to remember. Christ, yes.

Moshe did not answer Nana's question. He did not describe his mental and physical state. Well, not directly. He gave her a small lecture.

With his eyes averted, because that was a gesture of – no, not embarrassment – sincerity, Moshe said: 'Once I was with my parents in a small restron somewhere in Normandy. And from the window I saw this kind of mock-up of the Liberation, with a repro army marching through the streets.' But, and this was the thing, it could also have been the occupation. Maybe they were miming the occupation, said Moshe. Because somehow he could also see a chateau at the top of the village and blond men in dry-cleaned uniforms moving slowly, and a minuscule Moshe somehow or other mixed up in the whole affair.

And that was it. That was his contribution to the catastrophe – an anecdote of miniature Moshe, a secret fear, a novelty.

What was Moshe trying to say? I will tell you. He was trying to say he was sorry. He was asking Nana not to be angry. He was trying to make her pity him. He was saying that Moshe was scared of the Nazis.

But Nana was not angry. She was not a Nazi. She was just confused. She wondered if Moshe was embarrassed. She wondered what other explanations there could be for this set-up – Moshe the conversationalist in bed, telling her about his childhood fears, surrounded by sex aids.

6

Nana's arsehole was aching where Moshe's fingernail had scratched her. This made her wriggle. She tried to get comfortable. She wondered how far Moshe had got inside her arsehole before he. She wondered did this mean she was now infected.

He could see her looking at him – naked, on his back. He was exposed. Moshe worried that Nana was looking at his belly, and looked down and there was his penis. His penis looked silly and slick. It looked depressed. So he got up to find some clothes. It was only nine in the evening, but all he wanted was his pyjamas.

Moshe returned to his travesty of Jewishness. He said, 'Did you not like the Joosh thing? It was the best I could think of.'

Depressed, Moshe grinned.

She was looking at him, quiet. He was a comic visual diversion. 'What?' he said. And she grinned. She said, 'Cherub, you're only half Jewish.'

Moshe was standing in front of her with his body swaying slightly forward. He was resting his weight on his right leg, which was by now tartanly pyjama'd. The foot of his left leg was advanced a little. And his knee was gently bent. He was getting into his pyjamas.

Nana was wondering why she was happy, lying there as the street lights switched on, unequally.

'And you're not even circumcised,' she said.

'Let's not squabble,' he admonished her, as he hopped across the room in search of the left pyjama leg.

2

The principals

THIS HAS GONE far too far. I can see that.

Before this experiment with anal sex and bondage, Moshe and Nana met and fell in love. After *that* happened, but before the anal sex, they also tried the missionary position, ejaculation on Nana's face, oral sex, use of alternative personae, lesbianism, undinism, the threesome, and fisting. Not all of these were successful. In fact, few of these were successful.

In case this list worries you, perhaps I should explain. This book is not about sex. No. It is about goodness. This story is about being kind. In this book, my characters have sex, my characters do everything, for moral reasons.

After they fell in love but before they experimented with lesbianism and the threesome one of them fell for another girl.

By the end of this story one character will be dying from a brain tumour.

If only things were as simple as they looked. If only events occurred without a backstory.

2

So this was the beginning and the rest of it.

It was a play.

Her Papa had taken Nana to a one-off revival at the Donmar Warehouse. The play was Oscar Wilde's *Vera, or the Nihilists*. It was the opening production, explained Papa, in a tribute week of Oscar Wilde's complete works. This week had been crafted by the famous political playwright David Hare. It was designed to show that Oscar Wilde was our contemporary. He was twenty-first century. A homosexual man, Oscar understood that politics was everywhere.

Papa was on the board of the Donmar Warehouse, and so he had to see it. It was his job, he said. He had no choice. And he did not want to see it on his own. He wanted to see it with Nana. He said it was a treat. This was, he pleaded, a contemporary revival. David Hare had called the play *a classic*.

But it was not David Hare who persuaded Nana. No. It was Papa. She went because she loved him.

I should explain something here. Papa was a widower. Nana's mother had died when Nana was four. And Nana's mother is absent from this story. This is because she was also absent from the relationship of Nana and Papa. She was calmly absent. Nana simply saw her as Papa's best friend. Whenever Nana imagined her mother, she imagined her chatting to Papa. And Nana did not want to interrupt these conversations between her mother and Papa. She preferred the conversations to carry on without her.

That was why Nana and Papa were such a duo. It is why they went, as a couple, to *Vera, or the Nihilists*.

And that was the beginning, Nana used to think, later. That play was the beginning.

As the lights undimmed, privileged Papa took Nana behind the scenes. And there Moshe was, straddling a plastic chair, admitting that he was the, yes, the star of the show. But he was tired of it all. He was tired of all the schmoozing.

Moshe was an actor.

The first time Nana saw him was on stage – backlit, melodramatic. Except – she teased him later, when they were in love – she hadn't really seen him. Nana had almost dozed. She was bored by Oscar Wilde. Instead, she had looked round – at the lighting rig, the showy couple fingering each other on her left. She was annoyed by her bench-seat's straight back, the stifled coughs behind her.

So that was why when Moshe – the actor who had played Prince Paul Maraloffski – stood up afterwards, backstage, and grinned his Princely grin, she did not notice the allusion. All she saw was a patch of tartar on Moshe's front two upper teeth. One eye was oddly smaller than the other.

This might seem mean of her but it wasn't. Some people are beauties all the time and all people can be beauties sometimes but Moshe was something special. He was a cameo actor. This was partly because of his smallish five-foot-seven frame, and the gentle dip of his belly. It was mainly because of his comically mobile fleshy face and big brown unequal eyes. He was the sketchy one, the sardonic one, the oddball cool. Self-conscious of his uncared-for teeth, Moshe would faintly chew on the right-hand side of his lower lip. This made him somehow charming. It gave him a shy allure.

Moshe was not pretty, but he was charming. He had a playful grace.

3

It is often ordinary, even banal, when people meet their lover for the first time. Some people find this difficult. It is often too banal. This is especially difficult for people who believe in grandiose things like predestination and fate and twin souls.

It was, for instance, difficult for Nadezhda Mandelstam. Nadezhda was the wife of the Soviet poet Osip Mandelstam, who died in the Gulag. Nadezhda believed in grandiose things. She believed in predestination. This is how she described Osip. 'He never had any doubt of his predestination and accepted it just as simply as he did his subsequent fate.'

I am going to digress from this digression just for a moment.

What a lie! 'He never had any doubt of his predestination and accepted it just as simply as he did his subsequent fate.' I think this is immoral. Nadezhda is implying that Osip accepted that death in the Gulag was his fate. He was, she is saying, poetically happy to die in the Gulag. No, I do not understand this kind of posturing. It would be difficult,

I think, being Nadezhda's husband. It would be difficult to eat some pasta in peace. It would always be predestined pasta.

Anyway. In the first volume of her autobiography and memoir of her husband, *Hope Abandoned*, Nadezhda described how she met the great romantic poet Osip Mandelstam.

In the evenings, we gathered in the Junk Shop, a night-club for artists, writers, actors and musicians. It was in a cellar of the city's main hotel, which was being used to accommodate some officials of the second or third rank from Kharkov. M. had managed to get a place on the train that brought them, and so he was also put up, by mistake, in a very nice room in the same hotel. On the first evening he came down to the Junk Shop, and we at once took up with each other as though it were the most natural thing in the world. We always dated our life together from 1 May 1919, though we were forced to live apart for a year and a half after this.

If you redescribe this passage, you can get at the real story. It goes something like this. Osip turned up by accident. He wandered into his hotel bar and chatted to a few girls. He quite liked one of them. He didn't see this girl for a year or two and forgot all about her. When he bumped into her again, she didn't remember him. He had to remind her. They both indulged themselves and told each other it must have been fate that they had found each other again.

Now, none of my characters was this romantic. But they were, like everyone, a little romantic. So it seemed sad, they thought, that the first meeting was so ordinary. It seemed sad that they did not fall in love.

4

Papa smiled a winning smile. He questioned Moshe on the history of Prince Kropotkin. This might seem very learned. It might seem that Papa knew the historical background to Oscar Wilde's *Vera, or the Nihilists,* a play about Russian anarchism. But it was not learned. It only showed that Papa had read the programme notes.

Papa marvelled at the wonders he had discovered in Moshe's interpretation of the role of Prince Paul Maraloffski.

Moshe looked down, being modest, at Papa's twotone shoes, their textured curves of cloth and leather.

'Oh yeah,' said Moshe. 'It took ages for that scene to find.'

But was Moshe, truly, being modest? No, he was not. There was reddish eczema on the tips and backs of Moshe's fingers, which he concealed by clumping and arranging them. He made his hands invisible behind his back. And this limited his possible, prideful gestures. That was why Moshe was standing there, his head bowed forward a little, the hands tight behind his back – acknowledging his fundraiser's finesse.

Papa admired the gravitas, he admired the obvious savoir-faire in such a noble pose.

5

Moshe was a tired professional. He was tired of being back-stage. The dowdiness depressed him. And I can understand that. Fake finery is depressing. But there was another reason why Moshe felt mildly depressed. No member of the royal family was present.

The royal family?

Recently, one Saturday morning, Moshe had narrated Benjamin Britten's *The Young Person's Guide to the Orchestra*, at the Barbican Hall. This performance had been attended by the Queen Mother. And Moshe liked meeting Her Majesty. He liked meeting her a lot.

First, backstage, the performers lined themselves up in a horseshoe. Moshe, the novice, drifted to one tip of it. From the corridor, he could hear the Queen Mother's voice, chatting away. Well, he assumed it was the Queen Mother's voice. It was nasal. It was aristocratic. Then finally she arrived.

Moshe was nearest to the door. This was a catastrophe. It meant that Moshe was the first to be introduced to the Queen Mother. Untrained in regal etiquette, Moshe had planned on copying someone else. He had especially planned on looking out for the first violin. The first violin was wearing a dress shirt with a quilted pleated and ruffled front. Everyone else was wearing an ordinary M&S white shirt. The first violin, thought Moshe, would know how to address the Queen Mother.

But the first violin could not help Moshe now. Elizabeth, unstoppably, was tottering in, on a line below Moshe's nipples. She was about four foot two, he reckoned. This unnerved him even more. And Moshe just stood rigid. He did not bow.

Moshe shook her hand and said, 'Hi.'

The Queen Mother constructed a smile. Her lady-in-waiting, Lady Anne Screeche, stiffened.

As catastrophes go, it was a small one.

The thing about royalty, thought Moshe, amazed, is that they are royal. And he was right. The Queen Mother was the Queen Mother. She was the Queen Mother exactly.

Then the conversation began. At one end of the room the Queen Mother sat in a grand armchair, placed beside two lesser chairs. The Director of the Barbican chose two people for the two lesser chairs. Everyone else watched. They pretended not to watch, while eating caviar canapés, but they watched. At carefully selected intervals, orchestrated by the Director, one of the chairs would be vacated and refilled.

Moshe's conversational partner was the third clarinet. His name was Sanjiv and he lived in Harrow Weald. Moshe felt bored. Sanjiv asked if much had changed in the Queen Mother's hundred years of life. And she replied that ooh yes of course. She had thought she would never get used even to trams. Then she turned to Moshe and looked up into his big brown eyes with her small grey eyes and said, 'But one can get used to anything. Can't one?'

Is this flirting? Moshe thought, suddenly smitten, entranced by this melancholy woman of the world. He looked at her and wondered if he could find her attractive.

He could.

And what a girlfriend, thought Moshe. As the Queen Mother described her recent education in email, Moshe drifted off. He had a reverie.

He would be her toyboy. He would be the solace of her final years. He imagined the *Hello!* spread – a photographic record of the Queen Mother and her companion. There would be spreads not only in *Hello!* but also in *¡Hola!* Perhaps there would even be pieces in *Paris-Match*. Elizabeth and Moshe would travel the world together, in a unique love nest of a yacht. It would not be, he conceded, exactly sexual. Well, it could be. He would not mind. But he imagined that, realistically, it would simply be a *mutual infatuation*. And when it was revealed that her will had been altered in his favour, and unkind words had been said in the gutter press, those close to her would understand. Her lady-in-waiting, Lady Anne Screeche, would understand.

Moshe looked at Elizabeth Windsor, fondly. Indulgently, he observed the ragged points of her scuffed and skyblue shoes. *Time was running out*, he thought. He guessed at the enticements beneath her artfully draped chiffon. Her legs, he admitted, were odd. Her shins were thick with ulcers. They looked like plastic. She had the legs of an unusual Barbie doll. And her arms were cracked and bruised.

Moshe suddenly imagined the Queen Mother cooking heroin on a heavy silver spoon, while she tugged with her teeth on a silk tourniquet wrapped round her arm. Or perhaps Lady Anne Screeche did the tourniquet – perhaps Lady Anne did everything for her.

None of this seemed very likely.

And I think he was right. I do not think it is believable that the Queen Mother was a nymphomaniac drug addict. But Moshe was right to consider it. It is always important to reimagine the lives of the rich and famous. It is very good practice for kindness. It makes you more empathetic.

Oh, thought Moshe. Oh you sweetie.

25

And then, as if he wasn't delighted enough, the hand-written thank-you letter. Addressed to the Director of the Barbican, on six octavo sheets of Clarence House notepaper, embossed with a curly entwined ER topped with a crown, she wrote:

It always causes such delight and trepidation when I receive my invitation to the Barbican. Every concert is so perfect. But there is also trepidation and this is because it is always so perfect! Every year, I am so worried for the new performers. I am worried that it will be impossible to enjoy it as much as the year before.

But I did!

Perhaps you do not read Sir Max Beerbohm but he is one of my very favourite writers, and in his book *Zuleika Dobson* he describes how everyone falls in love with a young girl called Zuleika because she is so beautiful. Now of course it is not quite right to call you all Zuleika, when there are so many of you, and all so talented. But I have to say that every time I hear you play I feel awestruck like one of Zuleika's admirers.

Perhaps you find this letter too light-hearted for such an occasion but when I left you on Saturday I was feeling utterly exhilarated and I am afraid that I still feel exhilarated.

With my warm thanks I am, ever yours sincerely, Elizabeth R.

What a charmer, Moshe had thought, perusing his personal photocopy. What a doll. And after all, thought Moshe, what's wrong with politeness? And I agree with him. There is nothing wrong, after all, with virtue.

6

So that is why poor exhausted impatient Moshe, talking to Papa, yearned for regal politesse.

He knew all about these backstage meetings. He was bored by them. Unless there was a sexy widow, these parties made Moshe feel slightly aggrieved. Not the champagne and caviar canapés, but the people made him aggrieved. The board of directors annoyed him. There you were, grumbled Moshe to himself, and they wanted you to thank them. They wanted you to be intrigued by their insights into acting.

Moshe has his problems, as we all do. So he can be quite crude. Especially when he is tired or scared. Let us leave him be. Let us ignore this grumbling. Let us forgive the fact that he did not see Papa's personal politesse.

He may not have been regal, but Papa had an etiquette all of his own. There was something soulful about him. And although 'soulful' is not a word I like, it is a word that Papa liked. So I will call him soulful. In fact, I will go further. In homage to Papa and his otherworldly instincts, I will give him an image. Papa is the benevolent angel of this story.

There were two reasons for Papa's chattiness about Prince Kropotkin. This was Papa's first performance as a board member. So he was looking keen. He was impressing the board with his commitment. And also, he was being kind. Chatting to Moshe about Prince Kropotkin was intended to flatter Moshe. It was not a lecture. It was designed to show that Papa had been entranced by Moshe's performance. It was a compliment.

7

While Moshe was being depressed at Papa, Nana had sidled off. Difficult Moshe had made her shy. She felt shy with this man impressing her Papa. Whereas here was a pretty and talkative girl called Anjali who loved the shiny green bead mesh of Nana's bracelet. Anjali had a plastic diamond in her right ear. Nana said that oh the bracelet was quite uncomfortable. It looked okay but it crushed her wrist. She looked at Anjali, and Anjali smiled at her. Nana took off her small black glasses – rotating them from the right-hand earpiece with two fingers.

Anjali is the other heroine of this story.

Nana specially admired Anjali's make-up. So I will describe it. High up on her cheekbones, Anjali had pink blusher. She had smoothed it right up to the bottom of her eyes. Round the eye itself, she had smoky black eyeliner. On the eye-socket bone she had stroked on some soft brown eyeshadow, fading to her skin tone.

Nana liked this. Anjali had style.

Nana took a champagne. Then she took one mini blini with red caviar and sour cream. Then another mini blini topped with the mini croissant of a minute prawn. She clamped the precarious champagne between her third and fourth fingers.

She said, 'Thass a cool name, Anjli's cool.' She said, 'My name's Nana.'

Maybe I should explain about Nana's name. I can see that it sounds a bit odd. Her original name was Nina. But when Nina was a baby, Nina could only say Nana. So Nana's name was Nana.

They went quiet. Anjali pushed at her pockets, trying for

some cigarettes. She found one and angled it into her mouth. Nana said, 'Swhat other plays have you been in?'

It was just conversation. But conversations are not always equal. You really don't know what you might be getting. Sometimes you ask a gargantuan question and someone just agrees with you. Or you ask a small conversational question and you get a gargantuan reply.

In reply to Nana's question 'Swhat other plays have you been in?', Anjali offered Nana the story of Anjali's career.

So Anjali had been an actress. But what are beginnings anyway? Who's to say where something starts? No Anjali had started as an actress. Then she met, recently she had met a voice coach, a Polish girl. Well she was not a girl, she was a woman. She was the clichéd older woman. And this woman was passionate, she loved opera, she loved nineteenth-century bel canto. She loved singers more than actors. And Anjali hadn't wanted to be a singer. At school they had said she should try singing. But she hadn't tried until she fell in love. Now, this is the sad part – yes, Anjali had a sad sad story, laughed Anjali – because Anjali was a remarkable singer, truly magical. No truly. She was the perfect mezzo. Her timbre was the ring around the moon. Who'd have thought it? She had a ring-around-the-moon voice. But Zosia – this Polish girl was Zosia – only loved Bellini, the Italian composer Bellini. And Bellini isn't interested in mezzos. No, Bellini goes for sopranos. The lead is always a soprano. And Zosia wanted a romantic lead. She wanted a soprano Anjali – musky, bosomed. And well Anjali was, Anjali was in love with Zosia. So she practised. But all she got was somewhere in between – an intermezzo, laughed lonely Anjali. And the Polish girl left her for another girl. So anyway, she said. At least she had her speaking voice. And that was what she was, really – an actress. So everything was fine. So what she was *trying* to say, laughed Anjali, was that she hadn't been in plays, not recently. She was mainly doing film work now. Film work. Well actually mainly adverts. Adverts, she said, paid a bit better. She was just doing this play with Moshe as a. Have you met him? He was a good friend of hers. They'd been friends for oh ages. She was just doing this as a favour.

Gosh. Jeez.

It is really very exhausting, being a non-talker.

8

And Nana was a non-talker.

Perhaps it surprised you that Nana did not interrupt Anjali. She did not ask her any probing questions. If a pretty girl called Anjali began telling you about her lesbian love life, you reckon that you would say something. I can even imagine people thinking that Anjali's little speech was an invitation to question her.

But Nana was not a questioner. She was private. She was beautiful and shy.

Nana was a non-talker.

Most people who are not pretty, and most people are not pretty, think that pretty girls are powerful and haughty. But I think that this is wrong. More often, pretty girls are shy girls. They can be gawky, nervous, badly dressed. Often, they are surprised that they are called pretty at all.

Pretty girls are assumed to be haughty, I think, because

people believe that pretty girls are constantly pretty. This makes them the opposite of unpretty people – who are only occasionally pretty. But prettiness is variable too. No pretty girl is constantly pretty. Prettiness is even variable in age. Some people are pretty fourteen-year-olds and some people are scrumptious sixty-seven-year-olds. Some people are only pretty when they are four and that is a tragedy.

And Nana was pretty. Nana was beautiful.

But how beautiful was Nana really?

Nana couldn't *not* be beautiful. She tried not to be beautiful and she was still beautiful. That was how beautiful she was. Nana had attempted the long hair, the short hair, the wispy fringe, the bob, the feathered bob, the crew-cut, the scraped back ponytail, the highlights, and now the short asymmetrical fringe. Even, in a moment of retro glee, a month-long phase of a Marcel wave.

She couldn't not be beautiful.

In Director's Cut, on Edgware High Street, hairdressers wandered away from their wet unhappy clients so they could offer advice to Nana. Let us call these hairdressers Angelo and Paulo. Nana entranced them both. Angelo had a pencil moustache and black curls. It was her pallor, he said. Paulo thought that it was her pallor and the colour of her hair. They asked her if she had ever dyed her hair. Nana said no. They told her to never dye it. It was the most extraordinary colour. It was the strangest mixture of blonde and white.

Her hair was beautiful. Nana was tall, thin, pale, blonde, breasty. Her glasses were little black rectangles and she was still pretty.

But – and this was the thing – when she was young she

was ugly. When she was at school, Nana was the tallest one, the gangliest bespectacled one. She was mannish and severe. And this had repercussions. All through her childhood, Nana believed she was ugly. Everyone said she was ugly. So that, as a result, she did not like pretty people. Or rather, she did not think prettiness was valuable. Instead she became the clever one, the careful one, the quiet one.

When you're fourteen you're gangly and mannish. When you're twenty-five you're leggy and elegant. This is ironic. This is a psychological problem.

Now that she was beautiful, she was praised for being beautiful. And Nana was confused by all this praise. Angelo and Paulo upset her. It made her feel pointlessly favoured. She was a girl who hated her beauty. She distrusted it. Pretty made her powerful and that unsettled her. But what could she do? You cannot stop people when they tell you how pretty you are. You cannot tell people that you think looks are unimportant. If you do that, you sound pretentious. You sound hypocritical.

This was why Nana became a non-talker. It might have looked like haughtiness, or oddness, now that she was pretty. But it was not.

An uneasy prettiness – that is how I would describe Nana.

9

Meanwhile, Moshe and Papa were chatting. Moshe said, 'So you're in banking. Is that, I mean do you? Is that?' 'Well it depends what you mean by banking,' said Papa. 'Well, I don know,' said Moshe. 'It's not so much banking as risk,' said Papa. 'Right,' said Moshe. Papa said, 'There are the elements of risk management in a global context. Then the cleanliness of risk data. Credit-risk modelling. The innovations of GARP.' Moshe gawped. 'Garp?' he said. 'Generally Accepted Risk Principles,' said Papa. 'Not to be confused with GAAP. Generally Accepted Accounting Principles. People often confuse them.'

'I know,' said Moshe. 'GARP GAAP. Always annoys me.'

It did not get a laugh.

He tried again.

Moshe said, 'I know a banking joke.' Papa took another glass of champagne. Moshe said, 'What's the difference between an English and a Sicilian accountant?' He waited. 'No? Shall I tell you?' he said. 'Shall I tell you?' 'Tell me,' said Papa. 'The English one', said Moshe, 'can tell you how many people are going to die each year. The Sicilian can give you their names and addresses.'

It got a laugh. It got a polite laugh.

Papa said it was no joking matter though. Sadly he told Moshe that banking was a *recipe for crash and burn*. 'Do you know New York?' said Papa. 'New York's just insane. I used to think I'd have to bring my pillow into work and die right there in the conference room. When I worked at Banker's Trust a friend of mine, Charlie Borokowski, the sweetest guy, odd ties with Egyptian designs. With Egyptian designs. Where was I? Insane. New York's insane. Oh yes Charlie Borokowski. Charlie worked two days and nights preparing figures for audits, some business with capturing funds. He went to work on Monday morning and I literally carried him out on the Wednesday. He didn't even remember being there at that meeting. He had very white teeth,' said Papa. 'He said apples were why.'

Papa said, 'You know they want to make a deal when they say, they get on the phone and they say, "Hey hey friend." That's how you know they want to make a deal. They say, "Hey hey friend."'

'I like that,' said Moshe. 'Yes so do I,' said Papa.

Papa liked this actor. He liked Moshe very much.

10

Nana said, 'Have you met my father? I want you to meet my father.' Anjali said, 'Um um yes I.' 'Oh you must meet him,' said Nana. She walked Anjali over to Papa. She introduced Papa to Anjali. Papa introduced Nana to Moshe.

Papa and Anjali began to talk about Papa's gorgeous tie.

Nana said, 'Iss doing really well you must be pleased,' to which Moshe said, 'Oh it's just a paper house.'

This comment was meant to be charming, self-deprecating. It was meant to be a joke. Unfortunately, Moshe was incomprehensible. Nana had no idea what a paper house was. She eyed him, shyly. She said, 'What's a paper house?' She drank from her champagne glass and then realised it was empty. And Moshe pretended not to notice. Instead he explained about the machinations of theatres, their two-for-one offers, their bribes. She said, 'Oh.' Then she had a practical worry. She said, 'It must be ekzausting, learning all those lines. I hate having to learn things by heart.' She put on her glasses again.

Two things were charming Moshe. The main charm was this. She was one of the most beautiful girls he had ever seen. The secondary charm was this. She was lovable as well. She was worried about Moshe's health.

She must have a boyfriend, thought Moshe.

So Moshe tried to impress her. Ever the intellectual, he said, 'But it's such an, it's so intresting to act in it.' She nodded. Moshe said, 'It's really, just. So. Sa wonderful role. The lines aren't a problem.' Nana was musing. She said, 'But all those repetitive jokes. Some of the lines are terrible. "Methinks the spirit of Charlotte Corday has entered my soul now." That's horrible. It's so romantic.'

Moshe was wishing he had not said it was a great role. He was wishing he had just agreed with her.

He backtracked.

'It's true,' said Moshe. 'I mean, the play does turn class into fashion. It romanticises class.' The duo paused. The conversation paused. Neither of them understood. Moshe certainly did not understand. He swayed. He steadied himself. Nana looked at her empty champagne glass.

Pauses are very difficult. They require agility. Unfortunately, neither Moshe nor Nana was being agile.

Moshe nervously added, 'I mean isnit just propaganda by deed?' as Nana responded, in slow motion, repeating, 'Romanticises class.' Moshe lowered his eyebrows and pushed his lips forward to show her that he was troubled, intellectually. Then Moshe looked sideways at Papa.

Papa was chatting to Anjali about the racial politics of acting. He was promising reforms.

And that was the beginning. That conversation was the beginning of the romance of Nana and Moshe. But Nana hadn't noticed.

It is a pity, Nadezhda Mandelstam would have thought it was a pity, but as Nana returned to Edgware with Papa, she was not thinking about Moshe. She had almost forgotten him already. She was thinking about theatres.

Theatres nonplussed her.

There was the foyer. Relaxed in the foyer, Papa had chatted, his neck angled up to the taller fat men. And Nana listened to him, while she looked with compassion at the boy with a plastic box of programmes and Loseley Dairy ice cream harnessed to his neck. With compassion, Nana noticed how his gelled precise fringe draped over some acne.

And then the auditorium, the pretentious auditorium. She watched the small lights in the rig dim down. In husky whispers, people almost finished their conversations. While Nana counted the white fire-exit arrows, and then the white running men on green backlit backgrounds.

Papa taptouched Nana's right hand. He told her to put on her glasses, tucked up on her lap. He grinned at her.

And then the star arrived on stage, disguised as Prince Paul Maraloffski. His name was something, Moshe something, Papa muttered to himself, chinking the open programme towards the safety lights. Moshe, the socialist socialite, drawled his readymade jokes. 'In a good democracy, every man should be an aristocrat.' No one laughed. Prince Paul Maraloffski intoned his epigrams. 'Culture depends on cookery. For myself, the only immortality I desire is to invent a new sauce.'

Nana considered the ending of *Vera, or the Nihilists*. She was amazed by its sentimentality. Vera, tortured by love, saves Russia but kills herself. And Nana had turned to her dearest Papa. She hoped that he was smiling too.

Papa was not smiling. Papa was an angel. He was moved by the ending. He was, thought Nana, almost crying. But because she was a girl who cared about her Papa, she cared for him more than anything, Nana was not embarrassed by this. No, she just tried to look after him. 'It's okay, Papa. Sokay,' whispered Nana. 'Don worry. She's still breathing.'

Nana just didn't *get* theatres.

12

When Anjali went home, it was around midnight. She lived in a flat in Kentish Town with her brother. Her brother was called Vikram. You are never going to see Vikram in this story. But I am mentioning him just now in case you are worried. He is there to reassure you that Anjali was not a loner.

Anjali went into the kitchen and looked in the fridge. Then she closed the fridge. She took off her denim jacket and sat on the sofa in the living room. She got up for a piss. She came back to the kitchen and opened the freezer. She took out a small cardboard pot of Ben & Jerry's Phish Food ice cream. She opened it and left it on top of the freezer. Then she sat on the sofa and picked up a bulldog-clipped pile of papers, which were Anjali's copy of a new script by Gurinder Chadha. She almost read through her fourteen lines. A telltale sign that she did not do this was that she did not open the bulldog clip. She looked at the letter requesting Ms Sinha to accept this working copy. She sat. She stared at the blank TV.

She remembered the ice cream.

She got up and took a spoon out of a drawer. The ice cream was still solid. She returned to the sofa anyway with the ice cream and the spoon. Anjali prodded at the ice cream, bored. She licked the spoon. She tumbled to her hands and knees and got out a video, sent to her by her mother, of *Sholay*. She considered watching a four-hour film. She mused on how much she disliked serious Bollywood films. She only liked the frivolous ones. She laughed at her mother's taste, out loud. Laughing out loud made her feel weird. She pushed the video into the machine and pressed play. She turned on the TV and found channel 0.

She missed her ex. She missed Zosia.

She remembered going to the Belle Vue cinema in Edgware to the late-night Hindi films. The Belle Vue cinema was located close to Nana and Papa but Anjali did not know that yet. Anjali's family lived in Canons Park and they went to the flicks together. She wondered why they had always called them flicks. She remembered how she fancied Madhuri Dixit more than she fancied Amitabh Bachchan. She remembered them all eating samosas in the Belle Vue cinema, and her mother stuffing a ticklish paper napkin down Anjali's T-shirt. Anjali remembered her fondness for little comic Johnny Walker. She remembered Johnny in Guru Dutt's *Mr & Mrs '55*, especially the hit song 'Dil Par Hua Aisa Jadu', in which Johnny listens to Guru Dutt in love, from a bar to a bus stop to a bus to the road. Or there was Madhuri Dixit in *Devdas*, a diamond-shaped gold ingot pressed between her eyes. Anjali considered whether Bollywood masala films were a little untechnical. Their appeal was not exactly formal.

Anjali was a mildly successful actress with a mildly unsuccessful love life.

This is not a very strange set-up, I think.

After all, sex isn't everything.

II

3

They fall in love

I

NANA FELL IN love with Moshe on 28 April.

That was Moshe's theory. That was the date he remembered. On that day, thought Moshe, his performance in the living room had made Nana swoon.

This might not seem very plausible. And it was not very plausible. When you know what his performance was, it will seem especially implausible.

They were in Moshe's Finsbury flat. It was on the first floor of a Victorian house. And Moshe announced the cushion shtick. 'The what?' said Nana. 'Oh the cushion trick,' said Moshe.

This was the cushion trick. Moshe pushed the window open and then picked up a cushion. His grandmother had embroidered it with a large red velvet heart. He hugged the cushion. He cradled the cushion round the room. Moshe cooed and kissed, he tossed his baby up and caught it. The cushion's gold tassels flapped. Nana stared at Moshe. He

43

was in paternal bliss. But then suddenly and tragically the bubba slipped from Moshe's hands and tumbled out the window, clumping on the pavement. It lay there beside an empty box of Heineken. While Moshe mouthed his misery, keening for his child.

Obviously this could not have been the moment that Nana fell in love with him. There is never a climactic moment. And even if there had been, I do not think this would have been the one. But that was Moshe's conclusion. He concluded that his talent had charmed her.

This does not mean that Moshe was not talented. He was a good actor. It was just not his talent that charmed her.

You see, when Moshe showed off his cushion trick or shtick, Nana was not even watching. Well, she was watching but not concentrating. Instead, she was wondering why she was there, on a Sunday afternoon, with her MA thesis due. She was especially baffled because Moshe was behaving so oddly.

No, Moshe was wrong. It was not his talent that charmed her.

2

In fact, people's conclusions are often wrong. And I have a theory about this. Conclusions are often wrong because people's memories are so bad.

For instance, the first time Moshe called her mobile, Nana saw it was him. She had misspelt his name. 'Moysha mob', said her Nokia 6210e. But she did not answer it. She let it ring. This was because she was on the loo in the

Bloomsbury Pizza Express, seated in the brace position – feet splayed, head down, leaning forward. And she never remembered that phone call. But that was the first time he called her. It was a crucial stage in their love story and Nana, because it was embarrassing, because it was *unromantic*, never ever remembered.

But then everyone is slightly romantic. Everyone has bad memories. Moshe was a romantic too.

Because Moshe remembered so little, he concluded two things about the beginning of this affair. Both were wrong.

Conclusion number one was that it was a *seduction*. She was seduced by his talent. That was what he thought just after he kissed her. Conclusion number two was that it had been *pure love*. That was what he thought just after they broke up. Both conclusions made sense only because he had forgotten all the details. To get to conclusion one, he forgot Nana's lack of concentration and his nervousness in the living room. To get to conclusion two, he forgot their nervous small-talk backstage at the Donmar.

The first conclusion, the *seduction* conclusion, romanticised Moshe. The second conclusion, the *love* conclusion, romanticised the two of them.

3

The next time he called he was crafty. Moshe rang her from the theatre. 'Withheld number calling', said her Nokia 6210e. She assumed it was Papa. It was not Papa. Moshe asked her out for a drink. And shy happy Nana said, 'No no no I'm, m, no. Not tonigh.' She said, 'Bu why don you email me?'

He did not email her. He got shy, too.

At first, he accepted, his dramatic techniques seemed only to depress her. But he was always witty. He possessed a variety of conscious burps. He told her acting tips. But why she sat there listening, thought Moshe, was a mystery. He was not cool.

I think, actually, that Moshe was being unfair to himself. It is true he was not incredibly cool. In fact, none of my characters is really very cool. I like that about them. But he was still quite cool.

There was, however, one specific uncool aspect to Moshe. This was acting. Get him on acting, and Moshe had thoughts. He had theories. He had learning. He was, for instance, a student of the great eighteenth-century actor, David Garrick. The cushion trick, in fact, was a bit of a steal from David Garrick.

And this was another steal. Moshe told Nana that in the final scene of *Romeo and Juliet*, Juliet should wake up too soon, too late, just in time to see Romeo die. This was absolutely crucial. As Juliet struggles awake from her drugged sleep she should drowsily see Romeo put the death philtre to his lipsticked lips. This would make it truly tragic. Because it would make the audience think that Romeo and Juliet could have lived happily ever after, that there could have been a happy ending. This would make it a heart-breaking tragedy. Oh yes, the art of acting was to know all about the human heart, and he was the heart's connoisseur.

Then he called her as she was going down into the tube at Goodge Street and she said she'd call him back. She didn't.

But Moshe had still more skills. He could put his head through a door and in four or five seconds could change his expression from wild joy to mild joy, from joy to contentment, from contentment to shock, from shock to astonishment, from astonishment to sadness, from sadness to exhaustion, from exhaustion to fear, from fear to horror, from horror to despair. He could make his face descend to anything. In the Alphabet Bar on Beak Street, Moshe showed her. She seemed to like it. He offered to show her again.

She browsed through his books and when she got to a copy of Nick Cave lyrics he said, 'Oh no no no not that one,' and tried to take it away, smiling, but not before naughty Nana had seen the dedication from 'C' who would love 'Puppy' for ever.

He was, thought Nana, stubborn. And stubborn had its attractions. It showed, after all, that he liked her. There were good things in persistence.

And then, they remembered later, he called her and she was with one of her friends – 'You know,' said Moshe, 'with Cleo, or Naomi. Or Biff, or Scooter.' 'It was Cleo,' said Nana, 'no Tamsin, yeh Tamsin, and we were trying on bras in M&S.' 'You never tol me that,' he said. Moshe said, 'You told me it was shoes, you were trying on shoes. In L. K. Bennett.' 'Well I wasn going to tell you bras,' said Nana. She was trying on a bra and was rushed and flustered. So she said yes. So they got drunk.

And she said once, 'So dyou like Dario Fo's stuff?' and Moshe said, 'Dario?' 'Dario Fo,' she said. 'You've got lots of his plays.' 'Oh them,' said Moshe, 'no no no, actually no.' 'Oh,' she said. 'I just would imagine you'd like him. He's good, I think.' 'Really?' said Moshe. 'Well maybe.'

We are just so well matched, thought Nana, happily.

47

4

As for the sex, the history of sex between Nana and Moshe began with the giggles. For the second night running, they were sitting on the futon. They were sitting primly on the sofa talking about the state of contemporary theatre. Then Moshe got up to go and piss. This was two a.m. And when he came back Nana was not sitting primly. Not any more. She had stretched herself out, horizontal.

This must be my chance, thought Moshe. But he moved very slowly. Moshe moved ever so slowly. He did not want to be wrong about this. He did not want to misinterpret.

He did not want to misinterpret! She was horizontal!

He kissed her. She kissed him. She kissed him. He kissed her. She said 'You're lovely.' He said 'You're lovely too.' Then they both started giggling.

As you may have worked out already, Moshe was not without his nervous side. So he said, 'Would youvev said no?' And Nana said, 'When?' And Moshe said, 'If I'd asked to kiss you?' And Nana replied, 'If I'd said no it wouldv made you cocky. Youdv thought I was, I don know, scared of you. So I kissed you.'

And although this sounded true, thought Moshe, allconquering gorgeous exhilarated Moshe, he reckoned it must be a lie. So Moshe kissed her again.

5

I am going to backtrack a little. I am going to backtrack to Nana on her own.

Nana was in the café at the Architectural Association in

Bedford Square. At this point, she had met Moshe but had not yet kissed him. She was therefore about to fall in love. However, although she was about to fall in love with him, Nana was not thinking about Moshe. She was not brooding, like a heroine, on the nature of love.

She was thinking about the architect Mies van der Rohe.

This might be a surprise to you, I suppose. But you do not need to be surprised. There was a plausible reason why Nana was thinking about an architect, and not Moshe. Nana was an MA student in the one-year Histories and Theories programme at the Architectural Association School of Architecture. She was doing an MA in preparation for a doctorate. Mies van der Rohe was the subject of Nana's MA thesis.

She was a quiet girl – you know that. She wanted to be an academic. She wanted to be a historian of architecture.

Mies van der Rohe was the innovative architect who in 1921 invented the glass skyscraper. He was a revolutionary. He belonged to the Bauhaus movement. The Bauhaus movement was committed to the renovation of design and style, in accordance with the demands of a new socialist democracy. It despised all ornament. In 1930, Mies van der Rohe became the last director of the Bauhaus movement. Mies banned political activity of any kind. In 1933 the Bauhaus was disbanded by the new Nazi government. In 1937 Mies went to America.

This is not an essay on revolutionary architecture. Architecture can often be revolutionary, and I like that. I like the Bauhaus. But I am not interested in the Bauhaus here. I am interested in Nana.

As a historian, Nana believed in accuracy. Now I know that if you asked her to remember certain details of

Moshe's and her history, she would not have been able to. But it is difficult being accurate all the time. The point is that she tried.

Nana's MA thesis was on the critical reception of Mies van der Rohe in America. She disliked those who idealised him. Nana loved the man, no question, but she was also a girl who cared for precision.

First, she did not see a natural progression, based on democratic theory, from Mies's revolutionary housing in Berlin to his American skyscrapers. The connection was aesthetic. It was not political. And her second disagreement was with Mies himself when he was political. For example, following the theory of the Bauhaus, Mies was determined to use flat roofs. Pointed roofs, claimed the Bauhaus, were bourgeois. They symbolised kaiserly crowns. Whereas, thought Nana, pointed roofs were just necessary. They were practical. They kept the rain off. Germany is rainy.

She remembered her visit to the New National Gallery in Berlin, Mies van der Rohe's crowning achievement, where little pails and engorged mops, positioned at strategic intervals, cluttered the clean lines in every room.

I know Nana sounds geeky, but I like her. I approve of this care for particulars. Sometimes I do not think it gets enough recognition – this care for the facts. There is nothing wrong with being an accurate historian.

You see, when a party person thinks about architecture they can tell someone, immediately. When a party person stumbles on a new theory concerning the nature of public design in Weimar Germany, he or she has a receptive audience. Whereas the people who just sit and read and think – they can only be charming on their own. And Nana was this kind of person. She was a quiet person.

What a fucking waste of time, she thought, considering Mies's attempts to politicise, in 1962, the design of an art gallery. It was so fucking anachronistic. Maintaining a theory for thirty years was just so lazy, thought Nana. It was just a form of nostalgia.

You see? She was geeky, but she was charming.

6

But the sex, the sex took time. It took practice.

This, for example, was how they first had sex. It was a week after they had first kissed. It was three weeks after 28 April.

At midnight, in a Covent Garden hotel, Moshe and Nana were naked. They were naked in full view of a buzzing minibar.

They were in a hotel?

The hotel was Moshe's treat. His idea was that people respond to treats. But unfortunately, it was not an idea he could test. This was because he was very drunk. He was now perhaps too drunk to eat. He was certainly too drunk to appreciate the joy of sex.

An empty miniature Stolichnaya bottle dropped, a miniature thud, off the bed.

This was not a sex scene, not yet. I do not want anyone to get the wrong impression.

Moshe swayed above Nana's long and slender body. He lovingly stroked her stomach with the back of his hand. Now, the back of the hand may seem like an unorthodox sexual surface. And it was an unorthodox surface. But Moshe had given it thought. The back of the hand was inventively tender. That was one reason. There was also a sadder reason. He stroked her with the back of his hand so that Nana couldn't feel the roughage of the eczema on Moshe's pink tough fingers.

Nana held his penis hard in her hand. It was not an erect penis. And they looked at each other in the way they imagined they should – an earnest look, a determined look. It was a very serious look. Moshe glanced down. He was trying to see what his penis was up to. But instead he just saw the freckles on the back of Nana's right hand. He studied them, propped on his arms, his back curved, propped on his arms, he studied them. Then he noticed the hanging dip of his belly. While they both observed his inelegant penis, Moshe tried to hold his belly in.

Nana and Moshe's first sex scene was not a sex scene. It looked a bit like a sex scene but it was not. It was slapstick.

Moshe got off the bed – to get a drink or stand mysterious by the window or just do anything but look at his floppy belly and floppy penis – and tragically stepped on a mini can of slimline Schweppes. He staggered. His knees gave way. His mouth was open. Then finally, wobbling and steadying, he spoke, not at the beginning, but at the end of a breath, with a trembling voice. 'Fuchristfuckme,' he said.

Giggling, they tucked each other up. They snuggled in their single bed.

I know the single bed looks odd. The single bed surprised Nana. But there was an explanation. This explanation was financial. The double rooms, Moshe had explained to her sadly, were *astronomical*.

7

At four in the morning, Nana woke up. She was hung over. She yawned, she yawned, stood up. She picked up a glass of water and it slipped and spilled on the bed.

She was in love. I know it sounds girly but it was true. She thought it was wonderful that she was here, feeling nauseous, in a single room paid for by Moshe. She thought it was too gorgeous, that Moshe was sleeping and Nana was awake.

Let me describe this moment. Let me describe this night-time idyll.

If you looked from up above you'd see the bed and Nana standing while Moshe slept. Above the bed there was a copy of a Raoul Dufy print, in a clipframe, of a sunny landscape and a cascading pot of red geraniums on a window sill. Next to the print, there was rain framed in a window. But Nana did not see this glamorous arrangement, nor the fish tank behind her in the corner where one fish brushed another. So she could not see the goldfish moving flatly past or through her head. Interior decoration was not her priority.

Having drunk two bottles of wine and then four miniature Stolichnayas, three miniature Jim Beams and one miniature Gordon's gin, Nana needed desperately to piss.

8

The next event in this story is a blow job.

I suppose this could be seen as a good thing or a bad thing. Personally, I think it was a good thing. This is not because I think blow jobs are intrinsically a good thing. Well no, I do think blow jobs are a good thing, I am rarely averse to a blow job, but that is not why I think that a blow job was the right thing here. I have another explanation. A lot of love is dependent on sex. It is difficult for love to survive without sex. So in the end, if they are going to truly love each other, Nana and Moshe need to get to sex. That is my theory.

It was also Nana's theory.

And there was another, sneaky motive behind Nana's behaviour that morning. She was imagining the endless procession of Moshe's previous, highly trained lovers. No doubt about it, they were more highly trained than Nana. Nana was no competition to the sleek girls of Moshe's past. Unlike Nana, these perfect girls could walk in five-inch heels. Their breasts were braless yet buoyant. To their yoga-schooled limbs, no sexual position was alien.

This should be a lesson to us all. The sleek girls of Moshe's past. I don't know. That is the conclusion of a girl who did not believe in her attractiveness. That is the natural conclusion of a girl who did not pride herself on her sex appeal.

If only people never came to conclusions.

Nana gulped down some water. Then her sleepy head began its determined route down past the black mushroom cloud of Moshe's soft chest hair, and along the fainter vertical line of hair from his tummy button to his pubic hair, until she reached his penis. At this point, she opened her unsure lipbalmed lips and was very gentle around Moshe. Moshe grew, then grew. He sleepily woke up. He could feel some spit leaking warm then cold around his testicles. This made him feel very satisfied.

54

Some people may think, and I can understand this, that performing fellatio before intercourse had even taken place was against the rules of ordinary sexual etiquette. This blow job is a slight surprise, I admit that. It is almost a surprise to me. But sexual etiquette is variable. It has to adapt to the situation – which, in this case, was characterised by worry. And in sexual situations characterised by worry, people often resort to much more extreme practices than a gentle blow job. A preliminary act of fellatio was actually quite tame. And Nana was not intending to give Moshe a complete blow job. She was not in it till the orgasm. The blow job was just a taster.

Nana was trying to speed things up. In this nervous situation, both of them wanted to have sex. Actually, secretly, they wanted to have *had* sex. That was how nervous they were. Up above her, Moshe was nervous. Down below, Nana was nervous she was making him nervous.

She dragged her mouth up and off Moshe's penis. Then Nana crouched over Moshe, on her hands and knees, and ran the edge of her tongue across his fatly flat nipples, pink over pink. And she was being very brave, I think. It is difficult – silently improvising. And Moshe said to her, 'Tell mto fuck you.' Leery-eyed Nana just smiled. He said, 'Tell me.'

As everyone knows, sex is a game of domination.

Nana was looking at Moshe. She was wondering if Moshe was going too fast. But because she wanted her podgy sweetheart to be happy as well, she said, 'Fuck me.' She drawled it out. She said, 'Fuh me. Fu meee.'

And then, and then, Moshe was naughty. He slowed it down himself. Like a pro, he just insinuated a finger, touching her cunt where she was.

It made her happily close her eyes.

9

Nana happily closed her eyes. She told herself not to think about anything other than this. But thinking like that made her think of anything. She thought about the minibar. So she opened her eyes instead. She opened her eyes and looked at Moshe's lips. She looked at his parting lips, posed for the occasion, and it made her remember she needed a new lipstick, which made her remember her diminishing eyeshadow, which needed to be that shade of ochre because without it her eyebrows really looked unreal and she wasn't sure she had seen it recently, no not even in Pure Beauty.

Then Moshe turned, he turned her over, on to her back. He pushed himself in her. He stopped. Nana moaned the right noises, she moaned them with her lips shut, stifled. He pushed himself further in. She moaned some more.

It was sex! It was a sex scene!

Eventually, it finished. In fact, it finished quite soon. Like many men, Moshe was overexcited. This was particularly unfortunate because, not wanting to *tempt fate*, Moshe had not taken the precaution of a pre-sex wank.

Nana did not come. And this was not, I have to admit, a surprise. It was certainly not a surprise to Nana.

But this small inequality caused a number of feverish thoughts. It especially caused a lot of feverish thoughts for Moshe. As Nana held him contentedly tight, relieved, Moshe wondered what she was feeling. It might have been too much to expect a personal compliment, he understood that, but saying nothing at all to Moshe was a little unsettling. All she was doing, thought Moshe, disgruntled, was holding him.

Oh Moshe. Moshe, Moshe, Moshe. Can there not be

untalkative moments? Can there not be a mutual silence? Will you always be this afraid?

Unfortunately, I have to tell you, he will always be this afraid.

He could feel his penis shrinking out. So, to minimise this moment, Moshe moved by her side, rolling on to her outstretched left arm, which Nana extricated from under him.

As for Nana, at this point her feelings were a mixture of happy and uncomfortable. She was happy because of the sex. She was uncomfortable because there was semen being ticklish and sticky around her inner thighs. She considered going to the loo to wipe herself and then she decided that no, she had to stay. Wiping might look unentranced. And in a way, she thought, she quite liked the sticky feeling, she liked its persona. It made her feel jaded, used, debauched.

She liked debauched.

So she rubbed her wet thighs together and said, 'Do you think we'll both get jaded soon? Do you think we'll become people who can only have sex in car crashes, like that book by J.G. Ballard, what's it called, *Crash*?'

Moshe charmed and calmed her. He waited, pondering. Then he looked at her. He reassured her.

'I can't drive,' he said.

IO

I know that this was witty, and when a boy is witty he appears carefree, he appears masterful. But the truth was something else. Moshe was not insouciant. Moshe was not

57

carefree. He was thinking harsh and angry thoughts.

It is difficult being a boy during sex. There is a performative side to the act which is undeniably objective. Sadly, duration is objective. It is seventeen seconds or fifty-five minutes. It cannot be both at once. And it was because Moshe was thinking about the cruelly objective nature of duration that he was thinking harsh and angry thoughts.

It was Moshe's nagging hope that Nana had been somehow so embroiled in sex that her sense of time had evaporated. Unless her sense of time had drifted away, he thought, she would be thinking witty thoughts. That would be only natural. And Moshe did not want her to be thinking witty thoughts.

Of course, Nana was not thinking witty thoughts. Nana was just content that intravaginal penetration had reached an ordinary ending. Nana was perfectly pleased.

It was Moshe who was not pleased. In a Covent Garden hotel, Moshe was seeing the point of homosexuality. He was thinking that one plus of being gay was that you would know precisely what was a gentlemanly average. You would not be haunted by uncertainty. The trouble with heterosexuality, thought Moshe, was the secrecy of couples. There was no transparency. A boy's guide to boys was girls. And girls were not good enough. They were so moral they could not be trusted. They were always generous. Maybe not, he admitted, when talking to other people. But with Moshe, in bed, watching the poetic rain, they were always so kind and soothing. They told him that sex was wonderful. They praised Moshe's tenderness and length.

No, Moshe wanted boys. He wanted a frank discussion with other boys. This made him sad. It made him sad because he was not really sure if this could ever happen.

This might seem tangential, I suppose, but Moshe's ideal conversation did happen. It happened a long time ago, but it happened.

On 3 March 1928, Antonin Artaud, André Breton, Marcel Duhamel, Benjamin Péret, Jacques Prévert, Raymond Queneau, Yves Tanguy and Pierre Unik – they all sat down and chatted about sex. Not many of these people are famous individually, I know that. But they have an importance. They are not negligible. They were key members of the Surrealist group. They thought that talking honestly about sex was a necessary beginning to the creation of a just and perfect society. They thought it was the first political step.

If only Moshe had been there, I think it would have calmed him. I think it would have calmed a lot of boys.

II

Raymond Queneau You have not made love for some time. How long before you ejaculate from the moment you are alone with the woman?

Jacques Prévert Maybe five minutes, maybe an hour.

Marcel Duhamel I'm the same.

Benjamin Péret There are two parts. Before the sexual act itself, a period which can be quite long, perhaps half an hour according to my desire at the time. The second part, the sexual act: around five minutes.

André Breton The first part, a lot longer than half an hour. Almost indefinite. Two: twenty seconds maximum.

Marcel Duhamel To be more precise, during the second part, a minimum of five minutes.

Raymond Queneau The preliminary act: maximum twenty minutes. Two: less than a minute.

Yves Tanguy One: two hours. Two: two minutes.

Pierre Unik One: one hour. Two: between fifteen and forty seconds.

André Breton And the second time? Accepting that one makes love in the shortest possible time? Me? Three to five minutes for the sexual act.

Benjamin Péret The sexual act: around a quarter of an hour.

Yves Tanguy Ten minutes.

Marcel Duhamel I'm the same.

Pierre Unik It varies: between two and five minutes.

Raymond Queneau A quarter of an hour.

Jacques Prévert Three minutes or even twenty minutes. What do you think of a woman with a shaved sex?

André Breton Very beautiful, infinitely better. I have never seen it, but it must be magnificent.

12

I really do not think that Moshe needed to be so flustered by his performance. André Breton, the founder of the Surrealist movement, came in twenty seconds maximum. Raymond Queneau, a *novelist*, the author of *Zazie in the Metro*, would last less than a minute.

Whereas Moshe had come after six minutes and forty-seven seconds. In comparison with André Breton and Raymond Queneau he was a superman. He may only have been half Jewish, it may even have been the wrong half, but he still belonged to the chosen people.

And it was not just his sexual capacity that was remarkable. He was also a connoisseur of the 'shaved sex'. Yes, Moshe had seen a hairless vagina. When he was seventeen, as a birthday favour to Moshe, his first ever girlfriend, called Jade, removed all her pubic hair. She did this using a sensibly smeared layer of Immac Sensitive. She took him into the girls' toilet at the Fridge in Brixton, and put his hand down her trousers so that Moshe could feel her babyish smoothness and incontinent wetness.

Moshe was a sexual virtuoso. Moshe was a talent.

13

But I am worried we are ignoring Papa. And I am not going to ignore Papa. Now that Moshe and Nana have finally had sex, we can ignore them for a moment instead.

While his daughter was being satisfied by an unorthodox Jewish boy, Papa was having a suit adjusted. As it happened, he was having his suit adjusted by an Orthodox Jewish man.

Life is full of such ironies and coincidences.

Mr Blumenthal was Papa's tailor. He was a short and oblong seventy-five-year-old. He had no hair. He wore cardigans. He lived on the corner of Shakespeare Close and Milton Road, by the synagogue, in Hatch End. On the A-to-Z map of Greater London the synagogue was represented by a Star of David. He lived with his wife who was called Mrs Blumenthal. Mrs Blumenthal was a short square woman. She had a lot of hair. She did not wear cardigans.

In their mock-Tudor house on the corner of Shakespeare

Close and Milton Road, it was Sunday morning, and Papa was having the trousers taken up and the shoulders taken in.

Mr Blumenthal was kneeling down in Mr and Mrs Blumenthal's living room, bent over Papa's heather-mix socks, with a row of pins in his mouth. He was complimenting Papa on having an eye for such high-quality cloth. At the same time he was criticising the makers of the suit for the inept stitching of the seams.

Papa looked at the coffee-table book of Israeli photographic landscapes. He looked at the red padded frame, embroidered with swirls of gold thread, that surrounded a photograph of a boy in his garish bar-mitzvah shawl.

And what was Papa thinking about? As usual, Papa was trying not to think about Auschwitz.

Auschwitz?

This was not because he was sinister. No no. It was because he was kindly.

Papa had been to Auschwitz. On business in Cracow, he had made the journey to Auschwitz with a tour party of Israeli boys and girls. When Papa was there, Auschwitz was sunny and clean. The grass was cut. Three Japanese tourists posed for the camera beneath the gate's welded inscription – 'Arbeit Macht Frei'. A cleaner polished the glass of the cases which held luggage, children's clothes, hair. There were tonnes of hair. The Nazis had made hair heavy. And this, thought Papa, was an achievement. It was an achievement – making everything abnormal.

But, actually, everything was not abnormal. That was Papa's main sadness at Auschwitz. It would have been better, he thought, if it was. Instead, all the objects were just the right size. They were just like ordinary objects.

There was a plait which would brush a girl's shoulder if she turned. It would catch on the side of her neck. Everything was in proportion.

Really Papa should not have gone to Auschwitz. It only depressed him. It destroyed him. Because the thing about kindly people is that they are amazed by aggression. And this makes them so upset that they want to find out why. How, they say, how is it possible that people can be so cruel?

Papa just wanted to understand.

He had once got the brochure for the Holocaust holiday, organised by Midas Battlefield Tours, but had been too horrified by the wording. 'Day 3. This morning we drive out to the Death Camps of Treblinka, where up to 17,000 victims were murdered daily. Returning to Warsaw for the afternoon, we stroll through the pleasant and peaceful Lazienki Park, maybe to the strains of Chopin, and visit the Palace upon the Water. Return to our hotel for dinner.'

Papa was not crass. He was not ghoulish. He was just an innocent.

In his attempt to understand the nature of evil, Papa's bedtime reading at one time was *Commandant of Auschwitz* by Rudolf Hoess, with a blurb by Primo Levi. Primo was no PR supremo. This was his blurb to Rudolf Hoess: 'This book is filled with evil . . . it has no literary quality and reading it is agony.'

Rudolf Hoess bewildered Papa.

Rudolf just wanted to be a farmer. He wanted a pleasant career with a silo and machines. And he ended up running Auschwitz. If Rudolf had been contemporary, his dearest wish would have been to sit down with a cup of Lipton's Earl Grey and a HobNob, discussing the evils of Brussels bureaucrats in his MFI kitchen. He would have wanted the quiet life. The nearest Rudolf would have got to violence would have been the slaughter of a pig outside the Moreton-in-Marsh Budgens, in protest at French malpractice and misfeasance.

But no. He ran Auschwitz.

'What was Auschwitz like?' said Mr Blumenthal once, repeating Papa's innocent question. Mr Blumenthal looked across at Mrs Blumenthal. Papa and Mr Blumenthal observed the fat feet of Mrs Blumenthal wrapped in blue tights on her dark velvet electric recliner. 'What was it like?' said Mr Blumenthal. And what could he say? 'The food was bad,' he said. 'The food was *terrible*.'

Papa had not really known if this was funny. He had not quite managed a laugh. He had wanted to laugh and he got as far as the giggle. But a giggle is not a laugh.

'You,' said Mrs Blumenthal. 'One of these days you will get yourself into trouble with this talk.' 'What sort of trouble?' said Mr Blumenthal. 'Trouble,' said Mrs Blumenthal.

Papa liked Mr and Mrs Blumenthal. He liked them a lot. It just made him unhappy that when Mr Blumenthal knelt down in a white vest to push pins into his hem, Papa could see, in amongst the freckles on his wrist, a bluish tattooed five-digit number.

Perhaps you understand the importance of the number five here, but maybe you do not. Five digits meant that Mr Blumenthal was an early arrival at Auschwitz. He was only in the tens of thousands. He had longer to get through than most.

But something else made Papa unhappy too. It was not just the number. It was this. 'There is a schvartze next door now,' said Mrs Blumenthal. 'Oh really?' said Papa. 'Yes a schvartze,' said Mrs Blumenthal. 'That must be nice,' said Papa. 'Nice?' said Mr Blumenthal. 'A schvartze next door to a synagogue! Some meshuggener family next to shul? Of course it is not nice!'

The Blumenthals were noble. They had both survived the concentration camps. But also they were racist. They disliked blacks. And this, obviously, stymied Papa. He did not know what to think. The Blumenthals confused him. They were noble and despicable.

No question, the Blumenthals were tricky. They were morally ambiguous.

'And the girl?' said Mrs Blumenthal. 'How is Nina?' 'Nana,' said Papa. 'Nana,' said Mr Blumenthal. 'She has got a new boyfriend,' said Papa. 'That is good, a boyfriend,' said Mr Blumenthal. 'And what is this one like, the boyfriend? I do not think he will be good enough.' 'He's an actor,' said Papa. 'He is not good enough,' said Mr Blumenthal. 'And I think he's Jewish,' said Papa. 'Then he is certainly not good enough!' shrieked Mrs Blumenthal, finding her joke snortingly funny.

Papa managed a giggle. It was all just too bewildering, this constant unserious humour.

Me, I like that humour very much. But then, I am not kindly. I am not sweet. I am not sweet like Papa.

4

Romance

I

IN 1963 MY mother went to Prague on a school trip. In Prague, she stayed with a Jewish girl called Petra.

In fact, Petra was only half Jewish. Her mother was Jewish. When the Nazis occupied Prague, they informed Petra's father that he had to leave Petra's mother. He did not. So they sent him to the concentration camp at Terezín. They sent Petra's mother too. And they both survived. This was obviously quite unusual. Not many people survived Terezín. To celebrate, Petra's mother and father decided to have a second child. This child was Petra.

There were not many Jews left in Prague, after Terezín. Because of this, Petra felt particularly curious about Jewishness. So when she agreed to participate in a school exchange, she requested a Jewish girl. That was why my mother stayed with her. My mother is Jewish too.

Afterwards, Petra and my mother wrote to each other regularly. In 1968, after the Russians entered Prague, Petra came to London. She lived with my mother's family. A year later, however, the Russians announced that all Czechs living abroad had three weeks to decide if they wanted to come back. If they ever wanted to see their families again, they would have to come back now. And she went back.

Here are two facts about Petra. She never joined the Communist Party. That is the first fact. The second fact is this. She preferred Václav Havel's plays to the novels of Milan Kundera because Kundera left Czechoslovakia in 1975 and this was a betrayal of the resistance.

But Petra's decision to return in 1969 was not motivated by commitment to the resistance. Nor was it motivated by belief in the Communist cause. In 1969 Petra went back because a boy in London had broken up with her. That was why she returned. She always believed, however, that she went back because she could not abandon her family. She could not abandon her Jewish heritage. She had to do the good thing, the right thing. That was Petra's rationale.

But there was also a less romantic, more financial explanation. In London, Petra was working as a temp. In Prague, Petra's mother had negotiated a job for her in the American embassy. It was salaried. It was very well salaried. With this salary, Petra could afford a house in the old Jewish Quarter. And Petra had always dreamed of a house in the Jewish Quarter. This was not quite for religious reasons either. It was because she loved art nouveau. You see, Petra – who wore stonewashed narrow-leg jeans, skyblue polyester socks and black pumps with snakeskin-effect uppers – longed for style. She adored the tracery of the balustrades in the Jewish Quarter, the floral moulding round the ceilings.

Petra went back, then, for two reasons. Neither was the

obvious reason. She returned to Prague because of her love of early-twentieth-century interior decoration, and also because she had been dumped.

2

'Yeh yeh, yeh, yeh yeah,' said Anjali. 'You love that?' said Nana. 'You really?' 'Yeh yeah,' said Anjali. As she said this Anjali swept a rhetorical hand and knocked an empty glass that had once held a vodka tonic. It wobbled then luckily steadied.

Have I described what Anjali looks like? I do not think I have. Well, I've described her make-up, but not her clothes.

Anjali was slimmish, shortish, darkish. Her style was a mixture of clubby and sporty. A normal outfit for Anjali was her old denim jacket, which she had worn since she was fifteen, and a pair of red Perry Ellis trainers with black stitching. She had a small collection of freckles across her nose. She often wore a silver bangle on her wrist. There were pale lilac acne scars on her cheeks. Halfway down her back, on her spine, there was a mole.

Eventually, Nana would be bored by this mole.

But I am getting ahead of myself.

'I think that sometimes Mies is a little bit, a little bit too programmatic,' said Nana. 'Like his skyscrapers?' said Anjali. 'Oh no those are wonderful,' said Nana. 'Oh good,' said Anjali. 'They're so austere,' said Nana. 'I love that skyscraper, the Friedrichstrasse skyscraper, it's so beautiful,' said Anjali. 'The building all made of glass?' said Nana. 'Yeah that one,' said Anjali. 'Oh yes, that's beautiful,' said Nana.

As you can see, they were talking architecture. They were being highbrow. And Moshe was there too. It was just that he was not included in this discussion. He had disincluded himself. A slump on the red leather sofa, beside a two-foot test tube full of crumpled white lilies, Moshe was being quiet. Instead, he was getting his money's worth, eating £6.50 of Japanese mixture graciously provided in a white china bowl by the proprietors of mybar, in myhotel. Although not mine, thought Moshe, not fucking mine. It was not his idea to price a my mary at £6.50. It was not his personal price range.

He carried on eating, in crunchy munchy silence.

While Anjali and Nana got to know each other.

Nana said, 'I think what's intresting is how form is internaschnal. I think they were right, calling it the Internaschnal Style. I mean I think people think that with, with, with, with the Bauhaus it's all specific to Berlin. But then Mies van der Rohe goes to New York and he does the same designs. So it had nothing to do with Berlin. It was all to do with form.'

Anjali nodded. She rather liked being taught. She rather liked Moshe's new pretty girlfriend and her difficult monologues. It was fun that this girl was clever.

'But what about the roofs?' said Anjali. 'What do you mean?' said Nana. 'Well I thought there was some German reason for them,' said Anjali. 'Oh, designing buildings with flat roofs? Being anti pointed roofs?' said Nana. 'Yes,' said Anjali. 'Oh I think that's terrible,' said Nana. 'I hate that. It was all to do with Communism,' she said. 'With Communism?' said Anjali. 'They thought pointed rooves were like crowns,' said Nana. 'So they made their rooves flat.' 'Because of crowns?' said Anjali. 'Don't,' said Nana.

'But', said Anjali, 'what about when it rains? What about that?' 'Oh no exacly,' said Nana.

Nana nodded. She rather liked this girl. She rather liked Moshe's pretty friend. It was fun that this girl was clever.

Nana said, 'Mies also refused to let the blinds be uneven. He refyoosed. They were either up or down, he wanted. On the Seagram Building, in New York. The skyscraper. And then all the people inside complained. So Mies compromised. He added another position. So it was up or halfway or down. I mean.'

'Only three positions?' said Anjali. 'Oh I know,' said Nana. 'I know.'

3

I have a very simple theory about the romance of Nana and Moshe. It is this. Their romance was not romantic. Well, it was not ordinarily romantic.

For example, one element that is crucial to the conventional conception of a romance is that a romance is *couply*. Romance is the opposite of friends.

Friends often complain about this. 'Stacey', they say, 'has abandoned me. She only wants to see Henderson now, all the time.' On the other hand, Stacey, if we are going to stick with Stacey for the moment, thinks that her friends are *too clingy*. Maybe this example is a little abstract. It is a little abstract, I can see that. Let me add some detail. Stacey has mastered a lisp. This means that she talks more slowly than other people. She wears three multicoloured friendship bracelets on her right wrist. Henderson, her boyfriend, is younger than she is and this embarrasses her. She is nineteen, he is sixteen.

Anyway, Stacey thinks that her friends do not understand how important it is to devote time to a relationship. This is partly, of course, because she does not want her friends to meet Henderson too often. He is, as I have said, only sixteen.

As for Henderson, his friends also think his relationship is too exclusive. But they have their own theory for this. Henderson never lets them meet Stacey because of, they reckon, her size. Stacey is not the thinnest of girls. Henderson's friends tease him that he just wants a mother figure. He wants a mother figure with big tits. Henderson's penis, they say, is umbilically attached to Stacey.

Now, Nana and Moshe were obviously not the same as Stacey and Henderson. No romance is the same.

Nana and Moshe were an unromantic romance.

4

In a leather chair next to Anjali and Nana and Moshe, in the window at mybar, there was a girl. This girl had an olive bandanna and a plait. At the tip of the plait an electric-turquoise flannel scrunchie was wrapped tight.

She was French. She was French Algerian. She was chatting to another French Algerian friend. They were talking in French. 'Wah,' she said, 'wah. Egzagdemaw. Dans la vie. Wah.' Then she took off a thin olive jumper, revealing a sleeveless black top with a turquoise question mark whose dot was the symbol for a woman – a circle joined above a cross.

It was advertising. The girl hooked her black thready bra straps under her top. Nana looked. Anjali looked. Anjali looked at Nana looking.

But Nana was not a lesbian. She turned to her boyfriend. She asked him how he was.

Moshe was, it turned out, disconsolate. He was slightly nauseous with delicately spiced nibbles. He was sucking a stained finger. Anjali said to him, 'The thing that's sweet about you is how you really give complimentree food a chance. You really give it your all. Nothing goes to waste.' And Nana grinned and said, 'I know. It must be his puritancal side. Hating waste.'

Moshe opened out his arms in a gesture of 'Why pick on me?' He said, 'What's that style called – the one they used in India, you know the Lutyens thing?'

But Anjali had already said to Nana, 'I so love that bracelet? Did I tell you last time we, it's just so wonderful, really gorgeous.' She said, 'Where dyou get it?'

Moshe said, 'No what's it called?'

'Oh really?' said Nana to Anjali. 'Really? No you did say.' She said, 'I don't know where I, maybe Hoxton Boutique I think oh no no no, it was this little place, you know that yard, if you go a little bit down Brick Lane there's a yard, with little places. I think it was in one of those,' she said. 'And I got a sweatband as well, this really cool thing, a red and white and blue wristband saying "I love Paris" with little metal Eiffel Towers hanging off it. We should go there,' she said. 'Not Paris, I mean, Brick Lane.' 'Oh cool,' said Anjali. 'Thatd be cool.' 'Well maybe Paris as well,' said Nana, grinning.

Moshe said, 'Have I taken you to the Brick Lane bagel place?'

Nana said, 'Baygel? You say baygel?' And Moshe said,

'Yeh. Why? What do you say?' Anjali lit a cigarette. Nana said, 'Well bygel. Everyone used to say bygel.' He said, 'Well perhaps in Edgware they say "bygel" but me. No I say "baygel". And anyway,' he said.

Anjali blew out smoke at Nana then flyswatted it quickly away with her left hand. 'You're from Edgware?' she said. She said this to Nana. 'Yeah,' said Nana. 'Bu thass amazing,' said Anjali, 'I'm from Canons Park.' 'Really?' squeaked Nana.

'And anyway,' said Moshe. 'We should go there, to the Brick Lane Bakery. It's so cheap there it's I think fifty pence for a bagel or something. With cream cheese and salmon and evrething.'

Nana said, 'Oh yeah I know it.' Moshe said, 'Oh.' She said to Anjali, 'It's wonderful if you're there late after clubbing or something.' 'Yeah I know it too,' said Anjali.

Moshe said, 'Thass a nice street, Brick Lane, a nice place, with the bagels and what's that bar Two-nine-one no not Two-nine-one what is it One-nine-two no, no, fuck it, Ninety-three Feet East. And the curries,' he said. He said, 'Have you been to that restron there, Preem, oh it's Indo-Saracenic.'

Anjali said, 'What?' He said, 'It's Indo-Saracenic, the style, the Lutyens style. In India. The exotic Gothic thing. In New Delhi.' 'Oh yeh,' said Anjali. 'Yeh. Whata bout it?' 'Well nothing,' he said. 'Nothing. I mean I jus like it,' he said. 'I was jus trying to make conversation.'

'Did you know that the largest collection of Bauhaus-style buildings in the world is in Tel Aviv?' said Nana. 'They built flats for the workers.' 'No I didn't know that,' said Moshe. 'I didn't know that, darling.'

6

No, Moshe was not a serious Jewish boy. He was not committed to the history of the Jewish people. If he were asked to locate Tel Aviv on a map of Israel, I am not sure that Moshe could have done it.

I have a simple theory about nationality too. Like romance, nationality does not exist. In fact, nationality is a romance.

Occasionally Moshe enjoyed being overtly Jewish. Sometimes he felt loyal. But he was not inclined to worry about his nation. He did not worry about his Jewishness. This was partly because only his father was Jewish. It was also because his father was not a very Jewish Jew. In 1968 Moshe's father moved to Israel. By 1973, Moshe's father had moved back. He had had it with Israel. By 1975 he had joyfully married a girl, who was not Jewish, called Gloria.

At lunch one weekend, Moshe enjoyed telling Nana and lovable Papa how much he had hated Passover. He had only done Passover once, he said. But once was enough. He said, 'Do you know about Pesach? You have to hunt for the matzo, the youngest has to hunt for the matzo, and my grandpa hid it in the upstairs toilet, you know in the tank, with the ballcock. And then you have to eat it. So I had to eat it. It was terrible. I don know how he got up there,' said Moshe. 'My grandpa had Parkinson's. But he got up there.'

Papa thought this was quite funny. Nana thought this was very funny. She was laughing with her mouth closed and her head shaking backwards and forwards. This was because she had taken a large gulp of water.

'And then you have to sing this song,' continued Moshe. 'A song?' said Papa. Moshe sang it. '"One only kid, one only kid, my father bought for two zuzim, one only kid, one only kid." No it's fascinating,' said Moshe. 'There's the kid and the cat and the dog and the stick and the fire and the water and the ox and the butcher and then the angel of death kills the butcher and he kills the ox. No, the other way round. The butcher kills the ox and then the angel of death kills the butcher. It's just gripping.'

Sometimes he felt loyal. But, more often, he did not. He did not understand allegiance. When Papa at one point got sad about the trial of SS Lieutenant-Colonel Adolf Eichmann, Moshe agreed it was sad. It was sad, said Moshe, that there had been such a flagrant miscarriage of justice. But this was not why Papa was sad. Papa did not agree that the real person who should have stood trial was the maniac Nazi-hunter, Simon Wiesenthal. That was just Moshe's opinion.

No, Moshe did not have an easy relationship with Judaism.

For example, Moshe owned a 1996 Union of Jewish Students Haggadah. I also own this book. The Haggadah outlines the correct procedure for the Passover service. Imitating Hebrew, the UJS Haggadah begins at the back. You read it back to front. I think this is an affectation. Moshe also thought it was an affectation. Anyway, in this book, there is a section called 'Why Be Jewish?' The impetus for this section came from the chief rabbi of Britain, Dr Jonathan Sacks.

One of the illustrious Jewish figures interviewed – and these figures are illustrious, they include Kirk Douglas, Uri Geller, Roseanne, Steven Spielberg and Elie Wiesel – was the talkshow hostess Vanessa Feltz.

This was Vanessa Feltz's answer to Dr Sacks' question

'Why Be Jewish?' And, I have to say, at this point in his sceptical analysis of Judaism, I think I agree with Moshe. Both Moshe and I thought Vanessa's answer was a little unbalanced.

> Intermarriage robs us of our future. It callously dismisses as not worth preserving the 5,000 years of scholarship, persecution, humour and optimism which have made Jews an extraordinary people. Every marriage of Jew to gentile erodes the foundations which make us who we are. After all, without Jewish children there is no Jewish posterity. From my three-piece suite in Finchley, that feels like a tragedy.

Vanessa Feltz! Cuddly Vanessa Feltz! Two years later, in 1998, her Jewish husband left her. And Vanessa turned to another man. This man was not a Jewish man. Obviously, I approved of this miscegenation. And when the non-Jewish man left Vanessa Feltz, I did not approve. I worried that this mishap would put Vanessa off goyim for ever.

7

And what about Anjali? Was she more distressed by her ethnicity? Was British Asian Anjali vexed by the mix-up of her heritage? No. She was not. Well, she was not *distressed*. She cared much more about films.

But even films can be ethnically problematic. There was the time that Anjali and her schoolfriend Arjuna went to see Spike Lee's biopic *Malcolm X* when it came out in 1992. They saw it at the Staples Corner multiplex. No one in the audience was white. No one in the audience was strictly black, either. At least, they were not African Americans like Malcolm X. They were all like Arjuna and Anjali.

This embarrassed Anjali. Well, it was not this precisely that embarrassed Anjali. It was not the audience. It was the audience's attitude. Inexplicably, they all identified with Malcolm X. And this seemed silly. Surely you could like the film without thinking you were Malcolm X? thought Anjali. As they walked out of the Staples Corner multiplex, Anjali looked at Arjuna. She liked him. It wasn't that. It was just that in his navy-blue-rimmed glasses, with a small panda on each arm to indicate that the purchase of these glasses had gone some way to support the World Wide Fund, Arjuna did not seem like a Black Power freedom fighter. He seemed even less like a Black Power freedom fighter when his father arrived – in a white Mercedes with walnut veneer – to take them home to Canons Park.

Anjali could not understand it. *Malcolm X* was just a mediocre film. All she could remember was a 360-degree pan round Malcolm X in his hotel bedroom. That was the only significant shot.

But there was a complication, it is true. Get her on ethnicity, and Anjali could be touchy. She might not admit it, but Anjali was touchy. For instance, the only thing Anjali liked about India was Bollywood. And Anjali's love of Bollywood had a very simple explanation. Bollywood was un-Indian.

Un-Indian? Bollywood un-Indian? Well yes, because, for Anjali, India was cows. India was scaffolding and mud. India was full of families. Whereas a sentimental and musical film was the opposite of a family. Bollywood was Hollywood.

Classified according to some as a Second-Generation Non-Resident Indian, and according to others, including Anjali, as a resident UK citizen, Anjali enjoyed the masala flicks. She read with amused interest an interview with Shyam Benegal, who told the devoted readers of *CinéBlitz* that the 'current interest in us is all down to the diaspora. Without them, no one would be paying any interest.'

I think Shyam's word 'diaspora' is a bit odd. A diaspora is a people driven from its homeland. And India may have been cows and mud but cows and mud do not drive you from your homeland. Shyam was being a bit melodramatic. By 'diaspora', he meant Indians living abroad.

Anjali also thought that this word 'diaspora' was odd. She was not a diasporee. Educated on scholarships at North London Collegiate School and then Brasenose College, Oxford, Anjali was just a success story. She had nothing to do with exile.

Bollywood films were the opposite of diaspora. That was their appeal for Anjali. They had nothing to do with a homeland either. They were all about style.

Perhaps you think that Bollywood films have no style. Perhaps you think they are kitsch. Well, style is arguable. The crucial thing is this. If Anjali ever liked something Indian, she liked it for un-Indian reasons.

8

Actually, Anjali is often confusing. That is one of the reasons I like her. She is unpredictable. For example, it is not just Anjali's ethnic identity that is confusing. Oh no. It is also her sexual identity.

On Old Bond Street, Nana was being a blurry reflection beside the reflected blur of Anjali. They were admiring some Tanner Krolle luggage in a window. The luggage was pink.

Anjali said to Moshe, 'Look Mosh, look, it's so pretty.' And Moshe made a noise, he made an agreeing noise. He was not thinking about fashion. He was thinking about kissing Nana. But his mouth felt wretched from a recent Starbucks skinny latte. This made him stop wanting to kiss her. So he swayed his hips against her instead, hugging her from behind and nuzzling on her shoulder.

He said to Anjali, 'Nos pretty as you.' Then he smirked.

To Anjali? He said that to Anjali? Yes, yes. He was jokily flirting.

And Anjali smiled back. She was flirting too.

9

Oh shopping. Oh fashion.

Some people adore fashion simply because it is so expensive. This is not a likeable position. Luckily, it is not a position anyone admits to. Other people adore the workmanship, the craft of fashion. I rather like these people. These people are similar to the people who look at clothes as artworks. For them, clothes are aesthetic. They are opportunities to exercise technique. I have to say, I am not sure I ever really believe these people. I worry that these people secretly just adore fashion because of the expensiveness. You can never quite be sure. But basically I like them.

Then there are the people who care about fashion in an

abstract, magazine kind of way because they want to be hip and I really do not get those people.

And then there are people who despise fashion. They despise it because it is far too expensive. Or because it is materialistic. Or because it is really just ugly, or impractical.

Me, my attitude is a technical interest and respect combined with an amazed sarcasm. That is the unimpeachable position.

Among the three of them, there were different attitudes to fashion. And you need to know this because, at this point in the story, Nana and Moshe and Anjali were window-shopping on Old Bond Street and along Savile Row. They did not quite know how they had ended up there, but that is where they were now. They were in the heart of London's fashion world.

Nana liked fashion in an amused way. She was one of the people who are interested in the technicalities. She liked the intricacies of stitching. She also liked the effort made by designers to cater for the tall thin girl. Unsurprisingly, she liked the gawkiness of models. And she liked new materials. She applauded the search for innovation. But Nana disliked the prices. She disliked the nastiness of fashion. Fashion, to her, meant exclusion. And Nana hated exclusion. The seriousness and anxiety of fashion made her bored – the quiet foreign minions, eyeing you up for appropriate savvy as you swished open the light glass doors.

Anjali did not like fashion at all. She was much more bored than Nana. She was even more astounded by the prices. The prices made it simply unrealistic. To Anjali, fashion was hype. She never really thought about it.

This brought her and Moshe together.

Moshe was the most passionate. He was passionately

against. To Moshe, fashion was so much schlock. It was just nervous people intent on reproduction. It encouraged cults of the unoriginal. Fashion was conformity. That was his theory about fashion.

But every theory belongs to a particular person. In relation to Moshe, the theory that fashion was vacuous conformity may have expressed an inner moral gravitas. It may have been a theory based on disapproval of excessive care for ephemera. On the other hand, it may have been insecurity. It may have been that, because Moshe did not feel beautiful or rich enough for these sumptuous and delicate clothes, he decided to deride them.

Whatever – like Anjali, Moshe disliked fashion. It annoyed him.

10

But he tried. Honestly, Moshe tried. In Prada, yawning, he picked up a trainer and tried to look. This trainer was a jigsaw of a plastic black slipper, spotlit by an invisible halogen strip. Nana came over to him. She came over to look after Moshe. She stood beside him and touched up something that was floating and minuscule on a metal clanky hanger. Moshe tried to copy her. He made an ostentatious noise. The noise unnerved him.

They giggled.

Then a man came up behind them. His muscles stretched the elastic of his black T-shirt. There were diagonal rips on the arms. These were presumably deliberate. He was either, thought Moshe, a shop assistant or a model. Moshe could not tell.

While Moshe was wondering what his status was in the world of style, this man told Nana how much the little white shorts with the sailorstripe drawstring would suit her. He said she was really superb. So so sexy.

He was a shop assistant. Moshe hated him.

Are you flattered by your lover being flattered? considered Moshe. He did not consider the question for long. This was partly because he was depressed and jealous. It was also because he needed a shit. His intestines were leery with Starbucks coffee, and it was making him fart – small, furtive. As he juggled improbable panties on their slippy hangers, farting was anguish for Moshe. Each time he farted he had to keep on moving. He had to distance himself from his smell.

Moshe was regretting that morning's coffee. His stomach had not been well for some time, but he had thought it would be better by now. But it did not seem to be better. It had been very distressed by the coffee.

Moshe felt unflattered here, no question. He hated fashion. He trundled himself, trying to soften his breathing, up the stairs. Are these clothes for boys or girls? thought suddenly androgynous hermaphrodite Moshe. The shops he understood had areas for girls and areas for boys. They had separate floors for boys and girls.

And then there was Nana, eyeing a pinstripe suit, with Anjali beside her.

He said, 'It's a boyzuit,' to Anjali and Nana together. Nana frowned. She said, 'Valways wanted a boy's suit.' She said it really to the suit, miniaturely tenting out the silkiness with bunched fingertips. She said to herself, 'Erreckon it'd make me look taller.' 'Oh, taller,' intoned Moshe. 'Because that's important, I mean you certainly could do with being taller.'

Nana smiled at Moshe. She loved it when Moshe teased her.

Nana looked at the boyish business suit, constructed for an elegant day in the city. Anjali tried. She said, 'It's cool, it's got a nintresting cut.' And she was right. Anjali could have been in fashion. The right pocket was placed just slightly higher than the left, a deliberate mishap in the symmetry. So it was cool. Because cool is knowing what to do with form. You don't repeat yourself. Then Nana pushed some more hangers apart, to look at a pink shirt made of sewn-together sections, some crazy version of quilting.

Moshe said, 'Shall we go?' It was a statement, really, not a question. Although I have printed this with a question mark, Moshe did not say it with a question mark. He said 'Shall we go.'

Moshe turned round quickly and bumped into a boy in a V-neck tank top. The tank top had two patterns – one on the front, one on the back. The back was horizontal blue and yellow stripes. The front was chevroned multicoloured lines. But there was one thing, thought gloomy Moshe, that this odd boy must have loved. There was a crazy quirk that must have been the clincher. The back pattern started on the front. It began on the front at the left-hand side.

I don't know. Personally, I like the idea of this jumper. I am a little hurt that Moshe did not like it.

II

Nana said, 'Did I take my pill this morning? I can't remember did I take my pill?'

'Yeah yes you took it,' said Moshe.

'Oh,' said Anjali. 'What kind are you on?'

'Microgynon,' said Nana.

'And you like it?' said Anjali.

'Well yeah,' said Nana.

'It's just,' said Anjali, 'just the Pill makes me so depressed.'

'You take the Pill?' said Moshe.

'Well I did,' said Anjali. 'But I got this thing, I was going out with this boy, you remember, Torquil, and he, he. It's like a coil, called Marina, it releases the Pill. Like hormones,' she said.

'Why do you still take the Pill?' said Moshe.

'It's not the Pill,' said Anjali.

'Well whatever,' said Moshe. 'You don't have boysex any more, do you? What kind of sex are you having?'

'Me?' said Anjali. 'What kind of sex? I have none sex. You know that. That's the kind of sex I have.'

'I just thought,' said Moshe.

'But why do you want to know?' said Anjali.

'Well I just thought. I mean, if you're doing boys again,' said Moshe.

'And isn't it uncomfy?' said Nana.

'No no,' said Anjali, 'it's fine, I just leave it for I think five years. You should have it,' said Anjali to Nana, as Moshe pushed the door at Issey Miyake and so Anjali had to pull.

Clumsy Moshe.

12

Inside Issey Miyake, Nana was especially happy. She felt as if she were on holiday, reported chatty Nana to Moshe and Anjali. This duo, however, was being amused and amazed at a suit made entirely of small metal discs. Did she say she was going with Papa? Did she say they had booked a holiday, for the first week in September? Moshe pushed his lips out and nodded. She had been chatting to the clothes, and when she didn't hear a word, not a murmur, she looked round. Moshe and Anjali were giggling. Moshe pushed his lips out and nodded. Nana nodded and carried on talking.

I am going to stop for a tiny tiny moment. I do not want Nana to be misunderstood.

Perhaps you are finding Nana unsympathetic here. She does not seem to be caring about Moshe's dislike of fashion. As you know, Moshe disliked fashion. He only saw mock objects, overpriced and impractical. And Nana knew that this upset him. She agreed with him in a way. But Nana also understood Moshe. She understood the secret unhappiness that caused Moshe's grumpiness. These clothes made Moshe feel ugly. And Nana wanted him to realise that, although it may have been mawkish to say it, he was beautiful. There was no need to be depressed.

Nana being happy and playful in Issey Miyake was meant as a gesture of love for Moshe. Perhaps it was gauche, but it was also sincere and kind. It was meant to convince Moshe that they could play together. He was totally beautiful. He was not too ugly at all. She knew that at the moment it did not look like a gesture of love. But she thought that Moshe would see it that way. In the end, he would see it like love.

In Issey Miyake there was a creased greywhite dress with goldleaf and silverleaf appliqué. This dress was only wearable once.

'I'd love to see that on you!' said polysexual Nana to Moshe. And she was being honest. She was not teasing him. She loved the idea of Moshe in a dress. It would be, according to Nana, the sexiest thing.

Unfortunately, Moshe did not think it would be the sexiest thing. He was thinking much more about toilets than transvestites. He needed a toilet a lot. And this was making him distracted.

Suddenly theological, Moshe was musing on the cardinal sin of pride. He mused on the difference between pride and vanity. He could see the point of monasteries. He imagined a Moshe tonsured and robed, weeding a kitchen garden. He would grow cabbages. He would grow carrots. He did not think Issey Miyake had branched out into root vegetables.

They wandered, a zigzag, Moshe steering them out.

13

Let me return briefly to Henderson and Stacey.

For Henderson, the most entrancing moment in their romance was a surprise visit to London Zoo, when Stacey saw a giraffe for the very first time. That was his joyful romantic memory. But Stacey, on the other hand, does not remember much of the London Zoo visit. This is because she got her period that day and was too embarrassed to tell Henderson, given the early stage of their relationship. Having had a previous boyfriend who was revolted by menstruation, she did not know how Henderson might take it. Instead, Stacey remembers much more clearly and fondly the first night she found a small pencilled note from Henderson, in very shaky handwriting, concealed under her duvet. The writing was shaky because Henderson had written it in pencil using the pillow as a support. The note explained how much he loved her.

Romances are complicated. They involve more than one person. This means that every detail can be ambiguous. And I quite like that idea.

For instance, Moshe's favourite moment was, obviously, not their trip to Savile Row. Moshe's favourite memory was not the shopping. It was a blow job. It was a blow job administered when his penis was tight inside a strawberry flavoured and tinted condom.

14

One morning, bleary Moshe ventured down under the duvet. Inside the duvet it smelled. It smelled of sleepy farting hot and coital bodies. Nana was snuffling. She was dreaming of technicolor animals. They felt rubbery – but they were furry – when they nuzzled her and loved her.

Dreaming was not Moshe's business. His treat was to wake her, slowly, so she was half dreaming but happy – as he, so slowly, moved her legs apart. He moved them apart just enough so he could reach with his short and fuzzy tongue. And then he only breathed so she wasn't unsettled or woken. He breathed and breathed on her and watched as she slowly stretched, sleepy, still. Then he ingratiated his tongue. He pushed it and let it gently slide. She almost tasted of sweat. He could smell his breath. He tried not to smell his breath. The light was damped down pinkish on the inside from new sun.

Moshe with two fingers opened out her labia. The wrinkles were spotted with an odd, a sticky, a white, a what was it, ricotta?

This was not a romance. It was not a romantic romance. I said that.

Moshe was not disgusted. It was just that he preferred not to carry on. He had lost his taste for it. Unfortunately, this was just when Nana woke up. She said, 'What you, wha sweetheart?' 'Your cunt's strange,' said Moshe. 'Something's odd with your cunt.' He was not always tactful, Moshe. Nana pushed a finger round her labia. She brought it back and examined it. She sniffed it. 'It's thrush,' she said, 'it's just thrush.' And then she was embarrassed. She didn't know why, but that's the way it was. She was embarrassed.

Nana did not need to be embarrassed. I do not think thrush is embarrassing. It is certainly not embarrassing for the girl. Almost all girls get vaginal yeast infections from time to time. Yeast germs often grow in the vagina without causing infection. An infection occurs when the yeast overgrows. This only happens when the normal health of the vagina is disrupted. And we all know how the health of a vagina gets disrupted. Boys disrupt it.

No, it was much more embarrassing for Moshe. How else would the health of Nana's vagina be disrupted, except by Moshe's penis? And he knew that. 'In women with recurrent vaginal thrush,' say the manuals, 'it is often worth their partner using some treatment at the same time as them, as the infection may affect him without symptoms,

89

and be causing reinfection.' This is a polite way of pointing out that it is normally the boy who is to blame.

But by that evening, Moshe was not feeling remorse. I am sorry, but he was not feeling apologetic. He was happy. That evening, Moshe was treated to an erotics of nostalgia. He was allowed to see the gorgeousness of women's diagrams. Inside the packet of Nana's Canesten Once pessary – 'inserted at night so the cream can work whilst ("whilst"! grinned Moshe, adoring the posh vocabulary) you sleep' – was a leaflet of instructions. And Nana let Moshe announce the procedure to her, spread with the plastic equipment on the bed.

It was a perfect diagram. Against a skyblue background, like a TV-studio diorama, reclined a cross-section view of a woman, her limbs outlined with muddy green. The diagram included the clump of her belly. And all the squashy curves and lines, with arrows pointing modestly but precisely to Bladder, Womb, Vagina, Rectum. It was not a body that had ever changed. It was all the information Moshe needed. And Moshe read his lines. 'Carefully put the applicator as deep as is comfortable into the vagina.' He delighted in the sedate parenthesis, secreting so much pleasure. '(This is easiest when lying on your back with your knees bent up.)' So Nana bent them, for her concerned gynaecologist. 'Holding the applicator in place, slowly press the plunger until it stops so that the pre-measured dose of cream is deposited into the vagina. Remove the applicator. Dispose of the applicator in a safe place, out of the reach of children.'

She pushed the applicator in, like a porn star. It shortened, then the cream popped. 'You may observe a chalky residue,' added Moshe, gravely. 'This does not mean the treatment has not worked.'

Why was this Moshe's favourite moment in the romance? It was his favourite moment because, however thrushed and inviolable, Nana wanted to enjoy herself. Self-conscious of her body and its ways, she had made her decision. She wanted to be the fantasy girl. Her fantasy was being a fantasy. All through the medical rigmarole she had been eyeing up the multipack of flavoured condoms she had bought that lunchtime at Boots with the Canesten. Condoms were her new idea of keeping herself occasionally more clean. And she was in her Topshop gingham, its flappy checks and pinkness. She kneeled over to Moshe sprawling. Then she dressed his cock. She made him taste of strawberry.

This was Nana the little girl. And Moshe was her lollipop.

It was a romance. OK, in a way it was a romance. Romance, after all, is in the editing.

15

I do not want you to assume that I disapprove of Moshe. Not at all. I am not judging him. There are very few boys, I am sure, who have not given their girlfriends thrush. There are very few boys who have not sexually transmitted at least one disease. It can happen to all of us. It happened, for example, to Chairman Mao.

Perhaps you are surprised at this. Perhaps you are thinking 'Chairman Mao? The great Communist leader and thinker? The author of the lyrical works *A Single Spark Can Start a Prairie Fire* and *Be Concerned with the Well-Being of the Masses, Pay Attention to Methods of Work*? No, not Chairman Mao.' But, honestly, it is true. I am not making this up. You can find evidence in the memoirs of Mao's personal physician, Dr Zhisui Li.

In this book, Dr Li explains Mao's sexual preference. It was for frequent sex with as many young girls as possible, without ever coming himself. Of course, this was not due to some crackpot neurosis. No, no. Mao's sexual preference derived from the noble teachings of Daoism.

'The Daoist prescription for longevity', writes Dr Li, 'requires men to supplement their declining *yang* – the male essence that is the source of strength, power, and longevity – with *yin shui* – the water of *yin*, or vaginal secretions – of young women. Because *yang* is considered essential to health and power, it cannot be dissipated. Thus, when engaged in coitus, the male rarely ejaculates, drawing strength instead from the secretions of his female partners. The more *yin shui* is absorbed, the more male essence is strengthened. Frequent coition is therefore necessary.'

This was no ordinary sex life. This was a considered sex life. But – such is fate – disease can strike even here, even where life is purest. One young woman contracted *Trichomonas vaginalis*. She very quickly passed it to Mao, who in turn passed it to his other partners.

Like thrush, *Trichomonas vaginalis* is very painful for girls, but the boys feel nothing. This makes it more difficult to persuade a boy to have treatment. Boys are, sadly, very proud. They will not admit to a disease they cannot feel. Since Mao was the carrier, the presidential epidemic could be stopped only if Mao himself were treated. But it is difficult to persuade someone without any symptoms that they are carrying a sexually transmitted disease.

'The Chairman', writes Dr Li, 'scoffed at my suggestion.

"It's not hurting me," he said, "so it doesn't matter. Why are you getting so excited about it?" I suggested that he should at least allow himself to be washed and cleaned. Mao still received only nightly rubdowns with hot towels. He never actually bathed. His genitals were never cleaned but Mao refused to bathe. "I wash myself inside the bodies of my women," he retorted.'

Perhaps Mao's comments seem haughty and defensive. They do seem kind of mad. But maybe there is a more human side to Chairman Mao. Maybe he was just embarrassed. Nothing he said could not be explained by a perfectly natural embarrassment. It is not easy, admitting to your doctor that you are the carrier of a sexually transmitted disease. Even Moshe found it difficult, and Moshe is a much less public person than Mao. Perhaps this anecdote just demonstrates the necessity for tact when discussing someone's sexual health. 'I was nauseated,' writes Dr Li. 'Mao's sexual indulgences, his Daoist delusions, his sullying of so many naive and innocent young women, were almost more than I could bear.'

Now, I agree with everything Dr Li is saying. I just think it is more complicated. I am going to quote Dr Li one last time. 'The young women were proud to be infected,' he says. 'The illness, transmitted by Mao, was a badge of honour, testimony to their close relations with the Chairman.'

You see? You wouldn't have expected that, would you? I do not think it has been understood precisely enough, sexually transmitted disease. It can be romantic, sometimes.

16

And Nana and Moshe were romantic. They were romantic in their way. They loved each other. They said they loved each other. It was true.

And this was their first 'I love you'.

'Did you want to say enthing in paticyular?' Nana teased. Moshe said, 'No.' They sat there. He said, 'I really like you, you know.' 'You really like me?' she said. 'Yeh I like you,' he said. 'Wha do you like?' asked Nana. 'I like evrething about you,' said Moshe. 'I love your pubic hair,' said Moshe. 'I love the colour of your pubic hair. I love your, I love your. I just love you,' said Moshe.

'I didn't mean to say that,' said Moshe.

Even their first 'I love you' was unromantic. It was a mistake. That's how mean I am.

'Of course,' said Nana. 'I mean I can't,' said Moshe. 'Uhhuh,' said Nana. 'I mean we've only known each other what, a month, a coupla months,' said Moshe. 'Uhhuh,' said Nana.

Actually no, it was quite romantic. I take my meanness back. It is quite possible, I think, to have known someone for no more than two days but still believe that you could love them. You feel that you love them already. It is just not sayable. You just cannot say that you love them. So saying it, against all social laws, was romantic. Moshe and Nana's 'I love you' was romantic.

'Do you think you could?' said Nana. 'What?' said Moshe. 'Love me,' said Nana. 'What already?' said Moshe. 'I don't know,' said Nana. 'Well I don't know,' said Moshe. 'Maybe.' 'Maybe,' said Nana. 'Well alright,' said Moshe. 'Alright what?' said Nana. 'Well I kind of think that I love you,' said

Moshe. 'I kind of think I love you.' Nana wondered at 'kind of'.

She said, 'You know I do think you're so pretty?'

Nana thought Moshe was pretty! What a love story this is!

She said, 'Yeh, oh. Yes. I love you too.' 'You love me,' he said. 'Yeh,' she said. 'You love me,' he said. She kissed him. He kissed her. 'So,' said Moshe. Moshe was grinning. 'You're in love with me.' 'No, I don't love you,' said Nana. 'You don't love me?' said Moshe. 'Yes I do,' said Nana. 'But I,' said Moshe. 'Fuck you,' said Nana.

But Nana was not nasty. She said 'Fuck you,' and then she kissed him.

5

Intrigue

I

ONE EVENING, MOSHE was astride Nana's stomach. His legs were bent back on either side of her ribby chest. And he was giggling to himself. He was telling himself that it was crucial to stay calm. He looked at his penis. His penis was red.

Nana was staring at his maroon penis. She was thinking that dying was ever so melancholy.

This is a short chapter, but a necessary one. I am afraid we need another peek into Nana and Moshe's sex life. And I know what you are thinking. You are thinking that you have had quite enough of their sex life. You want something else entirely. You want a description of a mining community in Sakhalin, Siberia. You want more shopping. Well, I'm sorry. Their sex life was important.

Nana and Moshe were home alone, in Edgware. Their original plan had been eating. But then eating had somehow got sidetracked. After discovering a bottle of Hill's absinthe in Papa's stash behind the saucepans, eating had become drinking.

Absinthe, however, is a technical form of drinking.

The happy couple opened out the pine kitchen drawers, looking for Nana's limegreen lighter. They found it among the utensils, trapped inside a whisk. Then Nana draped the flame round the rim of a stainless-steel salad spoon, cooking the absinthe. The absinthe matched the limegreen lighter. It fizzed. There was a blue and white bag of Tate & Lyle caster sugar beside them, with its sticky crumpled flap. It was the sugar that was fizzing.

They got as far as the living room.

Moshe leaned, sexysleepy, against a leg of the sofa. He was nestling and snuggling against the curvy end of the cushion with his curvy neck. He looked very domesticated, lying there on a background of William Morris white chrysanthemums. And Nana fed him sips of absinthe.

It was a lustful situation – being spoonfed sugar-crunchy mouthfuls of lukewarm absinthe by *the girl of Moshe's dreams.*

Nana said, 'You, you, staring, what are, ystaring.' And Moshe replied with something weird, not a word, just a sound like 'Uuohoohyr', and then smiled. It made her happy. She was happy that Moshe was happy. And because she was happy, as a treat, Nana took off her bra.

It was a treat, no doubt about it.

Her nipples were dimples, inside out. Moshe kneeled over, wobbling on his arms, and embellished one nipple, her left nipple, with his mouth. It coned out, roughened, redder, tough. It looked like a strawberry Jellytot. Whereas her areolae were pale like skin. They faded from round her nipples.

Moshe stared at her.

He asked if she liked him looking. And Nana's reply was a smile that exposed her upper gum. It was not a satisfactory reply, she could see that, she saw that, slowly. So she curled her arm round Moshe and made him kiss her. Her mouth, wet with absinthe, stung Moshe's mouth. And this was how they both constructed a sex scene. Carefully, they looked after each other. They carefully calmed each other. They concentrated.

They were trying to have a sex life. They really were. But there was a complication.

3

Naively, many people think that sex is simple. They think it is animal passion and feral cries. But there are lots of reasons why a sex life might be complicated.

There is something I have not told you. There was something Nana had not told Moshe.

Nana was not a girl who had ever adored sex. Well no, that is not quite accurate. She always enjoyed it in a way. She just never quite understood it. This might explain, or be explained by, another fact. Moshe did not need to be told about this fact.

Nana had never come.

She had come on her own, yes yes. Lying on her right-hand side, pressing her thighs together round her squashed and repetitive right hand, it was easy for Nana to come. But with anyone else, orgasms were a problem. They were non-existent.

There was no obvious reason why this might be. It was true that Nana was a late starter. Nana first had a boyfriend, a small Turkish boy called Can, when she was eighteen. The first time she masturbated was when she was fifteen. She did this thirty-four minutes after finding a copy of *Emmanuelle 2*, the novel, underneath Papa's bed. She stole it. Papa, of course, never mentioned this theft. You can't ask your daughter to give back your porn. And Nana, of course, never mentioned it. She wanted *Emmanuelle 2* all to herself. *Emmanuelle 2* turned Nana on. It formed her masturbatory position. Nana masturbated on her side because that way she could read the book easily, spread out beside her on the pillow.

This, of course, did not explain why Nana could not come with other people. It did not follow that, being a shy late starter, who needed novels to come, Nana would not be able to come in company. But there it was.

I think this might explain Nana and Moshe's sexual nervousness. I think this might explain why they were concentrating. In her twenty-three previous sexual encounters with Moshe, let alone in her previous sexual encounters with four different men, Nana had never come.

I suppose this might especially explain Moshe's nervousness. He used to think that he was quite a talented lover, Moshe.

He did not think, not now, that he was a talented lover.

4

Instead, drunk on absinthe, Moshe was dozy and anxious. He was dozily anxious.

Let me give you an example of this dozy anxiety.

As Nana and Moshe kissed, Moshe was remembering that he had not moved his hands. This might not seem so bad. But lovers, Moshe thought, were meant to move their hands. So Moshe looked down to see what his hands were up to. They were crushed beneath Nana's ribs. He dragged them out from under her and stroked her. But lifting off his hands made Moshe heavy on top of Nana, his right hip in her stomach. So Nana shifted herself, she wriggled a little.

This made Moshe stop stroking.

In his effort to believe that he was still a talented lover, Moshe was not being entirely successful. He was experiencing yet another extra problem. This was the problem of simultaneity. As he stroked Nana lovingly, Moshe was simultaneously listening to Nana's question – 'You know I do think you're so pretty?' It was a phrase he had often returned to. That 'do' worried him. The whole question worried him.

The reason Nana's question worried him was this. It implied that Moshe's prettiness was in doubt. Because, just to ask the question, Nana must have assumed he was insecure about his prettiness. And naturally this assumption made Moshe insecure about his prettiness.

Perhaps this reaction does not seem very natural. Moshe was being quite precious, I understand that. Nana's question would not have made me insecure. I would not have brooded on it while I kissed my topless girlfriend. But then, I am not Moshe. This is not my psychology.

He let his left hand drift down, past her breasts towards her skirt. Then he hooked the reinforced satin pad of her gusset round his third finger and pushed down his second finger, on to and into her cunt. This rearrangement of Nana's knickers was not innocently passionate either. There was a sad reason too. This is the chapter of sad reasons. Moshe was cunningly gauging whether Nana was wet. He was rearranging Nana's underwear so that he could see how desirable he was.

Unfortunately, Moshe was not desirable. Nana was dry. There was sweat but Nana was not on heat, oh no. And Moshe thought to himself that this was surely the cruellest game, deciphering enjoyment. It was cruel because there was Moshe's enjoyment to think of too, pleaded Moshe to himself.

While he guessed and second-guessed, Moshe had been comfortably uncomfortable, erect. He wondered if and when Nana would get totally naked. He was an expert on his drunk penis, Moshe. He knew its ins and outs.

5

But Nana was enjoying herself! She felt, it is true, kind of drugged and melancholy. The absinthe made her feel melancholy. But melancholy, for now, felt sexy. She imagined she was almost dying. And she enjoyed that. She liked her vision of dying.

Everyone would be sorry, so so so so sorry, at the funeral.

She knew that her vision was not perfect. If this were perfect, thought Nana the methodical fantasist, then Nana should be dressed in a silk white negligée with scalloped lace trim. She should not be seen naked for the shame of it. So the fantasy was not perfect. Topless was not perfect.

But the essential detail was that she must not exert herself. And so Nana was happily passive. She was there to be touched. Her pleasure was being still, succumbing to the man's dreadful enjoyment. It was a new amusement.

And this way Nana was happy not coming. Coming was no longer an objective that evening. And that was a relief.

However, in this bedroom farce, Nana never thought that Moshe did not know her fantasy. She just assumed that he did. She looked at Moshe, looking in her face, and he seemed worried. He obviously knew she was dying. But of course Moshe did not know that Nana was dying, in the nineteenth century, of TB. How could he? How could Moshe know that Nana was a devastated lover, eking out her last tubercular pleasures?

Because of Nana's illness she may be touched but never entered. So she decided to devise a new pleasure. In sympathy for Moshe's sympathy for her distress, our heroine was pitiful.

'Ahwonyu to come on my face,' she said.

This was yet another complication.

She was not even wet and now she was trying to end it all, thought Moshe. She wanted him to schpritz her and end the palaver. So Moshe had been right all along. This flustered him. This sad realisation flustered him.

He said, 'Really?' And Nana nodded – speechless, desperate, imploring. So Moshe moved up over her, his testicles dangling between her flattened breasts.

Moshe was astride Nana's stomach. His legs were bent back on either side of her ribby chest. And he was giggling to himself. He was telling himself that it was crucial to stay calm. He looked at his penis. His penis was red.

Nana was staring at his maroon penis. She was thinking that dying was ever so melancholy.

Then Moshe began to masturbate. And Nana stared. She stared at his penis. He looked at Nana and Nana looked at his colourful penis. His penis was going warmly soft. Yes, the absinthe was finishing him off. But he carried on. He tried to carry on.

Because if he came, then this would be successful. If he came, the twenty-fourth sex act of Nana and Moshe would finally be over.

6

I do feel sorry for Nana and Moshe. It is not easy, being happy with sex. A lot of people are unhappy with sex. Even the famous, even film stars find sex difficult. Greta Garbo found sex difficult.

'I can use only one word to describe my sexual attitudes: confusion,' said Greta.

I don't think I could ever live with either a man or a woman for a long time. Male and female are attractive to my mind, but when it comes to the sexual act I am afraid. In every situation I need a lot of stimulation before I am conquered by the forces of passion and lust. But confusion, before and after, is the dominant factor.

This was why sex made Greta confused. She was not quite sure what sex she wanted. She didn't know if she wanted a boy or a girl.

I dreamed many times about a mature man with experience who would have the vigour of a boy but an adult's polished methods. Strangely enough, I also dreamed about women of my mother's age who were ideal lovers. These dreams came superimposed on one another. Sometimes the masculine element was dominant, sometimes the feminine one. At other times I wasn't sure. I saw a female body with male organs or a male body with female ones. These pictures, blended together in my mind, occasionally brought pleasure but more often pain.

I'm not implying that anguished bisexuality was the cause of Nana's sexual problem. No. I'm not saying that Nana was Greta Garbo. I'm not interested in Greta's reason itself. I'm interested in the fact that Greta thought there was a reason at all. I can see that it might be a relief, to imagine that there is a reason why you don't like sex. I can see that the last thing you want to seem is abnormal. And reasons make you normal. But I think that it's very possible there was no reason at all. I think that is normal too.

7

This chapter is in two halves. They are not equal halves. The first half was unhappy. It described an awkward complication. Whereas the second half is much shorter and is happier. It is a pastoral scene. It is a contemplation of the animal kingdom.

Nana and Papa were at the zoo.

Something squealed or bleated. It squealbleated. And it might have been, thought Papa, delighted, the mangy padding lion by its water trough and lettuce shreds, in front of him, or might have been, more plausibly, some other beast entirely.

Papa was not a man with a detailed knowledge of the animal kingdom.

Something, no something had definitely just been sick, he thought. He was looking at a panther, sceptically. And trying to decide if it was lavender or maybe heliotrope or purple or maroon or damson or even chocolate. Or even tobacco, he thought.

While Nana was a girl who adored the animal world. She loved the calmness of animals. She loved their sureness. They could only be good.

'Oh a monkey!' giggled Nana. 'A monkey!' 'It's stroking, it's stroking itself,' said Papa. Nana said, 'Do you know what I think I love about animals? It's that they're mute.' 'Uhhuh,' said Papa. Nana said, 'Do you think if animals had more nutritious foodstuffs they'd be happier? They'd have more time to play and think.

'Sorry,' said Nana. 'Sorry. I can see that's silly.'

They mooched round the zoo. They mooched and looked at the polar bears and penguins and Nana developed a fondness for pistachio ice cream. They bought Papa a pistachio ice cream.

Nana told Papa about her new amusing discovery called Elsa Schiaparelli.

You don't know about Elsa Schiaparelli. No one knows about Elsa Schiaparelli except Nana. Nana was that sort of girl.

Elsa Schiaparelli, said Nana, was a surrealist fashion

designer who despised the bourgeoisie's taste for ornament. She despised this taste so much that she made a black
jumper with a white scarf tied in a bow. The scarf was
knitted into the jumper. It was a fake scarf. And this was
symbolic. It was symbolic of bourgeois inauthenticity. And
Nana said, 'I really don't understand that sort of thing. It's
so. It's so.' Then her phone rang.

It was Moshe. Nana mouthed to Papa that it was Moshe.
Papa smiled.

This was the smiley scene. The motif for the scene was
the smile. Because this, thought Nana, was a conspiracy.

She said, 'Hi hi hi.'

An elephant bleated or squealed.

Nana said, 'Mat the zoo.' She said, 'I was. I said.' She
said, 'I was in college.' She said, 'No one.' She said, 'Till
now!' She said, 'Moshe! Moshe!' She said, 'What you doing
now?' She said, 'Uhhuh. Uhhuh.' She said, 'No I'm at the.'
She smiled. She said, 'Yeah I'm. Yeah call me.'

Meanwhile, Nana had hooked her handbag on to her
right wrist and rummaged and extricated her lip gloss,
which she unscrewed slowly, with her left-hand fingertips
slowly, and dabbed it on. Then she repeated the operation
in reverse.

She said, 'Okay.' She looked at Papa. She put her phone
back in her bag.

'That was Moshe,' said Nana. 'I know,' said Papa. Then
they smiled.

6

They fall in love

THEN THIS HAPPENED. They were in the Clinic on Gerrard Street, at the centre of Chinatown. It was Moshe and Nana and Anjali. But Moshe had moseyed off downstairs to the bar. So Nana was left with Anjali. For minutes neither looked at the other. They just dreamily swayed, they sashayed. And downstairs, a girl pushed Moshe aside. This was because he was blocking her view to a screen. The screen was showing an advert. She explained that she thought she was in that advert. Apologetic Moshe moved away.

Meanwhile, on the dance floor up above, Anjali moved closer in to Nana. 'Iz he okay? He's not sad?' she asked. She had to stretch her mouth up, breathily close to the arranged curls of Nana's left ear, its reddish clearer tip. Nana said, 'Wha?' So Anjali repeated herself and repeated her gentle gesture. And Nana said, 'Oh yeah. He's fine. He's got a tummy upset.' Anjali said, 'He's what?' Then

Nana said, 'He's got a tummy upset. He mustv gone to the loos.'

Anjali, reassured, nodded.

But Moshe was not in the loos. During this little exchange, he had prowled back upstairs. He was wandering round the dark loud crowd, pretending he was looking for someone. He was not, obviously, looking for someone. He was observing his two best friends. But it was difficult seeming casual. Accidental collisions occurred with strangers, who turned on him as Moshe crumpled and said sorry. It was like a ballet. Moshe was like a solo ballerina. He opened his big eyes wide and motioned, very apologetically, with his arms.

Ballet did not come naturally to Moshe. He decided to go back to the bar.

But before he had got down the narrow wet stairs, with the slippy steel ridges at each edge, a couple of girls who were prettier and ever so much younger than Moshe came triphopping up without seeing our hero. So he had to climb backwards, backwards was easier, squeezing himself next to the toilets. Anxious for solitude, air, just anything other than this, he wandered out on to the balcony. The balcony was a collection of black wrought-iron curlicues and florets. The floor was millioned with thin diamonds. There was some trio sharing a joint – two girls and a boy, a sarcastic cupid and his angelic hosts.

Moshe went back downstairs, down past the bar, out past the bouncers, then swivelled round into the Chinese restaurant beneath the Clinic.

2

At this point in the story it is important to be clear about Anjali's sexuality. There might be some confusion concerning Anjali's sexuality. She had been fitted at the Marie Stopes Clinic with a trendy version of the coil called Marina. She had at least one ex-boyfriend. This normally implies heterosexual orientation. She also had an ex-girlfriend. This normally implies homosexual orientation.

Well, Anjali was variable. She was an equable girl. Anjali could be interested in anyone. But basically, she was more gay than straight.

There, I've said it.

3

Back upstairs in the Clinic, while Moshe ordered Chinese, Nana and Anjali were dancing. Without anyone else to dance with, they were dancing as a couple. And it was fun being a pretend couple. It was being particularly fun, at this moment, for Nana. Nana was holding Anjali, lightly, her hand enjoying Anjali's strangeness. Anjali was *totally beautiful*, thought Nana. She had style. This was a whole new style.

But while Nana was musing on style, more pragmatic concerns were occupying Anjali. Anjali needed to piss. She shouted, 'Come to the loos with me? We could look for Moshe.' And Nana said yes. But Moshe was not there. And there was only one loo free. So pragmatic Anjali held Nana by the hand and took her in. As Anjali sat down backwards she pushed her knickers with her trousers and indifferent bored lascivious Nana saw a tuft, a stain of darker pubic hair. Anjali sat forward, grinning. Nana leaned her shoulder on the wall. The bass vibrations made her skin fuzz. She tried to pretend that she couldn't hear Anjali, sibilant, pissing. How it fanned out and then trickled. She looked at Anjali and Anjali was smiling at a vanishing point beyond the multicolour graffiti. Then Anjali stood up, holding in her stomach as she zipped up her trousers. She took Nana by the hand and pulled her out the loos. A girl with a wonky bulging nose and a pierced left eyebrow, a silver hoop through its corner, raised the other eyebrow, happily.

Concurrently Moshe, unloved and unlovable, was moving his mouth to the chopsticks and the chopsticks to his mouth, slurping a chilli beef chow mein. He shook out drops of extra-dark soy sauce from the bottle's red plastic cap. It was not a perfect night. There was an electric technicolor picture of a Chinese seascape in front of him, whose waves seemed to be moving for ever. He tried not to think. He read the menu's little blurb, sardonic, unamused – 'We trust you will enjoy them as much as we Did in collecting, testing and choosing the Best for you.' He didn't quite know why he was really down here, in a Chinese at one in the morning. He wasn't even hungry.

Moshe decided to go back in. But on the door the bouncers were amazed. No one who left got back in for free. You had to pay again. You had to pay extra now it was past eleven. So Moshe walked away, distressed, suddenly imagining ludicrous scenes of untold intimacy between his friends, the tenderness of each tendresse. He shuffled back over. He gave the bouncers their fifteen exorbitant quid. Then Moshe loped upstairs.

It turned out that his visions were not so ludicrous.

In the bar, Nana and Anjali were talking to a girl. Now, when I say girl I mean girl. She was, thought Moshe, seventeen at most. It was just that she had managed to look like she was a kiddy thirty-five. Her name was Verity. Verity was dressed in a pornographic combo of shirt and skew-whiff tie that was only, she said to bemused Moshe, a jumper. It was one of Bella Freud's tie jumpers. It was the whole *trompe l'œil* thing.

Verity was in fashion.

She explained to Moshe that her jumper was all very this season, what with Clements Ribeiro for Cacharel as well. Clements was doing these T-shirts pinned with costume jewellery and blouses with strings of pearls, trousers with chain belts, that kind of thing. It was a sort of homage to Chanel, she said. Nana said, 'Like, like Elsa Schiaparelli,' and Verity smiled happily.

I do like Nana. You know what she thought of Elsa Schiaparelli. But here she was, being polite. She was kind to this lonely girl.

Nana said, 'Thass cool.'

But Moshe did not think that this was cool. And I know what you are thinking. You are thinking he was jealous. And you are right. But Moshe was not only jealous. He was also sad. Moshe had a thing about girls like Verity. To understand this, you need to understand where Moshe came from.

Moshe had grown up on Ribblesdale Avenue in Friern Barnet. Many of you will not have heard of Friern Barnet. It is a hinterland, a suburb, an area of north North London. It is unusual because it is an in-between place. Sometimes, Moshe described Friern Barnet as Hampstead. This was a lie. At other times, he described it as Highgate. It is not Highgate either. Friern Barnet is Whetstone, Southgate, Palmers Green. These are less celebrated areas of London, but they are the ones that surround Friern Barnet. The enigma I am trying to identify is this. Friern Barnet was not quite rich, it was not quite dazzling, but it was in the area of richness.

Moshe had seen posh girls. He had seen them on buses. He had seen them on the 43, going into town from Highgate and Muswell Hill. He knew them. And these young posh girls made Moshe feel an unexpected emotion. Moshe romanticised girls like Verity. They made him sad. They were so young and yet so grown up. He saw in them a tragic ruined innocence.

'You know a disturbing thing,' mused Nana to Verity. 'All my style icons are men.' Then she asked Moshe where he had got to. He said he was going to buy champagne. Anjali started laughing because Moshe was really too. Just. So sweet. He said, 'Ohs just wandering round. I'm getting champagne for us.'

At the bar, with all the anxious boys and girls, clutching their twenty-pound notes rolled up in miniature batons, Moshe felt lonely. The bar was too small for everyone. Even Moshe felt hemmed in, and Moshe was not huge. It was *chaos*. But Moshe persisted, because he was lonely and melancholy, and a lonesome and melancholy Moshe was unfortunately prone to theatrical gestures. The cheapest champagne cost sixty-five pounds. He paid it. Of course he paid it. He took a glass for Verity.

In an appropriated nook by a bay window, with red leather sticky seats, she was telling Anjali, and Anjali's gorgeous friend, the sad story of her life.

'My mum died', she said, 'two yearz ago and that was just really unsettling. Bis been really really good since I started this, this therpy, I've been doing it a couple years now and I just feel this calmness?'

It was all too true. Verity was a tragedy. Moshe was right.

4

Then, however, Moshe's evening got worse.

Verity said, 'Oh look I've, I've got a spare pill. We could all. Dyou wan some?' She said, 'I've got a couple spare. You can have them for a fiver each.' And Moshe said, 'Oh no no no no no, we no no. Very bad for depression, that cauzes depression.' Verity looked at him. 'They've done studies,' he said.

Moshe suddenly regretted feeling kindly thoughts about Verity.

Nana said, 'Wha yeah.' She said to Anjali, 'Why don we just take a half?' Then she turned to Verity. 'Are you sure?' she said. 'Can you really?' she said. 'Yeah,' said Verity. 'I'd love you to.' Nana unwrapped the clingfilm and put it on the table then snapped the pill carefully, cleanly, and dabbed a half on Anjali's tongue so Anjali grinned while Nana tapped the other half inside her smiley mouth.

Sex and drugs and rock and roll was never Moshe's career choice.

He said, 'Dyou wan water? I'll get you water. You need water.' He told the dangerous girls all about the machinations of immoral nightclub owners, who turn off the water supply in clubs and sell overpriced miniature bottles of Evian. This was a *matter of life and death*. The dangerous

115

girls smiled at him. He said, 'Look you musn't drink alchol. Leave it um getting you water.'

He got them water. They drank the alcohol.

They sat there by the window. Nana was next to Anjali, who was next to Verity. Moshe was on the end. He was squashing one tense buttock on to the edge of the seat, trying not to touch Verity. He did not want to seem seedy.

In Moshe's opinion, the world had become far too touchyfeely. And once again, Moshe was right.

Nana and Anjali were melting, they were softening, into a girly couple. Nana's head was angling on to Anjali's face. And Nana was feeling small and warm and drugged. The world was the safest place.

Anjali was the prettiest, thought ecstatic Nana, because she was holding her. Anjali was stroking her bare stiff stomach. This movement made Nana shivery. All her feelings were soft. Anjali was making her soft. So everything was natural when she nuzzled and nibbled and kissed, and Moshe was there, he was watching, content, he was chatting about Friern Barnet. So Nana and her best friend Anjali could kiss, they just kissed. Because kissing was softest.

5

Has Nana just become a lesbian?

Of course not.

It was just a kiss. One girlongirl kiss does not make a girl a lesbian. There were reasons for Nana kissing Anjali, but they were not lesbian reasons.

The main explanation was this. As I have said before, Nana was not a girl for whom sex came easily.

But why should that make a girl a lesbian?

Hush hush. She was not a lesbian. But because Nana did not have a particular sexual obsession, she was always interested in other people's sexual obsessions. She was always interested in the way other people had sex. She wondered what it might feel like.

Nana was not hoping, really, for a new frisson when she kissed Anjali. No. She was curious. It was an unsexual interest in sex. You see, I am aware that at this point Nana might seem a little self-engrossed. And that would really be very unfair. The conclusion that Nana was selfish would be the conclusion of a sexual being. And a lot of my readers are sexual beings, I understand that. But Nana was not a sexual being. She was innocent.

That was the important reason.

There were also two extra reasons why Nana was feeling morally unworried. She was happy on Ecstasy. This limited her sense of naughtiness. The other explanation was this. Moshe was there, he was sitting beside them and chatting away. So Moshe was happy too. If Moshe had not been happy, none of this could have happened. Because then it would have been unfaithfulness. But it could not be unfaithfulness if he was watching.

So Nana kissed Anjali. Anjali was soft. It was softer than kissing Moshe.

But what was Anjali thinking? Was Anjali not thinking malicious and triumphant thoughts?

Of course not.

So Anjali was innocent too? Well kind of. Anjali was not innocent in the way that Nana was innocent. Anjali was ordinarily sexual. But Anjali was also thinking things through. She was not being selfish either. She was thinking about Nana and Moshe. She was happy on Ecstasy. She was thinking, if she was thinking at all, that this kiss showed how much Nana and Moshe loved each other. They were the most loving couple. They were not a couple wracked by jealousy.

For instance, to reassure you, compare Anjali with me. One of my bad traits is this. I can be very selfish. I know this might seem unbelievable, but it is true. This means that, a lot of the time, I want things just because other people want them. I am often a little worried that I might be missing out.

But Anjali was not thinking in this selfish way. It is a way that I could obviously understand, but it was not how Anjali was thinking. She was not motivated by acquisitive envy. She was just feeling happy. She was happy that her friends were happy. She was pleased they were in love. And it was true. Everything Nana and Moshe did was a loving gesture.

For example, just when Moshe was beginning to look a little glum and restless, Nana squeezed past Anjali. She kissed Moshe. She kissed him apologetically, kindly. It was more fun kissing Moshe. Then she stopped kissing him and looked into his big brown labrador eyes.

6

I am going to make this absolutely clear.

Anjali and Nana have kissed, but they have not done anything else that is sexual. But they will have sex in the end. I promise you that they will. And when they do, I will tell you! You are just going to have to wait. In the meantime, you can assume that they are getting more and more intimate. All three of them are becoming inseparable.

You will probably want to know the specific living arrangements of Nana and Moshe and Anjali. The living arrangements might start to seem important. So I will tell you now.

The three of them are not living together. I will tell you when they do.

7

To start with, let us look at Moshe's angle. I am going to investigate Moshe for a moment. The next part of this story, and it is an important part, was not an event. It was a series of micro-events. Often, the micro-event was not even a micro-event. It was just a feeling. The next part of this story is just smallness.

Moshe would wake up from his personal brand of tiring sleep and lie there. And while he lay there, he used to chat to himself about politics, sex, philosophy, art. Mostly sex. He abandoned his mind to each one of its libertine urges. He let it sniff at the first stupid or brilliant idea that came up, just as delinquent kids on the Cally Road dog some girl with laceless Nike trainers and dead eyes, a retroussé nose.

Had anyone behaved badly? Not at all. It was not infidelity, reasoned Moshe. And if it was not infidelity, then Moshe was not jealous. After all, he had been there when they kissed each other. If anything, it was sexy. He had to admit, he quite liked it. It was every boyfriend's dream.

He was an ethical thinker, Moshe.

But what was causing these philosophical thoughts? Why was a boy from Friern Barnet, whose adoring mother was called Gloria, pondering on the nature of goodness?

Sometimes Nana and Moshe and Anjali sat on the futon together under a duvet, with Anjali in the middle, watching videos and eating pizza delivered by the Go-Go Pizza Company. The Go-Go Pizza Company did a deal of a 14-inch Supreme pizza of your choice with two portions of garlic bread and a tub of Häagen-Dazs ice cream, all for £9.99 if ordered before 5.30. Five o'clock was, they all conceded, sometimes too early for pizza.

Or Anjali would come home with them after they had gone to the now discontinued Dub Club in Finsbury Park and stay the night because Nana and Moshe did not want her to schlep back to Kentish Town. And occasionally Anjali would wander back from her position on the futon into Nana and Moshe's room, after they had said good-night, and carry on chatting. She curled up on the bed while Moshe worried that – hunched like this under the duvet – his breasts looked like breasts.

These were not really events, you see. They were not really remarkable. But they were why Moshe had turned philosophical.

About a month later, after an all-day visit to the Embassy Bar on the Essex Road, they were standing at a bus stop. Nana was keeping her hands warm in Moshe's trouser pockets. And when Anjali coyly objected to this naked fondling, Nana responded by pushing Anjali's hand into Moshe's pocket. Anjali naughtily located his penis. She held it, slightly too tightly, thought excited and burgeoning Moshe.

Then the bus came.

There were minor moments of momentary kissing. Occasionally, Anjali and Nana kissed. But Moshe was always kissed too. It always became mutual kissing.

Anjali and Nana were not – let me repeat – a couple.

Moshe, poor thing, was happy.

8

Because he was happy, Moshe had taken to listing the various habits of Nana and Moshe. If he woke up on his own he remembered her wake-up games. He remembered how Nana snuggled and wouldn't talk. Nana would only mime hello, waving her hand, with her lips shut.

Her showers followed a precise routine: allover rinsing, hair shampooed twice, conditioned once, allover body soaping, a slight crouch to rub her crotch, pushing the foam in ovals round her breasts, stretching away and down to clean between her buttocks, then another rinse, then exfoliation with skyblue Body Shop wiry mittens, then allover rinse of the hair and body. She kept a Toulouse-Lautrec postcard by her bed because it looked like her and Moshe, two tucked up ten-year-olds. She used to scrunch up her eyes and he'd worry and pester her to wear her glasses and she'd say that she was fine. If she was sad she'd mooch and wear the Russian shapka that she discovered left behind in the cloakroom at Freedom on Wardour Street.

Sometimes Moshe wished he was a virgin, he felt so burdened with accumulated facts. But no, he had to admit it – virgins had facts too. He wished he was a baby. He wished he was a speechless baby.

Moshe listed his favourite fantasies. He lay there and wondered if a fantasy was a habit. Then he wondered why it mattered, decided that it didn't. He only ever imagined

Nana and Moshe in sunlight, in rooms with crumply beds and softest sunlight dimpled with reflections, on impossible holidays, drinking Voss water culled from an artesian well in bottles designed by Neil Kraft.

He tried to imagine himself without her and didn't want to.

He remembered going down on her with Duke Ellington bobbing in the other room. It was a syncopated sex scene. A big-band sex scene.

They talked together about sex. They worried about sex. They worried every evening about sex. Moshe told her just to think about what she found sexy. That was his exasperated advice. He said, 'What do you think about when you wank? Whaddayawankabout?' Nana looked sheepish. She couldn't say. She said, 'You.'

Sadly, this was true.

Whereas Moshe's fantasies came quickly. He had to slow them down. There was Nana in her schoolgirl pose, telling him, in gingham, all about her antics at gymkhanas. She described the feel of the pommel. She mentioned the word 'stirrups'. And Moshe imagined saying, 'Use me like a horse.' Or he would ponder on making her pregnant. It made him come more quickly. Often he had to make his dreams about Nana more abstract. He shied away from detail. Too much detail made him too excitable. Though there was the recurring vision of Nana in a bath, tightfitting her body, and in the clear water goldfish dotted round, swimming over her skin. And Nana would sprinkle fish food in her soft pubic hair, and let them gulp while Moshe studied her, his chin on the bath's cold rim.

If Nana had got up early to go to lectures, and Moshe was left alone, he would find the copy of a Louise Bagshawe novel that Anjali had got free with *Company* and left behind in his flat. Moshe would locate the sex scenes. The book began to fall open at the sex scenes. He would pad across to the toilet to get the toilet roll. Then, having arranged the four pillows in suitably supportive positions on the bed, he would recline and masturbate. His favourite passage was a description of a girl, who wanted to make it in the music business, being fucked quickly against a rough brick wall. The description was brief but evocative. He liked Louise Bagshawe's style. Moshe would come and then let the semen cool on his stomach until it ran thinly and unpleasantly down his sides. And Moshe would forget to put away the loo roll. When Nana came home she teased him.

Often people seem to be shocked by the idea of a boy masturbating, if he is in a relationship. But it is true. Masturbation is all too common. Moshe was a flagrant example. It was not that you would always find him backed against the headboard. But occasionally that was his pose.

Moshe remembered how Nana stood over the loo, a boyish girl, and trimmed her pubic hair with her curved cuticle scissors from a Boots manicure set that Papa had bought for her one Christmas. Or how he would wear her knickers all day, enjoying the tight light lace.

Moshe had once made up a fantasy of Nana licking Anjali from behind but now that felt weird. It felt a little loaded.

He listed her favourite foods. She loved purple sprouting broccoli. She loved pink sashimi salmon, which she ate jerkily, her head bobbing at the chopsticks. He marvelled at her calm in restaurants. Her calm was sexy. It had glamour. She called him from The Ivy, nonchalant, unfussed, because Papa had cancelled so maybe Moshe?

And Moshe, who possessed no ironing board, could then be found crawling on the tiled bathroom floor, ironing his only shirt, swearing, and jabbing, and swearing at the indents of the grouting.

He adored her. He adored everything about her. He even loved their weekends at Papa's house.

He would sit in the conservatory and pick up an old copy of, oh maybe *Risk Professional*. There was a pile of magazines in a magazine rack. The rack was twists and curls of glazed mahogany. It was like a pretzel. Moshe ruffled *Risk Professional*. He opened it at a two-page advert for Zurich Financial Services. 'Building relationships, solution by solution.' That was the motto of Zurich Financial Services. Then there was a quote in italics from William Hazlitt. 'You know more of a road by having travelled it than by all the conjectures and descriptions in the world.' Underneath the quote, there was a small photo of distressed-leather suitcases. The opposite page was a glossy of a dusty track. It was sunset. The light had gone misty with the melancholy of passing time. 'Drawing on years of experience to help you cover new ground.' That was the businesslike caption.

It was the last utopia on earth, thought Moshe, happy, looking round him at the photos on the upright piano – a smudged view of Lake Leman, Nana intent on a butterfly.

Moshe read a mauve leaflet enclosed in *Risk Professional*, advertising a Breakfast Briefing at the British Bankers Association. *Extremists – working towards a safer environment.*

> With the advent of globalisation, grows the voice of anti-capitalism, and it is becoming more sophisticated.

Dealing with terrorists and extremist mentality takes strategic planning, forethought and the complete implementation of a culture against this type of attack. Without preparation of this type, counter measures are hard to execute with any degree of success.

Moshe adored all this. He adored her.

He wondered what it felt like loving him. It was unimaginable.

He would lie there. He thought about threesomes. But there were no threesomes. He could not really think of any famous threesomes. They were oddly unusual. He thought about *Jules et Jim*. This thought did not last long because Moshe had never seen *Jules et Jim*.

9

But let us think about *Jules et Jim*. It is a film by François Truffaut. Of all the characters in this novel, apart from me, and I am not a character, only Papa has seen this film. The origin of François Truffaut's film *Jules et Jim* was Henri-Pierre Roché's novel *Jules et Jim*. Papa, an admirer of the film, somehow acquired a translation of this novel – 'The Classic French Love Story' – free with the compliments of *Options* magazine and Pavanne, in September 1983.

François Truffaut said that when he read this novel, he realised he had chanced on something new for the cinema. He had found a plot that was radically different from any other plot in a film. Up till then, a film's plot had good characters, whom the audience loved, and bad characters, whom the audience disliked. Everything was unambiguous.

Whereas in this special case, in *Jules et Jim*, the audience would be unable to choose between the main characters, because the audience is forced to love all of them equally. All three central characters are a little bit good and a little bit bad. It was that element, which he called 'anti-selectivity', said Truffaut, that struck him most forcibly in the plot of *Jules et Jim*.

Now, I am not sure that this actually happens in the film *Jules et Jim*. Personally, I never much liked the Jeanne Moreau character. I thought she seemed completely selfish and unattractive. But I like the point that François is making. I like the ideal.

Moshe dozed off. He listened to the city being busy. He gave Finsbury his blessing. Moshe blessed all the schnorrers.

The friendship of Jules and Jim had no equivalent in love. They accepted their differences. Everyone called them Don Quixote and Sancho Panza.

Everything was ambiguous.

10

But what was Nana thinking? Was Nana happy too? Was this truly domestic bliss?

Look. Nothing has happened yet. The two girls kissed each other, sometimes, but nothing else.

Of course this was domestic bliss.

One evening, in bed with Moshe, on their own in Edgware, Nana was looking at the three Miffy postcards whose hanging had been curated by ten-year-old Nana, above her Ikea pine desk.

These were:

Miffy looking at an artist's impression of a Mondrian.
Miffy looking in from a snowy window.
Miffy perched on the yellow crescent moon with yellow stars arranged around her in the dark blue sky.

And above the postcards there was Nana's Babar poster – in his green suit and jaunty trunk, in whose nip a bowler hat fitted snugly.

That was the decor.

She was thinking that this was domestic bliss. And it was domestic bliss. Nana was happy. She was particularly happy tonight because her name, just for now, was Bruno. Yes, Bruno. And what did Moshe think about this? No no, not Moshe. Moshe also had a new name in bed. Newly christened by Nana, Moshe's sex name was Teddy.

Alright?

Nana – Bruno. Moshe – Teddy.

Nana was happy. The girl scared by sex was confronting her fears. She had made up a scenario on her own. She was embarking on a life of perversion.

This was perversion?

Actually, I reckon it was perversion. There is something undeniably dirty about a twenty-five-year-old girl, in her childhood bedroom, being a ten-year-old boy. But it might be too dirty. Perhaps you need to keep sex in the realms of realism. If it is ridiculous, it becomes unsexual. It becomes bemusing.

Moshe was especially bemused. When Bruno told Teddy how much she loved Teddy's babyish arms, their talcum-powdered smoothness, prosaic unimaginative Teddy replied that they were soft because he washed in the bath with E45. He had eczema. Soap was bad for eczema.

Moshe was not brilliant at this fantasy. He was not sure what he was meant to say.

Moshe and Bruno and Teddy and Nana listened to the rain.

'I love lisning to the rain when I'm here in bed with you,' said Bruno, wriggling, being Teddy's best and closest friend. Bruno snuggled up, in her pyjama suit, cotton, with thin candystripes, flary at the ends. 'You're such a dorable creech,' she said.

This was a fantasy. So I should explain the details of the fantasy. Teddy and Bruno are prep-school boys. But they are not at the same school. They develop their education at separate schools. But in the holidays they can chat again. They chat and while they chat they pretend that they have never lived apart, or known about any other boys. No, whatever may have happened at school, it was always the holidays they looked forward to. They are loving kids. Brought up in mutual luxury, Teddy and Bruno are best friends. They are *soulmates*. That was the fantasy. That was the backstory.

Teddy read *The Little Prince* to Bruno. And because, insisted Nana, they were very naughty, they read in the dark with a torch, tented in the duvet. Did this qualify as *infantilism*? wondered Moshe. If it did, he was unfussed. He just liked Nana being happy. He liked Nana being sexual.

Well, Moshe at least presumed that this would end up sexual.

So Teddy talked to Bruno. He told Bruno how he was finding sleep difficult. Matron was worried about him. He lay down and he could hear his heart in his head. He said there was also the asthma. He couldn't breathe and it was asthma. Teddy confided in Bruno that every time when he was trying to make himself sleep, all he could imagine was that he was playing cricket. It sounded silly but it was true. He was batting. It was the same feeling as batting. It felt like he was standing there at the crease, hitting his bat in the mark, over and over, like they all do on TV. And his heart was all loud. Then Moshe went quiet. And Bruno piped up, 'That's an anxiety dream.'

He was a precocious kid, Bruno. He might have been seven but he had dipped into Freud.

They lay there in the bedroom with its chest full of toys. Inside the chest was a floppy busby, with fake plastic hairs, that Nana had received for being a brave soldier when she had her stitches in her forehead. All of Nana's music certificates from the Associated Board – her piano and flute, grades one to eight – were framed on the wall. Some of the frames had plastic giltpainted moulded curls at the edges. Some of them were clipframes.

And, 'Dyou remember', said Teddy, 'the way you used to fall off the side of the sofa, backwards onto the cushions, and you sort of felt your stomach disappear?'

Nana looked over Moshe's shoulders with their few thin hairs. His breasts were curved and squashed together, ovals. She said, 'Are you okay?' And Teddy, wailing an interior opera of love and lust and overpowering sex, whispered to Nana, 'Yehm fine.' He slumped on to his back, then slumped his head over towards her. His chins creased together. Then he kissed her. She kissed him. Nana said, 'Cool. If you say's cool then it's cool.'

If you had been down there on the street, beside a sleeping policeman, in the sodium fuzzy light, then nothing would have been obvious. You would not have got, say, a snapshot of Nana in her unbuttoned pyjama top, with just the merest slope of her left breast visible. No. You would have seen a bedroom. You would have seen lamplight. You would have seen a haven.

It was domestic bliss.

How, thought Moshe, how can you shift this from fondness to filth?

It was tricky. Neither of them were boys. Neither of them were gay. So filth, in the circumstances, was difficult. They had not had the practice at youthful gay sex.

He said, 'Should I touch you?' Because Teddy and Bruno, after all, were homosexual. He said, 'Do you want me to touch you?' And Moshe put his hand where Bruno's minute penis was. Nana held his hand. She held it there. She said, 'Oh no.'

When a prep-school boy says no, he means yes.

II

I can imagine that at this point you may be feeling a little confused. You may have a list of questions. Why are they not complaining? Why are they not wishing they were in a simple relationship? Why is Moshe playing along with this Teddy and Bruno scenario? And why is he not complaining that Nana is flirting with another girl? And why is Nana not complaining that Moshe is never jealous?

They are not complaining because complaining is difficult. They are not complaining because they are both happy to compromise. Complaining makes them more unhappy than compromising.

I know you are not convinced by this. You are unpersuaded. Where is the realism? you say. Where is the accuracy of the European novel? Where is the truth to nature of Balzac or Tolstoy?

Well, let us think about a European novelist. I am going to tell you a small story about the life of Mikhail Bulgakov. Bulgakov was a satirical novelist and playwright in Stalinist Russia.

On 28 March 1930, Mikhail wrote a letter to the government of the USSR.

12

After all my works were banned, many citizens who know me as a writer could be heard all offering the same advice:

Write a 'Communist play' and also send a repentant letter to the government of the USSR, recanting the views I had formerly expressed in my literary works, and giving assurances that henceforth I would work as a fellow-travelling writer who was devoted to the idea of Communism.

The purpose: to save myself from persecution, poverty and, ultimately, inevitable death.

I did not heed this advice.

My purpose is far more serious.

I can prove with documentary evidence in my possession that the entire press of the USSR has been asserting WITH EXCEPTIONAL VIRULENCE, ever since I started to write, that the works of Mikhail Bulgakov cannot exist in the USSR.

I wish to state that the Soviet Press is QUITE RIGHT.

ANY SATIRIST IN THE USSR MUST QUESTION THE SOVIET SYSTEM.

Am I conceivable in the Soviet system?

I AM REQUESTING THE GOVERNMENT OF THE USSR TO ORDER ME TO LEAVE THE COUNTRY IN THE SHORTEST POSSIBLE TIME, ACCOMPANIED BY MY WIFE.

If, nevertheless, that which I have written proves unconvincing and I am doomed to a lifetime's silence in the USSR, then I request the Soviet government to give me a job.

13

But, you say, that is entirely different. Bulgakov was living in Stalinist Russia. What is the connection between the pathos and courage of Bulgakov's letter, and the relationship of Nana and Moshe? Surely I am not saying that the relationship of Nana and Moshe and Anjali was equivalent to living under Stalinism? A flirtatious threesome is not Stalinist.

Well no. It is not Stalinist. If Stalinist only means totalitarian aggression, then it was not Stalinist. But in 1930, *Stalin* was not Stalinist. Stalin was rather friendly. According to an informer for the secret police, Stalin phoned Mikhail Bulgakov up.

'Are you comrade Bulgakov?' said an apparatchik. 'Yes,' said Mikhail. 'Comrade Stalin will now speak to you,' said the apparatchik.

Bulgakov was convinced that this was a hoax but he waited all the same. He looked at the sleeve of his brown velveteen cardigan. There was a grease stain with a piece of onion sticking to it. He tried to flick the piece of onion off. It stuck there. He peeled it off.

Two to three minutes later Mikhail heard a voice over the telephone. It was Stalin's voice. 'I'm very sorry, Comrade Bulgakov, that I was not able to reply quickly to your letter but I was very busy. I was very interested by your letter. I would like to have a talk with you. I don't know when it will be possible since, as I said, I am extremely occupied. But I shall let you know when I can see you. In any case, we shall try to do something for you.'

That was Stalin.

The informer for the secret police thought that this was a brilliant PR job by Stalin. According to this secret policeman – let's call him Igor – according to Igor, everyone was saying: 'Stalin really is an outstanding man and, just imagine, he's also simple and accessible!' Igor reported how Stalin's popularity had developed in an extraordinary form. He was spoken of, said Igor, *with warmth and affection*, and the legendary story of Bulgakov's letter was being retold in various forms. It was being told in every pub.

After this telephone call, Bulgakov was given a job at the Moscow Arts Theatre. And he never published again. But he had complained. He had resisted. He had just been stymied by Stalin's phone manner.

I think the two situations, of Bulgakov and Stalin, and Moshe and Nana and Anjali, are very similar. This might seem unlikely at first, but it's true. In case you had not noticed, in this book I am not interested in anything so small as the history of the USSR. I am not writing anything so limited. No, what I am interested in is friendliness. So I can see that if Stalinism means only totalitarian aggression, then describing Nana and Anjali and Moshe as Stalinist might seem borderline hysterical. But if Stalinism means politeness, then there is an obvious similarity. Let us call this type of Stalinism 'telephone Stalinism'.

Telephone Stalinism is the use of friendliness as a coercive technique. It enforces compromise.

Everyone, sometimes, is a telephone Stalinist.

In terms of friendliness, I cannot see a difference between the individual behaviour of Nana and Mikhail Bulgakov and Moshe and Anjali and Stalin.

14

Anjali walked into Moshe's living room. Nana was wrapped in a duvet on the futon. She was having a day off. She was watching *Trisha*. She was watching *Trisha* by looking up at the ceiling. This was because she was thinking about the issues raised by the strap line: My Boyfriend Told Me To Become An Erotic Dancer And Now He Wants Me To Stop. Nana did not think erotic dancing was erotic. When Gabrielle, who had long blonde hair and short fat legs and a purple diamanté G-string and bra, rotated in the lap of an applauding male in the audience, Nana looked away. It was more sad than erotic. She looked up at the ceiling. The light was a softer version of blue. She wondered why pale white wasn't paler than pale blue. She wondered why it was the same degree of paleness. That was how interested she was in the emotional fallout from erotic dancing.

Anjali sat snuggled on the futon beside her. She sat down and watched *Trisha*. Anjali liked the erotic dancer. She thought she seemed quirky. It was the boyfriend she disliked. She disliked his toupee.

'Oh, my God!' said Nana, staccato.

It was true. It was a toupee. The boyfriend was horrible. Nana agreed.

15

Anjali's attitude to this happy trio – that was not yet a three-some, not yet – was ambivalent. Mostly, she was sad. For Anjali, only a couple was love. The third person was always an extra. On the other hand, she did enjoy being the extra to a couple. It had its luxurious side.

Anjali mused on couples while she acted in an advert for Johnson's Baby Powder. Anjali was the straight girl to Anne Robinson. This advert was being made just as Anne's career was taking off. So now, when Anne made an advert, the advert followed the format of *The Weakest Link*. That was how successful she was. This advert for Johnson's Baby Powder was a spoof production of *The Weakest Link* for babies. There were four babies on blue plastic high chairs. Anne Robinson questioned them on the comfort and convenience of Johnson's Baby Powder. Anjali was the voiceover for one of the babies. She voiced its gurgled thoughts. The Anjali baby was the last baby left. She was the Strongest Link. This was because the Anjali baby preferred Johnson's Baby Powder to all other baby powders.

Oh in the end, thought Anjali, Anjali wanted to be in a couple. She wanted people to write anniversary cards to Anjali and. Anjali and Anouska. Anjali and Zebedee. It wasn't the name that mattered. She would give barbecues, thought Anjali. Barbecues, it seemed, were Anjali's ambition.

There was an explanation for this. Anjali was feeling upset about couples because of her ex-girlfriend, Zosia. Anjali had discovered, a week ago, that Zosia had recently married her girlfriend of three months, in a tender and moving ceremony on a Costa Rican beach. They were married in a makeshift hut made of yam wood.

Oh, Anjali. Look what Zosia has done to you. She has made you love the idea of barbecues. Your ex gets married in Costa Rica and you want to be a wife.

Whereas when Anjali was young, she had detested the idea of a couple. It was her mother who liked couples. Her mother had been very pro couples. She had been very pro marriage. Because of this bias, Anjali's mother had not always enjoyed their weekly family trip to the Belle Vue cinema in Edgware. These trips were not always pleasurable. They did not always end on a finale of heterosexual marriage. Sometimes the films seemed to see love as tragic. They made love grandiose and destructive.

This was still a difference between Anjali and her mother. They still did not enjoy the same films. For example, Anjali's favourite Bollywood film was a recent film called *Devdas*. *Devdas* is the most expensive Bollywood film ever made. After an improbable plot, the hero dies, outside the gates of his first, only and unrequited love, played by the former Miss World, Aishwarya Rai.

Devdas was Anjali's favourite film. She enjoyed the Bollywood endings. She liked their tragedy. She liked their garish style.

Maybe I need to be more accurate here. Anjali was, finally, not so different from her mother. She thought she was, but she was not. They were both in love with the idea of the perfect couple. It was just that her mother recognised only married couples as couples. Whereas Anjali would not limit the term in this way. That was the true difference between them. Because they were romantic, Anjali loved Bollywood endings. Because she was a romantic, Anjali's mother disliked Bollywood endings.

16

Nana was aware that Anjali felt left out of a couple. She was aware that Anjali felt like an accessory to the romance of Nana and Moshe. And Nana was not a girl who liked people to feel left out. She wanted everyone to be happy. She was not a selfish girl. She was a heroine.

Nana huddled her knees up, perching. She leaned in towards Anjali, and this made the duvet get stuck between them, so Nana had to push herself up slightly to get back near Anjali, close. Then Anjali turned her face. And Nana looked at Anjali's brown eyes. Then Nana's face dipped down, slowly.

Nana kissed her, a tiny suck or bite on her lips, then let her be. There was a silent confusion.

Why was there a confusion? It was not that unusual for Nana and Anjali to exchange little girly kisses. So why was this confusing?

It was confusing because every other time Nana and Anjali had kissed, Moshe had been there. But it was not until Nana kissed Anjali, this tiny suck or bite on her lips, that she realised that all their other kisses had been supervised kisses. She did not realise until it was too late.

Moshe was not in his living room in Finsbury because he was in the gym provided by the Cally Pool instead. He was rehearsing. He was toning his actor's body.

His career was taking off. He had been offered a lead at the Tricycle Theatre in Kilburn. He was playing Slobodan Milosevic in a new play called *Peacekeeping Force* by Richard Norton-Taylor, based on the early transcripts of the International Criminal Tribunal for the former Yugoslavia.

Moshe rather liked his role as Slobodan Milosevic. Slobodan was a moaner. He could identify with Slobodan. Slobodan was a comic genius. He had a gift for repetition. As Moshe lifted a thirty-kilo shoulder press for at least fifteen reps, he remembered the lines of his favourite monologue from *Peacekeeping Force*.

'As I have to get up at seven, I am ready by eight for transport and I get back, at the earliest, at six, so from six to eight thirty is the only time in which I can use the telephone, which means that I won't be able to use my two hours of fresh air per day, which is the right of every detainee, and the guards also complain of not having enough fresh air.'

It might not be obvious why, as the lead in a courtroom drama, Moshe's priority was weight training. But there was an explanation. I am a little ashamed to tell you, but I will tell you. Moshe was getting excited. He was imagining profiles in Sunday magazines. He was imagining more photo shoots in *Hello!* and *¡Hola!*. But he did not know if he had the body for a photo shoot. He was not a toned and bulging sight. Nervous and vain, Moshe was getting fit on the Caledonian Road.

18

Meanwhile, at the scuzzier end of Finsbury, Nana was thinking about Anjali's smell. Anjali smelt like Nana but different. On the other hand, she smelt more like Nana than Moshe.

She could compare their smells because Anjali and Nana were very close together.

Anjali was holding Nana's face with the palms of her hands. Her first uncertain kiss had made contact with Nana's bottom lip and the top of her chin. Then Anjali kissed her again. She swerved her arm round Nana's neck, with her fingers splayed tautly open. Then she closed her hand and touched Nana's lips with her tongue.

They paused.

In this pause, a woman in the audience of *Trisha* asked the erotic dancer's boyfriend why he objected – now that he had got what he wanted. Trisha agreed that this was the issue. This was *the crux of the matter*.

But Anjali and Nana had stopped watching *Trisha*. They had more important things to think about.

If an average heterosexual or homosexual couple has sex, it is rare for the sex to follow on immediately from their first kiss. It would be impolite to have sex so soon. There should be a wait. This wait signifies that it was not just sex that the twosome was after.

But Nana and Anjali were not an average couple. They were a secret couple.

When a clandestine couple kisses, it is much more likely that sex will immediately follow. This is because there is much more uncertainty for a clandestine couple. There is much more risk. Once you have kissed secretly, it is very difficult not to have sex. It would be impolite not to have sex. You have to show that you are serious about each other.

But Nana and Anjali were not even an average clandestine couple. They were only inadvertently clandestine. This made sex even more socially fraught. They had just kissed in secret – so they had to be passionate. They had just kissed in secret by accident – so they were still just good friends.

They paused again.

Then Anjali stretched herself out, elongating Nana above her. Beneath Anjali there was something that felt like a magazine or outsize book in the puffy duvet. She ignored it. While Nana thought to herself that this was *lesbian sex*. She was going to have lesbian sex. It was something she had to remember. The room was pale blue. She was going to have lesbian sex.

Nana was a novice in these matters.

The fashions sported by each participant in this particular variant on the sex act were as follows. Nana wears Moshe's Southwark Playhouse 1998 season T-shirt, daringly on its own. Anjali wears an M&S white G-string and an M&S white satin padded bra (because yes, Anjali was mildly unhappy with her smallish breasts) beneath a pale cream French Connection shift dress.

These are not redundant specifics. Not all of them.

Nana had two worries. Her main worry was Moshe. She was worried how she would tell him, how she would explain this. She did not really know how she was going to explain it.

That was her main worry. But it was such a genuine worry that she tried to ignore it. That worry was unsolvable. Instead she concentrated on her second worry. The second was more practical. Nana was scared that she was about to let Anjali down. She wanted this to be erotic, but erotic was not Nana's forte. Nana was afraid of sex, she was afraid of another disappointment.

In order to hide from Anjali the fact that she was worried, Nana relinquished foreplay. Relinquishing foreplay, she thought, would be a way of appearing to be on heat. Only neutral and familiar lovers obeyed the rituals of touching and kissing. Lovers like Nana and Anjali were passionate, ferocious.

Nana dragged her hand up Anjali's right thigh and pushed it in under her G-string. And Anjali was wet, she was wet! Nana lightly lightly touched Anjali, she used her fingers on her, and Anjali held her wrist and lifted her away.

Nana was chastened and sad. She was only a learner. But she was also, she thought, very keen. But she did not need to be worried. Anjali was not complaining. She was calming her new playmate down. For a while, everything was slow and nondescript. They slowly kissed.

But then, with Anjali's hand stroking and rubbing and entirely using Nana, a new sexual crisis developed. Nana, pleased with her progress, was becoming very excited. She was repeating to herself the word delirious. It was exotic. It was true sex, she thought. So she repeated her first sexual gesture. Nana dragged her hand up Anjali's right thigh and pushed it in up under Anjali's G-string.

And Anjali's G-string was hooked, the crotch of it was hooked round one of Nana's fingers as another pushed into her. And her finger was bliss for Anjali. It could have been more blissful, however, if Anjali's posture had been different. She was reclining but stretching up, tense. The G-string was cutting into her anus, her perineum – whatever, thought Anjali, unconcerned with anatomy, it hurt. But Anjali was now too excited to explain to Nana that she was in pain. She just wanted to come. She was in sex's serious stages. So Anjali said nothing.

Fuck that hurts, thought Anjali. Oh no, oh no, oh this is wrong, thought Nana, remembering Moshe.

Anjali, in desperation, pushed down her G-string with her right hand, then settled back. She pushed it further down with her feet. It finished on her left foot. It dangled from her left foot. And Nana continued to touch her. Looking at Anjali's closed eyes, Nana touched Anjali. And this was wonderful, thought Nana. As Anjali tightened and arched backwards, as she started to make small gasps, Nana was happy. Nana stared at Anjali's cunt. She had a shiny mole just above her pubic hair.

Then Anjali came.

She looked at Nana. She looked at the G-string flopping from her left foot. Anjali giggled.

I told you I would tell you. So here it is. Nana and Anjali have just had sex.

It is, I reckon, socially awkward – bringing one of your friends to orgasm. Nana looked down at Anjali. She was resting her chin on Anjali's head. But the main awkwardness for Nana was not psychological, not at the moment. It was physical.

Resting her chin on Anjali's head, Nana's mouth was closed. So she was breathing through her nose. This might not seem bad. But it was. Nana's breathing was difficult, because her nose was blocked.

Nana needed to pick her nose.

Nana crept her hand from Anjali's warm hair upwards to her inclined face. She pushed her face down towards her hand, moaning contentedly for happy Anjali. She was anxious with embarrassment. Then Nana upended the mucus from her nostril, she examined it, not now, she thought, on her little finger above Anjali's head – a curved fleck of blood glazed with mucus. Then Nana was furtive. She stroked Anjali. Her idea was that she should stroke her languidly, seeming exhausted. She did this while curving her little finger out, displaying the correct and polite method of holding a Delft teacup, deftly. Then Nana let her arm flop over the edge of the futon, like the image of abandon, and draped the snot under the wooden frame. She squashed it, wiping off the wetness.

That was Nana's solution to the immediate problem posed by infidelity.

It was obviously not the only problem. It may have been the first, but it was not the most important. Nana had been unfaithful. That was the most important problem.

But this is not really a story about unfaithfulness. Unfaithfulness was not why Nana was serious, not exactly.

This is a story about kindness.

If you are already in love with someone else, then you eventually decide what to do. For example, while Nana picks her nose in secret, let us have another look at the case of Stacey and Henderson. When Henderson was unfaithful with a girl of his own age called Beyonce, he decided in the end that he would leave Stacey for Beyonce. This was because Beyonce went down on him and Stacey thought that oral sex was crude. I am not defending Henderson. I am just stating facts. And this is one option available. You eventually decide to be cruel to someone else (Stacey) and kind to yourself (Henderson).

The irony of Stacey and Henderson's break-up was that, only a month before, Stacey had met an iron-welder called Barry. He was a member of the National Iron and Steel Foundation. Barry was a big man. And big, for Stacey, was sexy. But Stacey had decided that she could not leave Henderson for Barry. She decided that it would hurt Henderson too much. This is another option available to the unfaithful person. You decide to be cruel to yourself (Stacey) and kind to someone else (Henderson).

This is a much rarer option. There is often an extra reason. For instance, there was actually a truer, more chancy reason why Stacey did not leave Henderson for Barry. Just as Barry's penis glugged in and out of Stacey for the first and only time, Stacey's mobile rang. It was three a.m. It was Henderson. He was five minutes away and wondering if he should come up. And the shock of this made Stacey sadly but surely ask Barry to leave, for ever. On the other hand, it was only for ever because she forgot to find out his phone number.

But anyway, in both the options I have outlined, it is the third party, the interloper, who was disregarded. In both these options, the rights of Beyonce and Barry were ignored. But what if you want to be kind to someone else and also kind to the third party? What if you want to be kind to everyone? What if you want to be kind to Stacey and Beyonce, or Henderson and Barry?

Nana wanted to be kind to everyone. But if you want to be kind to everyone, it is problematic. The room was pale blue. Nana had just made Anjali come.

And this is serious.

7

They fall out of love

THIS IS GETTING more complicated. But I think that you
can cope.

To summarise:

Nana was in love with Moshe.

Anjali was in love with no one.

Moshe was in love with Nana.

At the same time, Anjali and Nana seem to have
embarked on an affair.

You can see it all now. This is the story of how Moshe
was abandoned by his girlfriend. She left him for his best
friend. Because that is the saddest, most obvious story.

2

And Papa was the benevolent angel of this story. He was
there, always just outside the central plot. He was the happy

147

character. Well, all the characters were happy characters. But Papa was the happiest character.

At this point in the story, it was August. (This story took just under a year. It began in March, and now it was August.)

Papa was sitting in his office on Old Broad Street, in the City. He was looking at the paperclip holder designed by Nana at the age of twelve in her Craft, Design & Technology class. Her Craft, Design & Technology teacher was called Mr Scarborough. Mr Scarborough was adored by the mothers. He was tanned, and had reconstructed a farmhouse in Provence. He was distrusted by the fathers. He was adored by Nana because he had made her paperclip holder and then told Papa that Nana had made it. Papa had pretended to believe them both. This paperclip holder was made of tin, with a jagged design scored into it. The lid was a circular piece of beech wood. On it, Nana herself had glued four enamel turquoise squares in a diamond pattern.

It was not the most beautiful object in the world. I don't think Papa would have ever said that it was beautiful. But it was Papa's most loved object.

Papa's office on Old Broad Street had a reduced waterfall falling down the back wall of the foyer, into a landscaped pool of ferns and water lilies. It made the foyer smell of chlorine. It was faintly like a swimming pool. And when ten-year-old Nana came to visit Papa she liked this swimming-pool smell. She liked curling up there on a leather sofa, watching the men watch their security TVs. Young Nana liked swimming. She imagined she could swim in the waterfall. She told Papa this. Papa explained that the pool at the bottom was not really deep enough.

In his office on Old Broad Street, Papa looked at Nana's

paperclip holder, filled diligently, as ever, with paperclips. He was happy because Nana was happy. His girl was in love and that made her happy. And that made Papa happy.

Papa is not a reliable guide to this story. He is not a good guide to the plot.

3

Meanwhile, Anjali was on a break from filming. She was having a cigarette. She was standing on a fire escape round the back of a studio on Leonard Street, trying to blow smoke rings.

Anjali was shooting another advert for Johnson's Baby Powder. The concept for this advert was to re-enact scenes from famous films. Anjali was in the final famous scene from *Casablanca*.

For those of you not in the know, the final scene of *Casablanca* hinges on Humphrey Bogart, playing Rick, making the stern and noble decision that Ingrid Bergman, playing Ilsa Lund, should leave Casablanca with her émigré Jewish husband, called Victor Laszlo, played by Paul Henreid. It is a stern and noble decision because Rick and Ilsa are in love. It is a film, then, that romanticises generosity. As the plane leaves, with Ilsa and Victor safely on board, Rick turns to Captain Louis Renault, played by Claude Rains, and says to him, 'Louis, I think this is the beginning of a beautiful friendship.' That is one of the film's two famous lines. The other line is 'Play it again, Sam' – except, as all you film connoisseurs know, there is no such line in *Casablanca*.

In this reconstruction, Anjali was standing in for Ingrid

Bergman. And the plot of the advert was this. Anjali Bergman was tempted to stay with another, lesser brand of baby powder. But affairs were not moral. They were not acceptable. Every baby should resist the temptation to leave Johnson's for a new thrill. So in the end the plane soared away with Anjali the baby safely on board. 'Johnson's and baby – a beautiful friendship.' That was the advert's strap line.

And I know. I know this was not accurate. I know that the beautiful friendship was not between Ingrid Bergman and Paul Henreid. It was not even between Ingrid Bergman and Humphrey Bogart. It was a homoerotic friendship. But that is not my fault. Blame Johnson's Baby Powder.

Interpretation is difficult. So often, interpretation is personal, subjective. It is not just the makers of Johnson's Baby Powder adverts who get things wrong. Anjali could get things wrong as well.

As Anjali lit and smoked her way through two Marlboro Lights, she remembered the whole delightful plot of *Casablanca*. It was the story of a famous threesome. It was a film about generosity. As she smoked, Anjali realised that she was Rick, she was Humphrey Bogart. So Anjali should behave like Rick. She should give Nana up. It was true, she did not want to give Nana up – but if she did not, well what then? Nana might leave Moshe for her. And Anjali did not want Nana to give Moshe up. It was difficult for Anjali – giving Nana up – but it would have been much more difficult watching Nana give up Moshe.

It was a tragedy. But tragedies, thought Anjali, were noble. It moved her so much that she almost began to cry, on a fire escape, near Old Street.

As for me, I have my own theory about the end of

Casablanca. I do not think it is a tragic ending. Me, I think it is a happy ending.

Victor Laszlo was a Czech and Jewish resistance fighter. He was a hardworking and courageous anti-Nazi intellectual. I do not think it was a tragic ending at all. Victor was fleeing for his life, and we are meant to feel sad that his wife has stayed with him instead of with the morose owner of an ex-pat bar in Casablanca. Now personally I do not think that is sad. I do not think love is this important. I do not think that melancholy is that attractive. There is no need to romanticise the love triangle.

4

As it happened, Anjali did not need to worry about the tragedy inherent in a love triangle, because Nana was not considering leaving Moshe. At this point, there was no tragic threesome, because Nana did not think she was in love with Anjali. Nana was in love with Moshe. She was in love with Moshe and she had been unfaithful once. That was Nana's position so far. Rather than feeling torn, she was just feeling guilty.

I do not think she needed to feel guilty. She was not having an affair. And it was not as if the situation was entirely her fault. Even Moshe could have foreseen this. But Nana thought it was all her fault, and this was making her nervous. It was making her cry.

A few evenings after her lesbian sex scene, Nana was crying. Actually, crying had become a feature for Nana. It had become regular. But I will go with one night in particular. Nana was in bed with Moshe and her toy leopard. She was crying soft grey mascara tears. These tears blackened the tip of the toy leopard's head. They smudged its sewn-in lines for claws. And while she cried, Moshe, who was almost asleep, cupped her from behind. He edged his penis into the fur of her bottom, and made no noise. It was three in the morning.

Moshe tried to wake up.

There are all sorts of funny moments when someone is crying in the middle of the night. There are all sorts of droll ironies. This might sound heartless and cold but really it is true.

Nana was feeling nervous. Meanwhile, Moshe was simply confused. His sensible girlfriend Nana had recently become tormented. You see? That's one droll irony already. She was not tormented at all – she was just nervous.

'Wha?' said Moshe. He was sleepy, sleepy. 'Yll be betten the mornung,' he drawled, touching the tips of her shoulders, softly. Then he let his hand drop. No question, Moshe was tired. Inside his head Moshe was drifting. But Nana was awake. Moshe said, 'Whas the matta?' He felt helpless. And the reason he felt helpless, thought Moshe, was that he was desperate with sleep.

But sleepiness was not really why Moshe felt helpless. I happen to know an extra fact. He felt helpless because Nana was crying. That was it. It was the simple fact of her crying. Due to some internal inadequacy, crying always left Moshe stymied. There are limited feelings, after all. You can only feel what you feel. It is not very fun, but that is how it is. It is very difficult, not repeating yourself, it is very tricky and not very fun.

It was not very fun for Moshe.

He slumped back, caring, useless. He listened to Nana.

He said, 'Doll maybe yshoud, mayb, o Iloveyou, you know?' 'Nana, Nana,' he crooned, a matinée idol at three o'clock.

Nana tried. She said, 'Umsorri I'm doon this. Iss just. Oh sorry.'

Moshe thought that this might be a rest. This might be the prelude to quietness, thought Moshe. When she understood the value of sleepysleep sleep. 'Dunma,' he said, 'it don matta.' But no. It was not the prelude to quietness. It was not the prelude to sleep. It was the prelude to trying again.

As Nana mumbled and chatted, Moshe fretted. He tried to see the invisible time, ticking somewhere on the bedside table. It must be nearly dawn, worried Moshe, it must be and if it was then Moshe was a destroyed tired man. He wondered if he could remember any of his lines. He tried to run through his lines. In his hysteria, Moshe could not remember any of Slobodan Milosevic's lines. He was panicking and blank.

It was the middle of the night and Moshe was scared. He felt unsafe.

Whereas when he was a boy and woke up in the middle of the night, scared by the shapes of his *objets trouvés* stored in a Homebase cabinet, Moshe knew for sure that he was safe. When he was a kid, Moshe was not distressed by his jumping beans, or his Russian doll, or his one-inch wooden elephant, which was orange with black spots. He was not afraid, because there was a ladder in the corner of the room. And all he had to do was stand on it and paradise was just up there, on a ledge around the walls two inches off the ceiling, where a line of wooden painted animals glistened in the dark. And if this failed, he knew that his mother would be guarding him, in her promised busby and red suit with gold new buttons, just outside the door.

But now it was the middle of the night and Moshe felt as if he were alone. He felt old. He was twenty-six years old. And his girlfriend called Nana was crying. 'Iss jus hol me?' she said. 'Please hol me, please.'

Oh Moshe. Moshe was scared. He was a grown-up. He was unable to cope with events.

5

Then, the next morning, guiltily, Nana was having sex with Moshe.

In case you have not understood, I want to make this clear. This is not their sex life. That is not what you are reading about. You are reading about their feelings. You are reading about their ethics.

As for Moshe, grown-up Moshe was not feeling guilty. He was just on top. He was making Nana's vagina belch and squelch as he altered, like a pro, the dippy angle. But this was not Moshe's ideal position. No, he wanted another position. He wanted his favourite thing. And what was Moshe's favourite thing? Wait, wait, I am going to tell you. His favourite thing was for Nana's legs to be bent backwards along her chest, her knees resting on her collarbones.

However, Moshe's favoured position was not, this morning, Nana's favourite thing. This morning was not a morning, thought Nana, for such prosaic acrobatics. No. She was feeling altruistic and remorseful. She was going to do something special for Moshe. She was going to do a thing she had always thought about. And Moshe always asked her to think about what she liked. She was going to lie there and be naughty.

Naughty equalled pissing.

She needed to go, said Nana, and she really did not know if she should go. Should she go? It was just she did not know if she could wait. She did not know if she could wait until a toilet.

Her name for this innovation was rudies. At this specialised moment, she said, 'Can I do rudies?' It seemed that Nana had blossomed out, that morning, into a boyish girl with toddler instincts. And instincts are uncontrollable, everyone knows that. Nana said, 'Uwanna go. Uv gotta go.' She said it to Moshe with her closed eyes and tight neck. She said, 'Please can I go.'

This was her treat. This was her apology.

Nana had been unfaithful. And infidelity makes everyone at least momentarily remorseful. But Nana felt additionally guilty, because she did not even have the ordinary excuse for infidelity – a tragically high sex drive. Nana was not highly sexed. She knew that, if she was going to get into sex, she could at least have got into it with Moshe. So Nana was doubly remorseful. That was why she decided to explore the sexiness of pissing. She was being altruistic.

I have to say, if this is altruistic, there are good things in altruistic. If only more people were altruistic, they might find their lives were more complicated. They might find their sexual repertoire piquantly extended.

Moshe said, 'Bu bu, Nana.'

Quite frankly, he was surprised.

6

I am not sure what the general attitude to pissing is. I do not know how most people view pissing as a sexual manoeuvre. Presumably, some people are not turned on by it. I assume that this group of people do not use visions of rustling entwined strands of clear and yellow streams as a masturbatory aid.

For other people, it is a gorgeous luxury. It is part of the whole sexual triumph. For these people, it is a delicious moment of abandonment, calling for the purchase of a rubber mattress protector, from Mothercare perhaps, or Asda.

As for reading about pissing during sex, each of these groups will have corresponding ideas about literary decorum. They will each find things to criticise in my description of Nana's exploration. They will experience problems of identification. Either it will be too explicit, or it will not be explicit enough. I know that. But I am not interested in that kind of reading. I am not interested in readers who want to identify with Moshe and Nana. I am interested in readers getting this right. I want them especially to get Moshe's position right.

Moshe's position, you see, was neither pro nor con. He was persuadable, that was Moshe's position.

At first, Moshe thought that pissing was just not his thing. He stopped moving and looked at her. But Nana would not let him be unsure. She was enjoying herself. She said, 'I don't think I can hold on.'

Yes, Nana wanted this.

There is a phenomenon perhaps underplayed by the propagandists for particular sexual practices. These propagandists believe that each particular sexual act needs to be longed for by each sexual participant. According to the propagandists, therefore, you cannot be a dilettante of anal fisting. You have to be committed. But as for me, I do not think this is true. If you do not share someone's sexual fantasy, there is a range of feelings available to you. Someone else's sexual fantasy can, of course, seem bizarre and disgusting. It is also true that it can simply seem boring. But another reaction is also just as common.

It is a turn on, when someone else is turned on.

It was a turn on for Moshe, when Nana was turned on. Just for that morning, pissing was Moshe's *dream come true*.

She had told him that she could not hold on. So Moshe said, 'You will have to hold on. You will absolutely have to hold on. I am not letting you soil this bed.'

He meant what he said. He was good at this fantasy. Moshe did not want Nana to piss in his bed, not entirely. This was because he had never bought a mattress protector. He had bought an expensive Dunlopillo mattress, but no mattress protector. So he was not absolutely keen on a naked Nana wetting herself.

Nana wailed. She wailed, 'Bu I can't. I can't.' And Moshe was more and more stern. He said, 'If you go, I will be very angry.' And Nana quavered, 'Oh, oh.' She seemed docile. He said, 'If you go I will be very upset with you.' And Nana did not want Moshe to be upset with her, but she was curious what he might resort to if displeased.

Underneath him, Nana was now wanking. Moshe could feel the back of her hand tight rubbing against his belly.

He said, 'If you go, if you go without permission, then I will have to punish you.' She said, 'Punish me?' He said, 'Punish you.' She said, 'Mmm.'

Moshe put his left-hand palm on Nana's furry pubic

mound. And Nana's eyes were shut. She was breathing, she was wheezing from her nose. She turned her head from side to side. He looked up at her. Her eyes were shut, her mouth was shut.

Then Moshe's palm was wet.

Nana had been naughty. She had been oh so cleverly naughty. The webbing between Moshe's fingers was stinging and wet. Nana pushed his hand with her hand against her wet cunt. Nana was dribbling it out.

Moshe worried about the effect of urine on eczema. He did not think it could be soothing. And he had to think what to do with the sheet. It was not that he wanted to look brisk. It was just that the mattress had been expensive. Dunlopillo was no mean brand. He wanted to whisk the sheet into the washing machine. He was especially worried because this was the morning. As every good undinist knows, piss in the morning is much much stronger than piss in the evening.

Nana opened her innocent eyes and looked at him. 'You disgust me,' said Moshe. Nana giggled.

7

This reminds me.

There is a short novel called *Thérèse the Philosopher*. It was the Marquis de Sade's favourite novel. It was published around 1750. No one knows exactly who wrote it. The novel is narrated by Thérèse. One episode describes how she watched Mlle Eradice uncovering her buttocks to receive the discipline of her priest, Father Dirrag. First the priest whips her with a bundle of birch rods. Then he tells her that he is going to mortify her with the true 'cord of St Francis'. The true cord of St Francis is his penis. She does not know it is his penis. Having thought about penetrating her anus, the priest in the end decides just to make love to Mlle Eradice from behind.

This is a quotation from *Thérèse the Philosopher*.

His head was bent and his glistening eyes were fixed on the work of his battering ram, whose thrusts he controlled in such a manner that, as it retracted, it did not leave its sheath completely and, as it shot forward, his stomach did not come into contact with the thighs of his charge, who might thus, upon reflection, have guessed the origin of this supposed cord. What presence of mind!

This quotation is important.

Eventually, Mlle Eradice comes. And she interprets her orgasm as a divine reward. "'Oh, yes, I'm feeling celestial happiness. I sense that my mind is completely detached from matter. Further, Father, further! Root out all that is impure in me . . .'"

I can see what the writer of *Thérèse the Philosopher* is up to. He – because of course it is a he – wants to attack corrupt priests. He also wants to satirise religious texts where virgins swoon in religious ecstasy. He wants to satirise the pretension to spirituality of spirituality. All the girl wanted, we understand, was a fuck.

I can see all that. I just think that, in his effort to be politically acute, the writer has missed an opportunity. In my rewrite, Mlle Eradice would know all along that she was being fucked by her priest. And she would *pretend* not to know. That would be the crucial change. Whereas in *Thérèse the Philosopher* Mlle Eradice really does not know. She is fooled. But surely this is unrealistic? It is unrealistic. And the writer knows that too. That is why he is so careful to tell us about the priest's masterly control of his penis's movements. That is why he is so insistent that only the priest's penis touched her. In his effort to prove his pointless point, he has falsified kinkiness.

I am therefore not surprised that when the Marquis de Sade, known to his closest friends as Donatien, decided to write his own political porn, *Story of Juliette*, in 1797, he singled out *Thérèse the Philosopher* as a model. He called it a 'charming work'. It was charming because it was the only book which 'agreeably linked luxuriousness with impiety'. In case this is a bit obscure, the cryptic Donatien just means that the book showed monks fucking. That's what Donatien wanted to read. It is what he wanted to write. He didn't want realistic kinkiness, he wanted political kinkiness.

But then the Marquis de Sade was not an expert in kinkiness. He was too theoretical. When it comes to kinkiness in prose, I am a better writer than the Marquis de Sade.

8

But that is enough, for the moment, of Nana and Moshe in bed. There is Anjali to think of too. Following her afternoon of passion with Nana, along with *Trisha* in the background, Anjali had become remorseful. *Stricken with remorse*, she had let Nana and Moshe be on their own for a while. She did not return phone calls. She did not reply to emails.

Anjali had taken to walking in Regent's Park. Because if you are a young woman on your own in a park, then you may seem romantic and beautifully lonely. For the last couple of weeks since being made to come by Nana, Anjali had gone on little walks, happily sad, deliciously melancholy.

There are two things you need to be sure about, when thinking about Anjali. Anjali had been seduced by Nana. This we know. But the second and key point is this. Anjali was occasionally sentimental.

This is my definition of sentimentality. Sentimentality is the valuing of feeling for its own sake. It is therefore the exaggeration of feeling. An example of this exaggeration is Anjali's generosity. On a fire escape near Old Street, Anjali had discovered a far greater seduction than Nana. This greater seduction was morality. It had taken her over.

For Anjali, her vision of noble Humphrey Bogartian generosity was more of a turn on than Nana. That was why she kept away, wandering round Regent's Park. It was more exciting to give Nana up than to keep her. It was just like living in wartime Casablanca.

9

But Nana, it seemed, did not think she was living in North Africa under the Nazis.

Nana said, 'I am so so so annoyed. I've just been to this lecture on the new Prada shop in New York, the one designed by Rem Koolhaas.' 'Rem Coolharse?' said Anjali. 'Yeah Rem Koolhaas,' said Nana. 'And this guy, this guy, this *guy*, he said that Prada was a new innovation in architecture. In arkitetcha. I mean. Listen. This is what Rem

Koolhaas said. "Architecture is not the satisfaction of the needs of the mediocre, it is not an environment for the petty happiness of the masses. Architecture is an affair of the elite." An affair of the elite! What do you mean an affair of the elite? It's a technique,' said Nana, angry.

As you might have guessed from this dialogue, Nana and Anjali were in the Architectural Association café. They were standing at the counter, waiting to be served. 'I'll have an ekspresso,' said Anjali, relieved. 'No I'm fine,' said Nana. 'No, I'll have a sparkling water.'

'And then', said Nana, 'this guy quoted him again. Rem Koolhaas said, I can't believe this, Rem Koolhaas said, "True architecture is an operation which deliberately abstains from prescriptions or from architecture." That deliberately refrains from architecture! Architecture should refrain from architecture!'

'God,' said Anjali. 'I don't think I understand.' 'Yeah no igzacly', said Nana. 'You're not men to. Because it's meaningless.'

Anjali sat down. Nana stuffed away her Pukka A4 pad.

Now, it is true that Nana was genuinely annoyed by her lecturer. She was also genuinely enraged by Rem Koolhaas. But Nana was not dominating the conversation architecturally purely because of her passionate attachment to urban design. No. Nana had a plan, she had a sexual plan. But she did not want to talk about this plan immediately. She wanted it to look casual. She wanted the conversation to be natural.

Nana was worried about Anjali. She thought she might be sad. That was Nana's interpretation of Anjali's odd absence. She did not know that for the last couple of weeks Anjali had been sentimental in parks. She thought she had been at home, moodily eating her way through trapezoid packets of Cadbury's Celebrations. And this was not what Nana wanted. She did not want Anjali to overeat on chocolate. She wanted Anjali to feel loved. Well, she wanted her to feel loved as long as Moshe felt loved too.

So Nana had arrived here in the Architectural Association café with a plan.

But Anjali felt loved. She felt too loved. She was simply stirring sugar into her espresso. She was wondering what Humphrey Bogart would have done.

10

Nana had a plan. She had another sexual suggestion. This next suggestion was a threesome.

I think it is amazing what people who dislike sex do to sex. They make it rational, they make it moral. Often the most perverse people are the ones who do not like sex. They are often the ones prepared to do anything. And Nana, as we know, was not a sexual monster. She was not highly sexed. And this made her, I reckon, more perverse.

You see, Nana did not think that Moshe was having the time of his sexual life. And it was true, he was not in sexual *seventh heaven*. But actually Moshe was happy with that. It was Nana who was not happy with Moshe's sex life. Because she was feeling guilty, she thought she should still invent ever newer delights for Moshe, her paramour. And she had thought of something.

She had thought of a threesome.

This was Nana's reasoning. Because he was a good and patient boy, Moshe deserved a threesome. It was every boy's ideal scenario. Moreover, Anjali would not feel left out if they had a threesome. She would not feel rejected. And as for Nana, she was equable about a threesome.

So Nana should orchestrate a threesome. That was the most rational solution.

II

But how do you propose a threesome in polite conversation? This was the question that Nana was pondering, while she watched Anjali sip her hot espresso. How do you broach a threesome?

Well, this is how Nana did it. You do it as a joke. You smuggle it in. You pretend you're not saying it at all.

First, she praised Anjali's sexual skill. She said, 'I so loved what we did, you know. I really loved it. It was really oh delicious.' This unsettled Anjali, because Anjali was flattered. She did not want to feel flattered. She wanted to feel aghast. Then Nana said, 'I liked it. I really did like it a lot.' Nana was smiling. She was smiling a lot. Anjali continued to feel flattered. She was not acting like Humphrey Bogart. By now, Humphrey would have grabbed the dame by the neck and told her that it was over.

Then Nana said, 'But I'm not sure we can.' Anjali said, 'Look of course.' She said, 'Look of course. It doesn't matter. Of course it was a one-off.' 'Oh,' said Nana. 'Oh but it's not that I wouldn't like to.' 'Uhhuh?' said Anjali. Nana said, 'I mean I spose one way of doing this. I mean. We could do it all three of us. I mean. What about all three of us?'

'All three of us? A threesome?' asked Anjali. She was smiling. She was smiling a lot. She liked this idea. That way, she could feel noble and also see Nana naked again.

Nana knew her stuff. She knew what people wanted.

'Was this his idea?' said Anjali. 'Um, no,' said Nana. 'Was mine. He doesn't know.' 'All three of us?' said Anjali. 'Well yeah,' said Nana. She was grinning. Anjali said, 'Uhhuh.' She was interested. She was grinning too.

12

But there was still the problem of telling the boy.

I reckon that the main difficulty when setting up a threesome is persuading the second girl. I reckon that most people's idea of the crux is the second girl. Once you have the extra girl, the boy should follow naturally.

But, as Nana knew, Moshe was not an ordinary boy. He was more gentle than other boys. He had ordinary lusts, it was true, but Moshe would also deny them. As Moshe's girlfriend, you could not just propose a threesome. You could not ask him directly. Moshe, I suppose, could not believe that any girl would like a threesome. He could not believe that a threesome was anything other than a selfish fantasy, a selfish boy's fantasy.

So Nana cunningly asked indirectly. She discussed it during sex. It was just like a fantasy. It was only a fantasy.

A couple of nights after her conversation in the Architectural Association café with Anjali, Nana was describing how there was another woman with them. She was asking if Moshe liked that.

You know that Nana was not really a girl who went for talking during sex. So you can understand the effort she was making here.

Moshe liked it. He liked this other woman being there.

Then Nana added some specifics. Nana was, by the way, lying on her back. She raised her knees, up to her breasts, and looked into Moshe's happy eyes. As she did this she said, very softly, smiling, 'And this girl's Anjali?'

It was a fantasy. They were having sex. So Moshe agreed to this scenario. I can't see anything odd or wrong about that. The point of a fantasy is that it is completely amoral. It has nothing to do with reality. Moshe grinned. He liked it when Nana described what Anjali was doing to his testicles. It sounded interesting. It sounded technically advanced. And it was making him come. So when Nana said, 'Why not?', he only nodded. When she said 'I mean really why not?', breathing deeply and happily Moshe nodded. He said, 'Yeah, yeah,' as Nana explained how she would sit on Anjali's face while Moshe licked Anjali.

He gasped. Nana explained what Anjali's tongue would be doing, and where Moshe would be positioned. He gasped. He said, 'Yeah we should do it,' and then he came.

He did not think it would be *for real*. He did not think that Nana was serious. I told you. It was not his style.

13

In real life, however, Moshe did not have to deal with such a fantasy threesome. No. It was more of a polite threesome. It was decorous.

Nana was looking scared, lying on the floor. And Anjali – because Anjali was that sort of girl, she was into aromatherapy – handed Moshe her pot of Aveda juniper massage oil.

This might seem obscure at first, I suppose, but I do not think it was obscure. It was very intelligent. Alone in Regent's Park she might have been prone to sentimentality but – on the floor in Finsbury – Anjali was being the most thoughtful.

The conventional view of a threesome, I think, is of blonde girls draping themselves around some toned and attractive boy. Or not even a toned and attractive boy. Two blondes, people think, will drape themselves round any man with money. But this is a very limited view of the threesome. A threesome is not this easy. It is certainly not this abstract. There are all sorts of possible mistakes to be made. A threesome is socially uncertain. The key, therefore, to a successful threesome is to keep everyone involved. And this was exactly what Anjali was thinking. Her plan was that she and Moshe would be gentle to Nana. They would massage her. A massage was not quite sexual, it was not frightening.

So Moshe and Anjali pushed smooth oil on Nana's legs and feet. And it worked. It relaxed her. 'Thass lovely,' she said, closing her eyes, like a starlet, 'really lovely.' She scooped her glass of wine up, Ernest & Julio Gallo Californian cabernet sauvignon, and it spilled on her blonde furry chin. Anjali licked it off. Moshe stared, excited wide-eyed scared. He stared.

But Moshe was not an expert masseur. Soon he became bored with massage oil. So while patient Anjali moved on to Nana's hands and fingers, he began to kiss Nana's stomach. I can see that this might seem forward. This might seem gauchely enthusiastic. And it was. But it also seemed to work. Nana was getting excitable. She said, 'Kiss me,' to Anjali, while Moshe stroked and scratched inside her legs.

Anjali put the pot of oil on the window sill and said, 'This okay? This okay?' She kissed Nana. She said, 'I like kissing you.' She nuzzled down to the base of Nana's neck, cheek to cheek. 'That tickled!' giggled Nana at Moshe. She looked down and grinned at Moshe. He grinned back. So Nana let her head flop back. She kissed Anjali, shutting her eyes.

This is slow, I know that. No one has even undressed. I know. But this is what sex is like. It is lots of thoughts and movements.

Anjali, for example, was wondering why she had never done this before – having sex with a couple. But then suddenly Nana stopped kissing her. Nana kissed her lightly on the forehead and then looked down at Moshe.

I do like Moshe. Moshe is really so sweet. He was doing his best to make stroking Nana's inside thigh a pleasure for him. But it was not easy. It was not easy to be that interested when he was feeling slightly sad. But he grinned. And Anjali curved her neck round and grinned at happy Moshe. She looked at Nana, grinning. And then Anjali knew what was wrong.

Nana was anxious for Moshe. She wanted to see Moshe with Anjali. She did not want Moshe to be abandoned. That was what Anjali thought.

And she could do that, thought Anjali. It was not what she had imagined. She had imagined just girl-girl action, while Moshe watched. But if this was what Nana wanted, thought Anjali, then she should be kind. After all, Moshe was not unappealing. If that was what Nana wanted, then Anjali would do it.

14

Oh, altruism.

Positioned at Nana's feet, Moshe was sad. He was expecting to be left out. He did not think that Anjali really liked boys. Now that they were in this extraordinary position, he would have liked this to be a trio. It would, he felt, be best if everyone were pleasured. But he was not expecting anything. Moshe just sadly assumed that this was the natural progression of all their mutual kissing and touching. This was what came of eating Go-Go Supreme Pizza deals at five in the afternoon. *He had only himself to blame.*

Moshe, you see, did not know what was going on. He thought this was the first time Nana and Anjali had become this intimate. In fact, he never found out that Anjali and Nana had had sex already. He thought that the threesome was their very first time.

But as well as feeling resigned, Moshe was also, as you can imagine, very turned on. And I do not think you can blame him for this. His girlfriend and another girl, who was in no way unattractive, were behaving homosexually in front of him. He was feeling generous, Moshe. But he was also wondering when the evening would get properly pornographic. Even if Moshe was not involved, it would still be fun to watch.

15

And just as Moshe was thinking that the evening needed pornography, Anjali – what synchronisation – stretched her arms up and crossed them, unwrapping her turquoise T-shirt. Then she pinched her bra clasp apart. The bra slid forward from under her breasts.

At last, some nakedness! Anjali was topless.

At this point, I am going to describe Anjali's breasts. This is not because I am seedy. No. The look of Anjali's breasts was important, because it was the opposite look to the look of Nana's breasts. As you may remember, Nana's breasts were large and entirely pale, with only the palest smudge for areolae, and the softest small pink circles for nipples. While Anjali's were smaller. Each breast was stained by an areola. Her nipples were thick and blackly maroon.

It is true, of course, that I am enjoying this description of Anjali's breasts. But this still does not mean I am seedy. There is a crucial psychological detail to be inferred from this comparison. It is crucial that Nana and Anjali had different kinds of breasts. It was a distinct turn on for Moshe, and a slight difficulty for Nana. Anjali's breasts made Nana feel faintly insecure. Anjali, thought Nana, was much more attractive than Nana.

Nana placed her hands at either side of Anjali's ribcage. She sucked at Anjali's blackly maroon nipples. Anjali leaned over to help her. This positioned Anjali face to face with Moshe. So above Nana's suckling mouth Moshe and Anjali started kissing.

Now the evening was sexual. Now they were having a threesome.

But Moshe pulled apart for a moment. He was finding it odd kissing Anjali, his lesbian friend. He wondered if this was really what she wanted. He could not quite believe it. So Moshe said, 'Iz this okay?' Anjali nodded and pulled him towards her from the back of his neck, and Moshe said no no no, was this really what she wanted. And Anjali kept nodding and kissed him. Then Moshe said to Nana, 'Iz this okay?' and Nana also nodded.

16

If I were a pornographer, what happened next would be a hitch. I have to describe my characters undressing. Undressing embarrasses pornographers. But luckily, I am not a pornographer. I hate pornography, I hate its magic realism. Me, I believe in nineteenth-century realism.

Undressing is no problem for me.

The three of them stood up. Anjali removed all her clothes. This did not take very long, because all she was wearing by now was a denim skirt and black knickers. She rolled them both off together. Nana took off her dress and bra and then felt coy about taking off her knickers too. For the moment she kept them on. Moshe had unbuttoned his shirt. He pushed his jeans and his Converse boxer shorts off. Then, with a curving erection sticking into his belly as he bent down, he struggled with his recalcitrant ribbed Gap socks.

Moshe joined his two girls who were kissing on his bed.

17

Anjali was sitting, like a cello, between Nana's legs, so that Nana could touch her from behind and kiss her neck. Moshe crawled across the bed and lay on Anjali and kissed her. But this was complicated. Nana, thin Nana, was squashed. So they arranged themselves differently. They moved back to the floor. There was more space on the floor.

Well, two of them moved to the floor. Nana just rolled on to her front and hung her head over the side of the bed.

From this position, Nana watched Moshe *get carried away*. He kissed Anjali, he kissed her roughly. Then he pushed her legs apart with his right knee, so his penis was hovering in front of Anjali's vagina. And when Moshe judged that the time was right he held his penis with his left hand and pushed it into Anjali. Then Anjali and Moshe started to have sex. Moshe reared. Anjali's breasts shook from side to side, flattened out over her ribs.

But this was not pornography. It was confused.

You see, Moshe was happy. He was having sex, legitimately, with another girl. And he was feeling particularly happy because Anjali was not as thin as Nana. Toned and elegant Nana had always made Moshe feel tubby. Whenever Moshe and Nana's bodies entwined and writhed, there always seemed to be more of Moshe than Nana. Whereas Anjali was the real physical thing. Anjali, thought Moshe, was uncompromisingly sexual. She was physical and uncomplicated and luscious.

Obviously, Moshe was wrong. Anjali was complicated.

Moshe had pushed himself into her without her deciding. And Anjali knew that not deciding was not the same as not consenting. It was just she wasn't sure that immediate sex was the correct scenario. She was not certain that this was Nana's plan. So she tried not to look at Nana. Anjali looked at the joins of the plaster where the ceiling became magnolia walls. She followed the ins and outs of the foliage of the dado. It was odd looking at a room from the floor. It made the room unusual. She could see a peeking patch of mustard yellow by the radiator.

And Anjali also felt aggrieved. She had expected more involvement from Nana. This was not what she had imagined. A threesome was not a prosy floor show. And this was just a floor show. Moshe was shoving her. This was meant to be more fun. It was meant to be more caring. This was not a threesome at all.

Lonely Anjali decided to hasten the fated end. And she knew what she was meant to do. 'Christ this is wunful!' Anjali exclaimed. 'Christ. Sweet Jesus. Oh Jesus that's good! No that's just so. Oh. Sweet fucking mother of.' She wrenched her hips round Moshe. She kissed the paler skin over the tendons on his veering neck, tightening the muscles in her cunt to make herself smaller for massive, so achemaking Moshe. 'Oh no that's no no yes oh that's. God,' she said.

This was the entertainment business.

Anjali pushed her feet up and down Moshe's back so Moshe could manoeuvre further in. She just wanted him to come. She just wanted the solace of all the objective signs. So she could curl up and be pretty.

OK, I will write some pornography. I will write one paragraph.

As he pulled out she made her cunt grip him like she was coming and whispered, 'Fuck me please fuck me hard.' And then she felt him, tight and thickening, so she cried out, 'Oh oh oh oh oh. Oh.' She was drifting. 'Oo,' she said. He was pulsing and ('mmm') she could feel it, she said to him, relieved.

She rubbed her cheek on his sharp face. Moshe felt heavy. He was a lot heavier than Zosia. He twitched, pushing his cock further in, for the last of it.

As for Nana, Nana was sad. Because, as you can see, multiple sex scenes don't work. I am not embarrassed to say so. The flaw in a threesome, Nana had discovered, was not exhaustion. Contrary to what she might have expected, the flaw was not the busyness. It was being unemployed. 'Threesome' was a euphemism. 'Threesome' was the word for infidelity. She was jealous.

Moshe was very proud. He felt weird, and he felt proud.

18

But what is infidelity?

On the night of 16/17 May 1934, the poet Osip Mandelstam was arrested. You know about Osip. You know about how he met his wife. The secret police knocked on his door when Osip was on the loo, despondently, his back straight and his neck back. He had been on the loo for the last fourteen minutes, trying to crap. As he heard the secret police arrive, he quickly wiped himself, although, even in his hurry, he still inspected the stain on the loo paper before flushing it away.

Osip was arrested because he had written a poem in which he had described Joseph Stalin like this: 'Fat fingers as oily as maggots, / Words sure as forty-pound weights, / With his leather-clad gleaming calves / And his large laughing cockroach eyes.' It was not a very friendly description. So Stalin had him arrested.

But they didn't arrest him just to be nasty to Osip. No. They wanted to know who had seen this poem too. They wanted to know what people had thought.

Osip is uniformly considered to be a hero. And he was a hero. I do not want you to think that I think anything else.

Obviously, if Osip had told them names, then the people he named would be in trouble too. So surely Osip did not tell the police these names? Surely he did not betray them?

He betrayed them.

Q. When this lampoon had been written, to whom did you recite it and to whom did you give written copies?

A. I recited it to: (1) my wife; (2) her brother Yevgeny Khazin, a writer of children's books; (3) my brother Alexander; (4) my wife's friend Emma Gershteyn, who works in the research-workers' section at the Central Council of Trade Unions; (5) Boris Kuzin, of the Zoological Museum; (6) the poet Vladimir Narbut; (7) the young poetess Maria Petrovikh; (8) the poetess Anna Akhmatova and (9) her son Lev Gumilyov.

I know that he was worried about the possibility of torture. I know that. Maybe there were even untranscribed pauses in this interrogation. But look at Osip. Look at him be extra helpful – 'my wife's friend Emma Gershteyn, who works in the research-workers' section at the Central Council of Trade Unions'. It is the extra detail I am interested in here. As well as being scared of torture, Osip was trying to be charming.

I am not getting at Osip. Honestly, I like him. Because I like him, I do not want to idealise him too much. If I had been in the Lubyanka prison, being interrogated by Stalin's secret police, I would have told everything. I would have been scared of torture too. I think I would have said much more than he did. Like Osip, I always want to appear helpful. Everyone does.

And this is what infidelity is. It is the selfish desire to be helpful to more than one person.

Infidelity is natural.

19

But why was Nana jealous? Was she jealous of Anjali or Moshe?

She was jealous of Anjali with Moshe. She was jealous of Anjali's sexual ability. Anjali, Nana had noted, came even quicker than Moshe. This made Nana feel sad. Anjali was every boy's favourite. Not only that, she was every girl's favourite. Anjali was simpatico.

'So that was good it was really good?' Nana said to Anjali. 'Was lovely, no it was really really good,' said confused and fractious Anjali. 'I din think, I haven't come like that oh well frages. It was just. I feel all tingly. Like it wasn't jus my cunt but all over?' she said. 'Mso glad,' said Nana. 'It sounded lovely,' she said.

Poor Nana. She hated sex. She hated its competitiveness. She was glad that Moshe and Anjali had enjoyed themselves. She was not feeling angry with them. She was angry with sex. She wished there were no more sex. She just wished that Moshe would hold her. But instead he was lying on the floor, looking blissful.

Anjali stood up, looking for tissues. There were some Kleenex on the floor by the bed. She crooked her legs and wiped herself, along the top of her thighs up to her pubic hair. She used one up then dragged out another. Then

Moshe got into bed with Nana. Clean dry Anjali got in too. They shuffled each other, happy.

But really only Moshe was happy. And even Moshe was nervous. He was nervous about what might happen next – the precise nature of future shenanigans.

You're offered it once, he thought, but that's just to keep you sweet. You do it once then they make you watch over and over again.

Moshe was no fool, you see. He needed more positive signs.

20

In August 2000, the Italian police intercepted some conversations in Arabic between Al Qaeda members.

A suspected Al Qaeda member from Yemen, called Mr Abdulrahman, told an Egyptian living in Italy that he was 'studying airplanes'. Then he added: 'God willing, I hope that I can bring you a window or piece of airplane the next time we meet.' According to the Italian version of the Arabic, he went on: 'We must only strike them, and hold our heads on high. Remember well: the danger in the airports.'

It is not easy, spotting clues.

Referring to America, Mr Abdulrahman said, 'We intermarry with Americans, and thus they study the Koran. They have the feeling they are lions, a world power; but we will do them this service, and then the fear will be seen.' He also said, 'There are big clouds in the sky, there in that country the fire has been lit, and awaits only the wind.'

The Italian police, speaking in their defence, said that

177

such images can often mean the opposite of what they appear to mean. And I have a lot of sympathy with these *carabinieri*. Mr Abdulrahman does not sound like an international terrorist. He sounds like an alcoholic. He sounds like my friends when they have taken a lot of drugs.

It is not easy, spotting clues. In retrospect, everything is so much clearer.

8

Romance

I

THE WEEKEND AFTER his first ever threesome, Moshe was excitable. He wanted to see what would happen next. He wanted to find out what sexual treats were in store for him. But unfortunately for Moshe, what happened next was not sex. It was not a sexual treat. It was, in fact, an absence of sexualness of any kind.

Nana went away on holiday. She went away with Papa for ten days.

This is not the best time for a digression, I know. But I cannot always choose the digressions. Some of them are inevitable. And this holiday was inevitable. Nana and Papa had booked their September holiday, if you remember, as early as the shopping trip to Savile Row in Chapter 4. It was Papa's treat to Nana for when she finished her MA. Papa had bought two Go flights to Venice. This was Nana's ideal holiday. They would fly to Venice and in the middle of their Venice holiday they would make one pilgrimage to a small town in Romania. It would be fun to travel on the Central European trains. Because although Papa quite wanted Benidorm, or Torremolinos, Nana wanted a cultural holiday.

That was what Nana was like. It was what she liked. I can't help that.

2

I do not know what your views of holidays are. Maybe the only place you have ever been to for a holiday is Mykonos. Maybe your definition of a holiday is to rent a small flat furnished with a wicker coffee table and a collection of Mills and Boon novels, and have sex with at least one boy a day. Or maybe the only place you would ever go to is a skiing resort. Unless you can ski all day, and have a quick tuna sandwich on the piste for lunch, then a holiday is not a holiday.

People are funny about holidays. Everybody has their theory of the perfect holiday. And I do not want your theory about the perfect holiday to influence your take on Nana and Papa's holiday.

I can imagine this would not be your ideal holiday. Perhaps it makes you question why anyone would like Nana. But you must not let your theory put you off Nana and Papa.

The point of Nana and Papa abroad is that this is the one section of true love in the book. It may seem dowdy and geeky, it may not seem like your kind of holiday at all, but this was love. It was purely altruistic.

You must not misinterpret.

No. In this book, Nana and Papa are true love. That is what I want you to remember. So the title of this chapter is true and not true. If, for you, a romance is always sexual, then the title is not a true title. But if romance means perfect love, then it is true.

3

In Venice, the two of them stumbled off a rocking water taxi at Arsenale, and walked along the quay to the Hotel Bucintoro. Nana had chosen the hotel from the *Time Out* website. It was small and had an ochre front wall and views of the lagoon. It was also where the painter James McNeill Whistler stayed at the end of the nineteenth century. This appealed to scholarly Nana.

They checked in, then walked up the red and green floral carpet to their room. Nana sat on one of the beds and tugged her sandals off, while Papa stood, a silhouette, at the window. He leaned against the window, happily. And Nana walked across to join him. There was a large standing fan by the window. Nana switched it off. She stood next to Papa, and leaned her head on the frame beside him, so they were symmetrical. Nana's bare feet were cold on the cheap terrazzo floor, a glazed terrine of grey and black splinters. She noted the brush lines in the frame's paintwork, the embedded bristles in the gloss. They watched the water lighten, and darken, repeatedly.

It was beautiful.

Venice is beautiful, it really is. Some people think it is too beautiful, whatever that means, and some people think it is not beautiful at all, they think people say Venice is beautiful only because it is old, and all these people are just completely wrong.

Venice is beautiful.

'It's byootiful,' said Nana, 'really byootiful.' Papa said, 'And what's that?' She said, 'That, that's the Dogana. That's the customs house.' 'Uhhuh,' said Papa. 'And is that beautiful?' 'No,' said Nana. 'That's not beautiful. Well it's okay. It's oh kay. It's not unbeautiful.' 'And what about that, what's that?' said Papa. 'That's the church, that's Salute,' said Nana. 'It's beautiful,' said Papa. 'No it's not,' said Nana. 'It is definitely not beautiful.' 'Why not?' said Papa. 'It just isn't,' said Nana. 'But why not?' said Papa. 'You are going to take me to Florian's,' said Nana, 'and then I will tell you what is beautiful.' Then she kissed him. 'I want a hot chocolate,' she said.

As they walked down the stairs to the foyer, they could hear the unmistakable sounds of a woman on holiday faking or reaching an orgasm.

Both of them ignored these sounds.

4

In case you are worried, that is the only moment where sex will intrude on this chapter. There is no sex in this chapter. In this chapter, Nana is at her happiest.

Sometimes I think that this book is an attack on sex. Sometimes I think that it is prudish. It might be. And if it is, then some people, maybe even a lot of people, will think that this is wrong. They will think that being prudish is indefensible.

But me, I do not think that prudishness is indefensible. I really don't.

Caffé Florian is a coffee shop on St Mark's Square in Venice. It is a very old coffee shop. This means that now it is very very expensive. If Moshe had been there, it would have upset him. It was maybe four pounds for a coffee. It was maybe five pounds for a hot chocolate.

But Nana and Papa were not going to worry about the price. They were on holiday. They loved the kitsch charm of Florian. Delighted, they sat at their miniature heptagonal table. Perhaps 'miniature' does not quite convey how small this table was. It was an eighteenth-century table. It was premised on the notion that a giant human was five foot five. And it looked like something, thought uncomfortably folded six-foot Nana. It was like something but no, she, no, she could not remember.

Nana looked out the window at the multicoloured domes of St Mark's Cathedral. St Mark's Cathedral is the most famous building in Venice. And this made Nana happy. She was happy she could see St Mark's Cathedral, while she sipped an eighteenth-century hot chocolate. She loved being a tourist. And here, I completely agree with Nana. I love being a tourist too.

She said, 'I so love that cathedral.' She said, 'I just love the way it's so colourful.' She said, 'I love the shapes.' She poured out some thick chocolate from a porcelain jug, and the faint lines dribbled from beneath its lip, each ending in a dense clot. It was darker than chocolate, almost black. 'It's just so cool,' she said.

It's like a backgammon board! she thought, relieved. Yes, the table was like her old backgammon board.

Nana was happy. Nana was nostalgic.

She was looking at Papa and remembering how, when she was young, she would get up and sleepily walk downstairs. She could hear Papa chatting on the phone. The French windows would be open. She'd get up in the morning and the living room would be cold and Nana would be able to hear the motorway noise, the start of the M1 in the blurry distance.

She loved being a tourist. Tourism was restful. Tourism was just like home.

6

For example, this was one of their conversations in Venice.

'What's that?' said Papa. 'What?' said Nana. 'That,' said Papa. 'That is eighteenth century,' said Nana. 'Really,' said Papa. 'Yup,' said Nana. 'That is the architecture of the eighteenth century.' 'How do you know?' said Papa, suspiciously. 'Because I, because of the, because of the bricks,' said Nana. 'But you can't see the bricks,' pointed out Papa. 'Yes I can,' said Nana. 'No you can't,' said Papa. 'Yes I can,' said Nana. 'And they're eighteenth sentry.'

'And what about that?' said Papa. 'That is, that is the Dogeez Palis,' said Nana. 'And that is the Bridge of Sighs.' 'It is not the Bridge of Sighs,' said Papa. 'I have seen the Bridge of Sighs on a postcard and that is not the Bridge of Sighs.' 'No,' said Nana. 'No. You're right. It's the Ponte dei Pugni.' 'The what?' said Papa. 'The Ponte dei Pugni,' said Nana. 'Never heard of it,' said Papa. 'I read about it in the *Rough Guide*,' said Nana. 'Architecture, it's architectral histry you're doing, isn't it?' said Papa. 'That's right,' said Nana. 'You know that.' 'Only teasing,' grinned Papa.

He wasn't teasing. He couldn't remember. But I am teasing you too – just you wait. You'll see why I'm teasing you later.

On a gondola, in the dark, drinking demi-sec Cava from the bottle, Papa and Nana were happy together.

7

Three days later, in the middle of their study of the Venetian Renaissance, Nana and Papa set off for Târgu Jiu. Târgu Jiu is a small industrial town in western Romania. It was Nana's special sightseeing treat.

Nana was no conventional tourist.

In Venice railway station, a man in a ticket booth told them the train times from Venice to Budapest. He did this by reading the times off a grid, using a ruler illustrated with the sights of Turkey. Then from Budapest they got a train to Craiova, in Romania, and from Craiova to Târgu Jiu.

But why was this unpronounceable Romanian town Nana's special sightseeing treat? Because there are three Brancusi monuments in Târgu Jiu. But who is Brancusi?

Brancusi was a sculptor at the start of the twentieth century. He was Romanian, but he lived in Paris. In Romanian, Brancusi's name is pronounced 'Brunkoosh'. But I don't think that matters. Calling him 'Brunkoosh' is quite pretentious. In this book, you can stick to 'Brankoozy'.

This is getting quite cultural, I know. But cultural tourism is inescapably cultural. I can't help that. If Nana and Papa had chosen to go to Benidorm, then obviously I would not have had to bring Brancusi into this. But they are not in Benidorm. They have just arrived in Târgu Jiu, a small industrial town in western Romania.

Anyway, it is not that cultural. Brancusi was a sculptor in the twentieth century. He was Nana's favourite sculptor. He was the subject of her proposed Ph.D. That is all you need to know.

The frontage of the kiosks at Târgu Jiu station was a collage of adverts. There were adverts for Wrigley's Spearmint and adverts for Snickers. The adverts for Marathon bars were still there also, although Marathon bars, thought Nana, must have been discontinued at least ten years ago. The air hurt Nana's skin. It hurt to breathe. As I've said, this was a small industrial town. Her dress stuck to her. Papa strode out to the row of taxis and drivers outside the station. He demanded Hotel Europa. A driver smiled.

There was an arrangement of faded multicoloured beads draped over the driver's seat, like a poncho, and Sellotaped to its back was a felt-tip note occasionally in capitals concerning his children and his unending belief in God. His God was portrayed in a hologram. Nana stared out the smudged window. Half an hour later, twenty pounds lighter, they arrived at the Hotel Europa. This hotel was on a main road, with some Coke parasols on a thin concrete terrace. Papa thanked his driver, as he turned, tugging the suitcase out the boot, and saw the adverts for Spearmint and Snickers, at an angle of thirty degrees on the other side of the station road.

Papa tried not to look downcast. He tried not to be angry. Regaining his poise, in the dark lobby of the post-Communist Hotel Europa, Papa spoke French. He handed over their passports. He marched Nana down the empty corridors. There was a mop with its handle angled into a door. He located their room, on the seventh floor of the empty hotel. Its wallpaper was flowers. It was crimson roses embedded in green leaves.

They dropped the bags then left.

Nana and Papa walked past the Manhatten Martini bar where is always cocktail hour. They reached the main square. In the square, four loudspeakers were playing local radio. And Papa and Nana paraded, scared. They were looking for the park.

This is the cultural bit. In 1935, the president of the Romanian National League of Women, who happened to be the Romanian Prime Minister's wife, commissioned a war memorial from the famous Romanian sculptor Brancusi. This memorial would be built in Târgu Jiu. For this memorial, Brancusi constructed a Gate of the Kiss, a Table of Silence, and an Unending Column. Brancusi was a sculptor with a repertoire. He repeated himself. He repeated himself with variations.

Brancusi's 'Gate of the Kiss' was in the municipal park at Târgu Jiu. The gate looked like a dolmen. A dolmen is two vertical stones on which a horizontal stone balances. The 'Table of Silence' was in the park too. This was a large block of stone, two metres in diameter, with twelve stone seats. Twelve was symbolic. It was the number of months in a year, and also the number of guests at a traditional Romanian funeral.

Nana stopped at the 'Table of Silence'. Standing by the table, if she looked back, the 'Gate of the Kiss' was at the opposite end of the park. Beneath it, a girl and a boy were kissing. The boy's hair was sideparted and slick. And if Nana turned round there was a calm lake of oily water.

She was feeling just a tiny bit scared. This was an adventure, and she liked adventure. It was just that it was getting dark. And she wanted to see the last Brancusi before it got dark.

So, after they had chomped and swallowed at speed a hot dog from a stall, Nana and Papa reached the final object – Brancusi's 'Unending Column', twenty-nine metres high. As they walked there, Nana told Papa all about Brancusi's home movie of the column, which he filmed when he put the column up in Târgu Jiu. He recorded, said Nana, how the clouds and the light changed the column's shape. They seemed to change its shape, she explained, because the column was a corrugated pole, with endless indentations.

But when they arrived at the column there was a difference. The 'Unending Column' wobbled between two racks of scaffolding. The crane next to it was higher. It was in a recreation ground, off a road in the village suburbs. And this all made Nana sad. She tried to imagine that the scaffolding wasn't there.

It is sad, but sometimes even tourism is not restful.

Papa said, 'No I like this. I can see what this has to do with architecture. I mean I. I.' He was trying to be nice. And Nana said, 'Brancusi said that architecture was just inhabited sculpture.' 'Yes of course,' said Papa. 'So you see?' said Nana. 'Of course sweetie,' said Papa. 'He organised his things like architecture,' said Nana. 'Uhhuh,' said Papa. 'This is architecture,' said Nana. 'It's organised so that you see that church behind.'

It was true. If you looked very hard, in the twilight, you could just see a small bronze dome.

'I've got a headache,' said Papa. 'No I really have.'

They walked back to the Hotel Europa.

Papa went into the minuscule bathroom and locked it. Coy about the sounds he made, he turned on the hot tap in the bath while he pissed. Then he turned on the cold as well, brushing his hand through the water, and squeezed in the non-fitting rubber plug. He sat down on the loo seat. He stood up and trod off his shoes via each ridged heel. Then he stared into the smeary mirror. He had a headache.

8

Nana and Papa returned to Venice for the last four days. This was Papa's part of the holiday. It was his non-cultural time. For the last four days, they were both going to sit and eat and drink. They would not look at art. They would not look at architecture.

Papa and Nana went walking, looking for bars. The squares they crossed were almost deserted. From time to time a late courier came past, on a water bike. Boxes of avocados were being unloaded on to a gondola, supervised by a man with a list Biroed on the back of a receipt. There was one open window in an office and a woman sitting in front of the fluorescent mauve pod of an Apple iMac had turned away from it and looked thoughtfully out at Nana and Papa as they passed.

This is an idyll. This whole chapter is an idyll.

For instance, in the Paradiso Perduto bar, Nana had just taught Papa how to roll and smoke a joint. She was teaching him about marijuana because she was worried about his headaches. She thought that hash might be a cure. That was how idyllic it was.

Nana said, 'Do you remember that restron, that one

called My Old Dutch, and you'd take me there after the dentist.' She said, 'I don't understand why pancakes. And anyway. Now lick it. Lick the paper. Yeah. And the pancakes were just so much huger than the plates and the plates were huge enough.' Papa said, 'That was when you were a vegetarian, so I became a vegetarian.'

This is what she loved, thought Nana. She loved remembering.

She said, 'That was a cool place.'

Then there was a pause. It is difficult to express a pause. It can be expressed only by what happens simultaneously. For instance, this pause was long enough for Nana to watch Papa tear off a piece of card from a box of Paradiso Perduto matches, try to squeeze it in as a roach, and then tear it in half so that it was smaller.

She said, 'I think I might.' She said, 'I was thinking I might move in with Moshe.'

She was moving in with Moshe? She was moving in with Moshe?!

It was true. She had made a decision. I have kept it from you like this so that you can be surprised too. You can compare your own reaction with Papa's reaction.

Papa's reaction was happiness. He was happy. He was purely happy for Nana.

Now obviously, Papa had not been a witness to a threesome. He did not know all the facts. He did not know about Nana and Anjali. He did not know, for example, that Nana had started to enjoy the phrase '*ménage à trois*'.

In celebration of Nana's happiness, Papa, the benevolent angel of this story, lit up and took a long drag on his fat and badly made spliff.

9

When it was the night before Christmas, when Nana was still young enough for proper Christmas, Papa would sit on the edge of her bed and read to Nana. He read to her *The Night Before Christmas*. It was a poem. In this poem, Nana found out what preparations had been made in Lapland for Father Christmas's journey to the end of the night, delivering Christmas presents. Nana knew all about each reindeer. She knew their names. When she was older, she could only remember Rudolph – of course she could remember Rudolph – and Dasher and Prancer and Donna and Blitzen. There were more reindeer, but those were the ones she remembered. When Papa read the poem, he seemed very serious. It was not just a story. He seemed very concerned and grave. And Nana loved Papa's seriousness. She thought that this was right. It was the most serious thing – how Father Christmas would get to Nana.

It was Nana's favourite memory. She loved Papa's reading voice.

9

Intrigue

Conventionally, the *ménage à trois* is seen as sexually uncon-
ventional. It is edgy. Couples can be obscene, it is true, but
in the end they are still just couples. They are still ordinary.
Whereas a *ménage à trois* is bohemian. It can't help being
bohemian.

In case this incontestable point needs proving, take the
film *Cabaret*. Produced in New York in the early seventies,
Cabaret has a trashy glam-rock glamour. Set in Berlin in
the early thirties, this film tells the story of an American
cabaret singer called Sally (played by the young Liza
Minelli), and a British writer called Brian. Sally and Brian
are girlfriend and boyfriend. Then they meet Maximilian.
Maximilian is a German count. You can imagine what
happens. Sally falls for Maximilian. Brian also falls for
Maximilian. Maximilian falls for both of them.

The threesome is the hallmark of a glam-rock plot. It
wouldn't be bohemian without a *ménage à trois*.

For instance, the most famous line in the film is this. 'Twosy beats onesy, but nothing beats three.' The line is sung with a leer by the rouged and male MC of the Kit Kat Club, in evening dress, flanked by two buxom women. And that is the conventional view of the threesome. The threesome is virulently sexual. It is pre-Nazi decadence. It is sex personified.

I know all that. I know that this is how lots of people think about the *ménage à trois*, if they think about it at all. I just think this view of the *ménage* is inaccurate. It misses out so many of the facts.

It was autumn. As she had told Papa, Nana moved in with Moshe. She began a new term at the Architectural Association, to begin her Ph.D. in Architectural Theory. Moshe came to the end of his run as Slobodan Milosevic in Richard Norton-Taylor's play, *Peacekeeping Force*, at the Tricycle Theatre in Kilburn. Anjali completed her year's contract of Johnson's Baby Powder adverts. Anjali kind of moved in with Moshe too. She had a key cut. So she popped in and out. She stayed there every weekend.

I hope you are happy now. I hope you are clear about the living arrangements.

They were a contemporary *ménage à trois*. They were definitely a *ménage à trois*. It was undeniable. They had sex in twos and three.

2

But a *ménage* is not just a sexual thing. It is not just a pre-Nazi decadent thing. Like everything else, it is also domestic. Nana and Anjali and Moshe played depraved

194

sexual games, of course, but the three of them also went swimming. On Saturday mornings, Moshe and his two girl-friends went swimming in the Oasis Pool on High Holborn. And I want to watch them swim. I especially want to watch Moshe at the swimming pool.

Swimming was mostly pure bliss for Moshe. But there were some complications. Some of these were minor, one of them was not.

These were the minor complications.

He was put out by the separate changing rooms. Gender segregation seemed unfair. He felt a little jealous. As he took off his low-cut H&M jeans, keeping his feet dry by standing on his socks and shoes, he had no idea what was going on in the girls' changing rooms. Morosely, Moshe stared at other men's penises. He disliked them. He only liked breasts. Carefully, without seeming gay, pretending to extract wax from his ears with a blue cotton bud, he compared his penis to the other penises. It seemed all right. It did not seem specially wonderful, but it seemed all right.

Moshe got into his navy Adidas trunks, dipped his feet in viscous disinfectant, and walked through to the pool. He stepped down, clinging bravely to the stainless-steel steps. The pool, at its deepest point, was three metres. This slightly scared Moshe. He did not know his height exactly, he did not know his height in metres, but he reckoned that three metres must be double. It must be at least double how tall he was.

Moshe looked round and saw a white cage containing bendy sponge floats, candy-striped rafts and orange inflat-able armbands. He wondered if it might be possible to use this large array of floats and rafts and armbands. He decided not. Anyone else could come in. A pretty sixteen-year-old girl could come in. And if a pretty sixteen-year-old girl joined him in the pool, Moshe did not want to be clutching a blue-and-white-striped polystyrene float.

Moshe hovered in the shallow end, looking at the entrance to the girls' changing room. He thought about the tricks they played on him. One morning, Nana and Anjali fitted Moshe up with water wings and carried him. Or Nana and Anjali swam away and kissed, treading water, in the deep end. Nana and Anjali were much better swimmers than Moshe. They teased him. He imagined them porno-graphically soaping each other's tits in the pre-swimming shower. This gave him an erection, trapped in his tight trunks. So he stood there, leaning his elbows on the greasy bobbled tiles, looking nonchalant and pensive. And he was being pensive. He was thinking about his coffee afterwards in his favourite café called the Mustard Seed in Finsbury. In the Mustard Seed, Moshe could dab Vaseline on to the chlorinated sores and welts of his fingers' eczema. The Mustard Seed was his rest cure, his urban retreat.

3

While he waits for his erection to subside and thinks about cappuccino, let us consider Moshe. We have considered all the minor complications that made Moshe's domestic routine problematic. But now let us consider his erotic nature. His erotic nature was the major complication.

The thing is, Moshe was not a Don Juan type. If he had been a Don Juan type, he would have seen his current sexual situation as a conquest. He would have seen two girls at once as a sexual victory. But Moshe did not see it this way. And I can understand this. I am not a Don Juan type either.

Moshe was moral. He loved Nana. He loved her virtuously. And this virtuous love meant that he could not really enjoy it, the *ménage à trois*.

In the glam film *Cabaret*, there is a fraught conversation between Sally and Brian, the original girlfriend and boyfriend. Brian shouts, 'Oh screw Maximilian!' to which Sally replies, 'I do.' Then Brian, after a little pause, quietly says, 'So do I.'

I very much like this snippet of conversation. It summarises neatly the underlying relationships in a *ménage à trois*. The *ménage*, as Moshe was finding out, was based on mutual infidelity. A threesome was three different couples. And one of these couples was Anjali and Moshe. This did not make Moshe very happy. He enjoyed it, he enjoyed all the sex with Anjali. He was just not sure that he approved. It was, in the end, infidelity.

Moshe was not a Don Juan. He was not cool. He was a romantic. Now, my definition of a romantic is this. A romantic is a person who needs a love affair to be a moral affair as well. And Moshe did not think that a *ménage à trois* was moral.

Moshe was too nice for a *ménage à trois*.

4

However, you can think two things at once. He felt uneasy, and that feeling is important. But Moshe was only human. In addition to feeling uneasy, he could also acknowledge the obvious perks of having two girlfriends.

For instance, in the Oasis Pool, the *ménage* was normally domestic. It was normally a series of invigorating lengths up and down the pool. But on this particular Saturday swim, it was naughty. Anjali's bikini top was flopping undone. That was why Anjali and Nana were late. They emerged from the changing room, giggling, with Anjali's arms crossed over her chest. The catch, she explained, was broken. And it was true. As she breasted the waters, her breasts appeared. It was, she told Moshe, a new bikini. She had bought it last week in Topshop. She had worn it once, said wide-eyed Anjali, without any problems. It was just that now it was useless.

They were a naughty threesome and they improvised. As you may remember, I like it when people improvise. Artfully concealed by orange water wings, Anjali's arms were kept close to her chest. This did for a bikini top. But it did not solve the dilemma of the decorous morning swim. The three of them stood in the shallow end, by the water filter, confused.

I am ashamed to admit it, but the odd feeling of abandon caused by her naked breasts had just given Anjali an idea. Even though she is one of my heroines, she did not want a decorous swim. She suddenly wanted a louche swim. She wanted to make Moshe come in the water. So with Nana standing behind him, Anjali stooped lowish in the water and gathered Moshe's penis inside his Adidas trunks. Even with the weight of a swimming pool on it, his penis grew. It grew and grew. And considerate Anjali promised Moshe that nothing would get spilled. At the critical moment, she would lean down and Nana would raise him up enough for his penis to break the water and meet her mouth. So everything was fine.

Moshe's eyes looked frightened. They expressed fear of police. As Anjali explained that in an emergency the water filter would eliminate all other traces of evidence, Moshe stood rigid and was scared. This does not seem to me unreasonable. They were tightly wedged into the corner of a public swimming pool, one of them apparently dressed only in a pair of water wings. It was not, reasoned Moshe, unsuspicious. It would probably not go unnoticed by the lifeguard.

It did not go unnoticed by the lifeguard. He was strolling over to assist this group of non-swimmers in the shallow end, one of whom needed water wings. The lifeguard was a tall and gorgeous man. All six abdominal muscles were clearly visible. He was very beautiful. He was starkly handsome. He made Moshe feel undernourished. And sadly, Anjali Moshe and Nana never found out his name. But I will tell you this lifeguard's name. His name was Ade.

Ade said, 'Hi.' Moshe replied brightly, 'Hi.' He was wondering what Ade could see. Ade could see enough. Ade said, 'You okay with those?' He was talking about the water wings. 'Yes yes yes we're fine,' said Moshe, wondering what his relatives would say when the *Jewish Chronicle* picked the story up. Anjali smiled at Ade. Nana looked away, abashed. And Ade smiled.

You see, even a lifeguard was charmed by a threesome. Even a lifeguard saw a threesome as the essence of edgy cool. Ade winked. He walked away.

Perhaps Anjali's behaviour seems unusually exhibitionist. I can see that it might need explaining. The thing is, Anjali and Moshe were not particularly relaxed being sexual together. In the course of the *ménage*, they always remained friends who, inexplicably, also had sex. They had sex because they were meant to have sex. They were, after all, two-thirds of a *ménage à trois*. But dutiful sex is, well, dutiful. Dutiful sex is boring.

I think that this was a pity. In many ways a threesome is the ultimate sexual unit. It is the socialist utopia of sex. One advantage of a threesome is that sexual responsibilities can be shared out equally. Sexual positions can be redistributed. Anjali, for example, had always felt unhappy asking a girl to use a dildo on her. With girls, Anjali coyly felt that begging for a dildo seemed to indicate an excessive interest in penetration. But obviously, in the *ménage*, she felt no such inhibition asking Moshe to use his penis on her. And Moshe was pleased to use his penis on her. The one position that Nana disliked was the girl on all fours, fucked from behind. She said Moshe hurt her when he did that. She could feel him almost in her stomach and it hurt her. Whereas Anjali was happy to crouch there.

Redistribution worked. It worked sexually. Anjali loved it when Moshe pushed into her, deeply. She *came*.

As for Moshe, one regret he felt when thinking about his sexual repertoire with Nana was the difficulty of the sexual position '69'. This position is simultaneous oral sex. It rarely featured in Nana and Moshe's sex life because Nana was six foot. And Moshe was not. In order for the position to be truly successful, Moshe's penis would have had to extend inversely, backwards. Instead, in real life, either Nana's back was painfully arched, or her mouth could only suckle on his inner thigh, close to his knee. Or Moshe could lick Nana's tummy button. Whereas Anjali, Anjali was smaller than Moshe. Her mouth was in just the right place. Everything was in the right place.

So why, if it was sexual utopia, was a threesome not perfect? I am going to explain with an illustration. Well, an imaginary illustration. You will have to imagine a sketch. This sketch shows Anjali on all fours, and Moshe kneeling behind her. If you want, you can imagine a small jutting prong veering from Moshe's waist. Anyway, the interest of this sketch is not the prong. It is the thought balloons.

You know what they are feeling. They are feeling enjoyably fucked. It is what they are thinking that is the problem. You already know what would be written inside Moshe's thought balloon. 'Nana,' he would be moaning in this sketch, 'darling Nana.' His thought balloon was soppy and romantic. Anjali's thought balloon was different. It was soppy and romantic, that is true. But it was lesbianly romantic. It was full of lesbian memories. 'Zosia,' she was thinking, 'Zosia.' She was remembering her ex. And even, oh no no no, she was occasionally thinking 'Nana'. She was occasionally remembering more recent lesbian moments, like the time that Nana had made her come in Camden Library on the Euston Road, in the Ordnance Survey area, leaning against Wales and Northern Ireland.

You see, as I have mentioned before, Anjali was more bisexual than most. And she was a proficient bisexual girl. She had a gift for every sexual permutation. She had a talent. But in the end she was not really that into boys. Not as much as she was into girls.

Anjali did girls. She fell for girls.

6

So, as you can see, this *ménage à trois* was ambiguous. It was less bohemian than it looked. You know that Moshe was not that happy. And it does not seem that Anjali was very happy either. A *ménage*, you see, is not pre-Nazi decadence. Not at all.

Even the sleeping arrangements were difficult.

Ordinary couples often develop particular sides of the bed. In the doomed relationship of Stacey and Henderson, for example, Stacey always slept on the left. But in a threesome, sleeping positions are more complex. They are not neutral. They are symbolic.

For instance, to celebrate the close of *Peacekeeping Force*'s triumphant run at the Tricycle, Nana and Moshe and Anjali went to Le Caprice for lunch. Nana and Moshe and Anjali did not, however, remember much of their expensive lunch. They were not gourmets. They drank. They got noisily drunk and talked about themselves. They got drunk and tetchy.

It was so glamorous, thought Moshe.

But this was the conversation. The conversation was not glamorous.

'You won mind, will you, if I sleep in the middle tonigh?' said Nana. 'Jus for tonigh?' asked puzzled Moshe. 'Well I really can't go on sleeping on the end,' said Nana. 'I wake up every morning when those men come for the bottles and then I can't get back to sleep and then you get up and I'm sleepy all day. You don mind, dyou?'

And Moshe said 'No, um, no, iss fine.'

Let me sketch out a quick diagram. Normally in bed it had been

Nana, Moshe, Anjali.

Now Nana wanted

Moshe, Nana, Anjali.

There was a subtle difference. Look who was next to whom. And Moshe understood this difference.

'And also,' she said, 'there's the window.' 'The window?' said Moshe. 'Yeah well I thought I'd get used to it I mean,' said Nana, 'I often sleep badly and maybe if. I don know. It's just so cold.' 'Well less just stop sleeping with the window open,' said Anjali. 'From now on', said Anjali, 'iss shut. I prefer it shut too.'

Moshe stared at his steamed sea bass, wrapped in a wilted leaf.

'Or you could sleep on the end and I'll go in the middle,' said Anjali. 'If you go on the other end then you won't be near the window.'

In Anjali's revised diagram, the bedding arrangement went

Moshe, Anjali, Nana.

Nana liked this arrangement. Moshe did not like this arrangement at all.

Moshe leaned round and grabbed the wine from its silver stand behind him – which placed him full frontal with a black-and-white glossy of Elvis Costello. Elvis Costello, it turned out, was a regular at Le Caprice. He belonged to the glittering people. Moshe glared. He suddenly hated Elvis Costello. He hated glitzy happy people.

'You never said,' he said to Nana. 'Did she say?' he said to Anjali. 'I don't want you to,' he said to Anjali and Nana.

And Nana said, 'Well I could sleep on the futon tonigh, I suppose. I could jus sleep there.' 'The futon?' said Moshe. 'Why the futon? Why can't we just shut the window?' 'We could shut the window,' said Anjali, to Nana. 'No no, why should Moshe be put out?' said Nana to Anjali. 'I mean it's your flat isnit?' she said to Moshe. 'And you've always said you feel too hot with the window shut. So I should just sleep on the futon tonight.' 'Look,' said Moshe, 'akshully iss nothing. Really nothing. It's not much of a sacrifice,' grinned Moshe.

Nana said, 'What did you say?' She said, 'Sorry I didn't hear that. I thought my phone was ringing.'

He said, 'It's no sacrifice.' But Nana said, 'No no. Msleeping on the futon.' 'But wha if I say I don want you to?' said Moshe. 'I mean, you don like sleeping on your own. I know that. Why don you sleep in the bedroom with me and Anji? You don like it on your own.'

Two waiters were at the table beside them, crumbing down.

'Look you're being so silly,' said Nana. 'I mean. I spose I mean if Anjali prefers the window shut. I can sleep there with Anjali.' 'Bu bu, I just said we could close the window,' said Moshe. 'Oh babes,' said Nana, 'it's not going to be for ever. I'm juss not sleeping,' she said. 'Za good idea,' said Anjali.

'Because when you get up you won't have to mind about waking me up.' 'I wake you up?' said Moshe. 'Yeah, yeh,' said Anjali. 'In the mornings. When you climb over me.'

Nana shook the small ice cluttering her sparkling water. Moshe went to piss.

There was a man at a table near the stairs to the loos who had hair, thought Moshe, that he must have consciously designed himself. It had been tightly waved that morning with a round horsehair prickly brush. This man was showing photos to his companion, his male companion. His companion had a darkly yellow tan, glistening red dyed hair and gold Hugo Boss glasses with metal lines that swooped horizontally across and past the top. He had a wart and a moustache.

For some reason these two men made Moshe feel bitter. They made him feel very bitter. And although Moshe would not admit it, I can tell you the reason. It was because they were two men together. They had a homosexual look.

It is sad, but yes, one of the heroes of my book has become momentarily homophobic.

The men's loos, however, were calmer. Luckily, there were no men. The urinals were one long urinal. This urinal had sloping frosted glass at its base, to allow the last weak and shaken drops to smooth away. Moshe bent backwards, scooping his penis out of his paisley-print boxer shorts. He tugged a pubic hair from his foreskin. Then he pissed. It felt nicer, thought Moshe, in the toilets, with the dimmed-down light and a black soft carpet. He looked at the rows of *Armitage Shanks* in discreet handwritten grey italics. He watched the way an empty circle spread around the point where his piss hit the porcelain. He shook the last weak drops away. Then he tucked his penis back in, it dribbled a little, zipped himself up, and ruffled his hair with water. The water fell out densely smooth with bubbles from the tap.

When he got back, the bill was on the table, in a leatherette wallet. Nana and Anjali were kissing. They were kissing little kisses.

Moshe, thought Moshe, had a problem.

7

Moshe's problem was entertainingly similar to the problem of dissent in a capitalist society. As many left-wing critics have pointed out, it is very difficult to object to capitalism. One person who tried to explain this was Antonio Gramsci. Antonio Gramsci was an Italian Marxist. In 1926, he was arrested by the Fascist government, and put in prison. In 1928 he was sentenced to twenty years, four months, and five days. He died from a stroke in 1937. At this point, he was also suffering from arterio-sclerosis, a tubercular infection of the back, and pulmonary tuberculosis. However, it was not all bad. He had written his *Prison Notebooks*.

In these notebooks, Antonio outlined lots of theories. One of these theories was about how to be revolutionary when you live in a capitalist society. Revolution was tricky, thought Antonio, because of a thing called 'hegemony'. Hegemony was 'the combination of force and consent, which balance each other reciprocally, without force predominating excessively over consent. Indeed, the attempt is always made to ensure that force will appear to be based on the consent of the majority, expressed by the

so-called organs of public opinion – newspapers and asso-
ciations . . .'

Phew.

Antonio, basically, was saying that no one ever cared
when you disagreed with capitalism. The capitalists rigged
it so no one noticed.

I, however, have a different theory why no one cares
when someone attacks capitalism. You always look like a
poseur. If you are rich, and you complain, people assume
you are hypocritical. If you are poor, and you complain,
people assume you are envious.

Similarly, if Moshe complained that a threesome was not
ideal, you would assume he was being hypocritical. A grown
man complaining about two girls in bed with him. The idea
of it! But if he held your wrist, looked into your pretty blue
eyes, and insisted that it was really not ideal, then you would
assume that his objection to the threesome was pure jealousy. He was not getting the extraordinary sexual encounters, the dual sexual attention, that he had expected.

Sexually, I reckon you'd think, Moshe was poor.

8

A *ménage à trois*, then, is a mixture of domestics and sex.
It is much more similar to a couple than people think. It is
just a more complicated couple. For example, you still have
to buy milk. So, on a Saturday or Sunday morning, Nana
and Anjali would walk to the cute dairy shop on Amwell
Street.

I am going to describe this milk-buying. It was a significant habit.

Lloyds & Son ~Dairy Farmers~First Class Dairy Products was painted in slanting gilt italics on the shop front. Lloyds & Son~Dairy Farmers~First Class Dairy Products was always full of wives. It was also full of fathers. This made Nana giggle. It made her giggle because she could imagine what the fathers and wives were thinking when they looked at Nana and Anjali. The fathers and wives were confused, thought Nana, by two girls coming into the shop, hand in hand. And what Nana really liked was that, although she and Anjali were apparently avant-garde, although they were apparently bohemian, they were bohemian by accident. Nana felt just as wifely as the wives in the Amwell Dairy. She felt totally like a married woman. It was just that she had a wife as well as a husband. That was the only difference.

Obviously, Anjali felt differently about husbands and wives. She was much more interested in the wife.

The decor of the dairy was a delight. There were ochre pots of Colman's mustard arranged in a pyramid, like circus acrobats. There was a poster from the fifties of a pretty, happy woman with her favourite Jersey milk. Her hair curled round her perfect curled ears. Nana liked this old-time charm. Beside the doorstep, an untipped cigar of dogshit had been carefully brushed to one side. Nana patted the fake green grass on the inside edge of the window display, waiting in the queue. She liked the prickly softness. She liked the fakeness.

As for Anjali, Anjali gossiped. She said, 'Do you know why they split up? I know. And they seemed such a happy couple. I mean only last week did you read it that interview that one in *Heat* where she said. I know. That's so true.' Or, 'And apparently he didn't even look Palestinian. He looked,

I mean he was dressed in a suit.' And Anjali asked for the milk, then she tried to find some money. 'I need a quid,' said Anjali, 'have you got a quid, I need a quid?' Then they left, slaloming and grinning past the toddlers and the shopping bags.

That was the routine. Anjali and Nana walked back on to Lloyd Baker Street off Amwell Street. Nana loved looking up at the windows with net curtains and yuccas, a peeling 'I love Washington' sticker, a plastic moulded Noddy. And sometimes she imagined a girl stretching one leg on top of the duvet, in a Bhs nightie with an awkward scratchy label. Or another time she would see a woman standing next to a girl with pigtails, in a black velvet dress, whose hands pressed down on to an invisible piano.

Houses made Nana think about babies. They made her think about families. And families, in the end, for Nana, were heterosexual families. I feel I should make that clear.

Meanwhile, at about this point in the journey to get milk on a Sunday morning, Anjali would say, 'I love you so much.'

That is why milk was significant.

It is important to remember that there is more than one way of saying 'I love you'. There is the 'I love you' of engorged and ravishing love. But there is also the 'I love you' of casual happy friendship. And Anjali was using the phrase in this second way. Well, no, she started by using the phrase in this way. It was just that gradually this phrase was becoming more and more serious. In case you hadn't guessed, Anjali was becoming rather fond of Nana. Her use of the phrase 'I love you' was more and more becoming an example of engorged and ravishing love.

And maybe there was another reason too. Anjali was not

really sure that this arrangement was going to work out for her. She was still feeling left out of the central couple. The threesome was always uncertain. So maybe her 'I love you', on her own with Nana, was an example of insecurity too. She was asking Nana to reassure her.

Because after all, thought Anjali, she was the one who was going to get hurt here. If anyone was going to be left out and devastated, that person would be Anjali.

No one falls in love immediately. It takes time. It develops, sometimes, because of delicate, unnoticed reasons. From early October to mid-November, Anjali developed a milk routine with Nana and simultaneously fell in love.

But Nana did not know this. She thought that Anjali's 'I love you' was just a phrase of casual happy friendship. On this occasion, in November, distractedly Nana looked at a girl with a buggy, chatting to a girl with a buggy. One of them was saying, 'Cos I'm a nigger, black, proud. You know like Michael Jackson when he was young when he had that afro?' The two fat babies slouched and watched the plastic creased sky. And Nana nodded and kissed her, she kissed Anjali in public. It was Sunday morning. They went shopping for milk. It was domestic.

Nana was happy. She was thinking about happy families.

9

One night in 1936, the film actress Renée Muller was alone in the German Chancellery with the German Chancellor. At that time the Chancellor was Adolf Hitler. Because it was late, and they were alone, Renée was sure that Adolf wanted to have sex. And it seemed that she was right. He started to undress her. But just as they were about to get into bed, Adolf fell on the floor and begged Renée Muller to kick him.

Initially, Renée demurred. It was quite embarrassing, having the naked Chancellor on all fours, begging to be kicked. But Adolf pleaded. He said he was unworthy, just a worm, a simpleton, a brute who deserved no better treatment than a dog, a bad little boy who needed punishment.

Adolf grovelled. Sexually, he grovelled at Renée.

It is a funny thing about being embarrassed that in the end you prefer to do the thing that has been embarrassing you all along, rather than continue to be embarrassed. You get it over with. In the end, Renée Muller kicked Adolf. She kicked him quite gently, but she still kicked him. And this turned Adolf on. He begged for more. He begged and begged for more. 'You worm,' said Renée, 'you degenerate rat.' Adolf was really enjoying himself. He told Renée how generous she was being, how much more he was receiving than he deserved, that really she should not reward him with the benefits of so much discipline. He was not even worthy to be in the same room as her, said Adolf.

The amusing thing was that by this point Renée was also enjoying herself. She had never been a dominatrix before, but this was fun. Far from being embarrassed, the film actress Renée Muller had just discovered the abiding sexual fascination of her life. She kicked him very hard. She started to beat Adolf up.

How few sexual permutations there are. Poor Adolf, wanting to be kicked. Poor thing, coming out with lines like: 'I am not worthy to be in the same room as you.' I rather warm to Adolf. And poor Renée, entranced so quickly by the role of the dominatrix. In their innocence, neither Adolf nor Renée made their sex life specific. There were no minute orders from Adolf, concerning the exact order and strength of Renée's kicks. There was just a general wish. There was just a general kicking.

Adolf and Renée had just encountered a central human predicament. It is this. Sex is not specific. It is not original. You might think your perversions are all your own, but no. Perversion is general. Perversions are universal. You have to make them specific.

IO

Anjali was on the Internet. She was having a look at free porn, sitting on her own in Moshe's living room, one morning. She was roaming around a thumbnail gallery offered by eroticamateurz.com. In case you have never heard of a thumbnail gallery, a thumbnail is a picture. It is a pornographic picture, no bigger than a thumbnail. It expands, however, if you click on it.

This is crucial to the narrative. Honestly.

Anjali was masturbating.

A girl dressed in a jet necklace and black fishnets was pushing her hand into her vagina, so that all her fingers were submerged. Or, alternatively, set against what looked like a Jackson Pollock drip painting, executed in black and purple, she was on all fours leaning over a quartered maroon and navy cushion. A man's arm was also in this picture. His hand was not. This was because it was in a white surgical glove and his fingers were submerged. Anjali could not tell exactly where they were submerged. It seemed likely they were submerged in the girl's anus. It was difficult to tell.

Having exhausted the fisting gallery, Anjali was offered 29 snaps of horny babe cucking lover off in back of class, 30 zooms of gorgous sexy hottie opening fat bald beaver, 12 clips of baby got ass chicken showing raw pink pussy, 23 peeks at lucious titt girls with very small but juicy cuntz, and 20 snips of a hot pussy babe in leather with a gun to her meat.

This list bored Anjali.

The thing about pornography, which is also the thing about sex in general, is that you need imagination. You need to be precise. And it is difficult being precise. So often, you borrow other people's plots. You can't help borrowing other people's plots.

For instance, class and family were the main stories that Anjali could see. There were 28 zooms of sexy blonde spreading delicious bush for mom's lover. That was family. Or 16 stills of rough rider babes in the saddle on pony all day. That was class. Or 27 slides of neices visiting uncle and attacking size 12 rod, and 25 slides of dad tucking in favorite daughter for the evening. Family. Or 28 looks at fine wine blonde modeling her gorgous shapely ass, and 16 pix of career girls playing with their snatch after work. Class. Then again, there were 16 slides of little slut who piss on cock before blowing stud, and this was more unusual. It was not Anjali's thing – it is not my thing, actually – but it showed some imagination.

In fact, thought Anjali, only one description showed potential. This was 18 looks at neighbor boy fucking grandma after mowing her grass. It was the mown grass that was good. It showed such a homely appreciation of context.

Now, the reason Anjali was roaming the Internet was a sad one. But it was also one that could have been predicted. She was not hugely enjoying all the sexual responsibilities of a *ménage*. They were not all pleasures.

She was feeling, in other words, a lack of precise imagination in her sex life. And I know the reason for this. You know this reason too. She had fallen for Nana.

So she had had it, thought Anjali, with boys.

II

Nana's feelings have been glossed over in this description of the *ménage à trois*. Perhaps some of you are thinking that this is a serious omission. But I have ignored Nana for a reason. I wanted you to observe two facts before I got to Nana. The first fact was this. Anjali and Moshe had good sex. Physically they had good sex. And this was because Anjali was a sexual talent. But there was also a second fact. Neither Anjali nor Moshe were emotionally happy with the sex. This was because they were both attached to Nana.

Nana, however, was feeling unhappy too.

At first, Nana had been glad that the three of them seemed happy. It was not what she had imagined when she first met Moshe, but it was what had happened. And I applaud this pragmatism. I applaud this lack of self-pity.

But there were worries. The sex worried Nana. It worried her more and more.

What a hopeless *ménage*! It was the most sexual arrangement possible, but none of them was happy about sex. Moshe was feeling guilty. Anjali was feeling frustrated. And now it turns out that Nana was feeling uneasy.

She was feeling envious of Anjali. She was feeling jealous of Moshe. The reason for this was that Nana was not a sexual talent. She was sexually complicated. And it made her sad, being in the same room as Moshe and Anjali, while Moshe and Anjali had sex deliriously and skilfully. It was difficult to stay amused by this. It was a social effort.

That is why I wanted to gloss over Nana's feelings. I wanted you to appreciate how wrong she was to be worried and sad. I wanted you to see the irony. Moshe and Anjali thought that their sex life was a difficult sham. Nana thought that their sex life was ecstatic, Kama Sutric. She was worried and sad. She was depressed by her pedestrian libido.

There was another irony here too. In order to counter her feeling that she was the sexual anomaly in the *ménage*, Nana wanted to display willing. She wanted to be Anjali's equal. She did not do this, however, simply by having sex with Moshe. She did that, of course, she had sex with Moshe. But more importantly, she experimented with Anjali. She agreed to all of Anjali's suggestions. And Anjali's requests were becoming quite intense. As Anjali became less and less heterosexual, her requests became more specific and outlandish.

I don't know how outlandish Nana may seem. I assume she does not seem very outlandish. In sex, the one thing Nana liked — and we know all too well that sex was not Nana's favourite topic — was intimacy. She at least liked feeling cared for. Whereas Anjali was becoming ferocious. This made Nana feel a little uncomfortable. But what could she do? She did not want to seem prudish.

12

That is why, one day, Anjali's first, second and third fingers were inside Nana's vagina, just below the knuckle. They were slick with Johnson's KY Jelly, whose blue tube with a white flip-cap was somewhere in the duvet.

Into their domestic repertoire, Anjali and Nana had introduced the sexual practice known as fisting. They domesticated fist fucking. And that is an achievement, I think, domesticating fist fucking. They did this, led by Anjali, using tips culled from Internet pornography and lesbian film classics such as *How to Fuck in High Heels* and *Femme II*.

For those of you who may like to experiment too, or who simply find it difficult to imagine this, I shall try to give you a guide.

First, Anjali warmed Nana up. She pressed her tongue slowly against Nana's clitoris. Anjali lapped the mucus from Nana's vagina. She spread it round her wrinkled doughy labia. And Nana let her head go sideways, raising up her vulva against Anjali's tongue. This gesture gave Anjali ideas. Anjali pushed her finger round Nana's arsehole, dabbing it, then pushed it up and round and in. It made Nana snugly oddly full. And this was what Nana enjoyed, Anjali knew that. But unfortunately, Nana was not herself this morning. She wriggled. She wriggled. Anjali's finger was slightly uncomfortable. But Anjali interpreted Nana's wriggle not as a wriggle of discomfort, but a wriggle of pleasure. It was, thought Anjali, a request for something deeper. So Anjali pushed further in. She could feel the scraps of Nana's shit.

Nana said, 'Aahyoourrr.'

It was an ambiguous noise. I do not think you could have known without me telling you that this was a noise of pain. It could also have been a moan of pleasure. But no, it was a noise of pain.

Anjali looked up.

The reason why this unique episode of lesbian fisting did not end prematurely, in a crisis of nerves, before it was even fisting, was that Anjali was still deceived. She did not know Nana was not on heat. She thought it was a moan of pleasure. She thought Nana was begging for more. She thought she was bored with just one finger. She wanted the whole shebang.

Anjali picked up her tube of Johnson & Johnson's KY Jelly, for internal lubrication, which she had received as part of her complimentary pack of Johnson's goodies. She squeezed some jelly on her fingers and rubbed it on to Nana.

Nana, in case you are wondering, was petrified. She was glad that Anjali's hands were the smallest she had ever seen, but even so, it was still scary. And I am with her on this. I would have been scared. Even scarier, however, was the article she remembered, perhaps from *Marie Claire*, that informed its readers that only an orgasm could release a fist from the vagina. This put pressure on a girl like Nana.

Anjali had by now spread a large amount of KY Jelly outside and inside Nana's vagina. She had spread clear strands of it on to her right hand. She was very much enjoying herself. Frankly, this does not surprise me. A six-foot blonde girl with pale pubic hair was a wet mess, reclining, in front of her. It was not an unappealing sight.

Anjali, with the palm facing up, as she had observed in her educational photos, introduced the first and second fingers of her right hand. She did this very slowly. She moved very very slowly. She got nearly as deep as the knuckle. And simultaneously, with a delicate first finger of her left hand, she delicately touched Nana's clitoris. This went on for minutes. Then she slid in her third finger. It slid in surprisingly quickly. It slid in so quickly that Anjali decided to add the thumb in too. The thumb should be lain flat above the fingers, in a position known as the 'duckbill'. Anjali formed the duckbill. Nana moaned. She moaned, this time, in pleasure. It was, she thought, the most extraordinary thing. And Anjali pushed. She slowly pushed, curving her little finger inside as well.

Gradually, gradually, Anjali's right hand slipped in. Her hand was inside Nana up to the base of the fingers. She was finally fisting her.

Then Moshe walked in.

They all carried on as normal.

Moshe sat on the wooden desk chair by his little black Formica desk. He sat on the chair and picked up the nearest book – unconcerned, frightened, turned on. He began to read. The nearest book turned out to be the hardback *Collected Stories* of Saul Bellow, as recommended, according to Anjali, by *Elle*. Moshe did not buy books. He thought they were too expensive. He might browse and quite like one in a bookshop but then he would look at the price and that was it. Moshe would put the book down. He glanced at the dust-jacket flap of Saul Bellow's *Collected Stories*. Twenty pounds! he thought, astonished. Twenty pounds! But he read it. He read about the life of the Jewish male in America.

Nana, being fisted, looked at the picture of a Cadillac, snowbound, in Chicago, on the cover of Saul Bellow's collected stories. It was something else to think about. She grunted. Anjali was unfolding and clenching her fingers in Nana's vagina. And this was a fundamental pleasure for Nana. She grunted. Anjali smiled approvingly.

But Nana was finding it hard to relax with her boyfriend reading contemporary American literature while she was being fisted. And she was worried about the orgasm. She was worried that now was not the time for her to reach her first ever sociable orgasm. Anjali was pleasurable but also painful. So Nana decided that, for an experiment, they had done remarkably well. They had discovered a special treat. But now it was time to stop. 'I think that's enough,' said Nana. She gasped it. And Anjali, because Anjali is gentle, I do not want you to think she was not gentle, smiled at Nana and nodded. She tucked a finger from her left hand into Nana's vagina, at the base, underneath Anjali's own right hand. And she pushed down on Nana's vagina. This was to let some air out. This was to release the vacuum.

Moshe put Saul Bellow down. He laid out his arms on the arms of the chair, then let them drop over, uncomfortable, heavy. He went to make everyone tea.

13

A while ago, I mentioned the surrealists. I mentioned their conversations about sex. Perhaps surrealism is creeping in here again. This kind of situation – where a boy watches his girlfriend being fisted by another girl, while reading Saul Bellow, and then makes three cups of tea – is often called surreal. A different raconteur from me might say 'It was all so surreal.' In fact, that was exactly what both

Moshe and Anjali were thinking. As Moshe made tea, and Anjali relaxed, they were both wryly thinking that this was very surreal.

But what is surreal?

The person who coined the word 'surrealism' was Guillaume Apollinaire. Guillaume was a French poet at the start of the twentieth century. He coined it in a programme note for the ballet *Parade* – with scenario by Jean Cocteau, choreography by Léonide Massine, decor by Pablo Picasso, and music by Erik Satie. Six weeks later, he used the word again, in a programme note to his own play, *The Breasts of Tiresias*. This was his definition of a surrealist: 'When man wanted to imitate walking, he invented the wheel, which does not look like a leg. Without knowing it, he was a Surrealist.'

I am not sure this definition gets us very far. According to this definition, Anjali and Moshe were probably wrong. It does not seem very similar to the invention of the wheel – a boy making tea for his girlfriend and her girlfriend, having watched them fisting.

Apart from his poems, the most famous thing written by Guillaume Apollinaire was a porn novel, called *The Eleven Thousand Rods*. In *The Eleven Thousand Rods*, lots of people get psychopathically raped whipped and killed by a human sexual automaton, called Mony. It is not a very good novel. In it, there are lots of sentences like this: 'When he had reached the climax, he took the sabre and, clenching his teeth and without ceasing the buggery, cut the head off the little Chinese boy, whose last spasms procured him a huge ejaculation while blood spouted from his neck like water from a fountain.'

However, some people reckon that this porn novel also

defines surrealism. Apparently, this novel shows how, in reality, there is no such thing as psychological motivation, or moral consideration. It shows that, if we were authentic, we would realise that the world is, in essence, surreal.

I think that these people are stupid. Did Guillaume Apollinaire deflower Chinese boys anally and then behead them? No. This is because there was a fatal flaw in the whole argument of surrealism. It is this.

Nothing in reality is surreal. Only the 'surreal' is surreal.

For instance, the day after Nana was ferociously fisted by Anjali, when the *ménage* had lasted for about two months, Papa had a stroke.

Now, I can imagine that you were not expecting this. I imagine that this comes as a sad surprise. It is difficult to expect illness. But I do think that it was possible to guess. There were Papa's headaches on holiday. There was the clue I gave you on the gondola in Venice. There was his dizziness. I even mentioned it at the start of Chapter 2.

But whatever it was, it was not surreal. No. Nothing is surreal.

Guillaume Apollinaire, for example, did not die after a sadistic homosexual rape. No. He died of flu.

14

'Look can you talk,' said Nana. 'Yeah yeah yeah,' said Moshe. 'Well for five minutes. Mon a break.' 'Well he's fine now,' she said. 'They're saying he's fine.' 'No wait I can't hear you,' he said. 'Wait. Well what happened?' said Moshe.

'It might be a tumour,' she said. 'A tumour a fucking a tumour?' screeched Moshe. 'Christ,' he said.

'It might be,' she said. Moshe said, 'Really? What? But how long's he?' And she said, 'The doctors won't say. They don't know. But he hadn't felt like himself for a bit, he said. Well he was starting to do all sorts of funny things. I mean at least this explains it. All the headaches,' she said.

Moshe inadvertently checked whether he had a headache. He could not help it. He, yes, he no no no, he, no.

'I mean,' she said, 'he phoned me that time – I told you – and said he couldn't make a cup of tea. I said "What do you mean?" He said "The tea bag's gone." I said "What do you mean?"' 'Where are you?' said Moshe. 'I'm in resepshon,' she said. 'I said "What do you mean?" He'd put the tea bag in the kettle, hadn't he?' She said, 'It was funny he was more himself after they'd operated. He was naughtier. He kept flirting with a nurse.' Moshe said, 'But he's fine.' She said, 'He's naughtier. He kept complaining that the doctor only cared about her date stamp.' 'Her date stamp?' said Moshe. 'I know,' she said.

He said, 'Well what, shall I come and find you?' 'Look you don't need to look after me,' she said. 'Snot looking after you,' he said. 'I want to.' 'You don't need to,' she said. 'Look I'm your boyfriend,' he said. 'I want to. I love you.'

And it was true, she thought. She was his girlfriend. It made her happy. But she was lovely, Nana. Feeling happy made her feel sad for Anjali. So Nana reconsidered. It was possible, she thought, to be two girlfriends at once.

'So it's cancer,' he said. 'Christ. Nana,' he said. 'Nana,' he said. 'Nana are you?' 'Yehm, I'm here. Well they don know if it's cancer,' she said. 'So what happens now,' he said, 'keemo?' 'Yes yes yes,' she said. 'Well first they do X-rays and then they do keemo. It's his choice but he's going to have it. Then they do keemo. I mean I'll make him if he doesn't.'

'Look,' he said, 'Christ look I'm going to have to go. They've all gone, they've all gone in.' 'I can't hear you,' she said. 'They've all gone in,' shouted Moshe. 'Look I'm. Look I'll call you when I'm out,' he said. 'Shall I just come up and find you?' 'What, what do you mean,' she said. 'Well shall I? I can get to the station, I can get to Edgware by six,' he said. 'No get the Thameslink,' she said. 'The what?' he said. 'Get the Thameslink,' she said. 'What's that?' said Moshe. 'You get it. Get on at King's Cross and get off at Elstree. Then get a cab,' she said. 'It's quicker,' she said. 'No wait I can't hear you,' he said. 'Oh ask Anjali,' said Nana, 'she said she's coming.' 'What?' he said. 'What what I can't,' he said. 'Ask Anjali,' said Nana.

And then she hung up.

15

It was at this point in the story, at the end of Chapter 9, that Chapter 1 occurred. About a week later, Nana and Moshe tried to have anal sex. You will remember, hopefully you will remember, that it did not quite work out. As Moshe tried, gently, to tighten the pink fluffy handcuffs surrounding his girlfriend's wrists, he noticed a tiny frown. Et cetera.

I am sure that by now you can understand all the well-meaning complicated thoughts and compromises that led to their mutual decision to indulge in bondage and anal sex.

And when the episode was over, you will also remember, Moshe carried on his travesty of Jewishness. He said, 'Did

223

you not like the Joosh thing? It was the best I could think of.'

Depressed, Moshe grinned.

She was looking at him, quiet. He was a comic visual diversion. 'What?' he said. And she grinned. She said, 'Cherub, you're only half Jewish.'

Moshe was standing in front of her with his body swaying slightly forward. He was resting his weight on his right leg, which was by now tartanly pyjama'd. The foot of his left leg was advanced a little. And his knee was gently bent. He was getting into his pyjamas.

Nana was wondering why she was happy, lying there as the street lights switched on, unequally.

'And you're not even circumcised,' she said.

'Let's not squabble,' he admonished her, as he hopped across the room in search of the left pyjama leg.

Moshe was not happy. He was depressed. Nana and Moshe, he thought, were not a success. Nothing was ever successful. He was brooding and dissecting the bad effects on a relationship of becoming a *ménage à trois*. He was thinking angry thoughts. He was wishing that it was just the two of them again.

If only Nana knew that! But she did not. Instead, Nana was happy. And she had worked out why she was happy. She was happy because she had realised she no longer had to try to have Kama Sutric sex. She no longer had to watch Anjali and Moshe together, being more proficient and excited. This was because she should make a noble decision. Nana should go back home and be with Papa. She should leave Moshe. Moshe did not need her. He was *better off without her*. Whereas Papa needed her.

You see, in case you have been wondering at the

propriety of planning unnatural sex acts while one's father is in hospital for a suspected brain tumour, you should understand that Papa was not in hospital. They were really not sure it was a tumour. They thought it could just be a small stroke. So Papa had been made an outpatient. He was sent back home while they analysed his scans.

Papa was sitting at home, happily, and resting. It was possible that he had recovered. Everything seemed calm.

But calm was no reason not to nurse him, thought Nana. Nana loved her Papa. She missed being at home with Papa. So she was going to show him how much she adored him.

A gesture of love – that was what Nana decided.

10

They fall out of love

1

LET ME MAKE this entirely clear. Nana wanted out. She had decided that she wanted out for ever.

There was one egotistic reason for this. She did not want to be part of the sexual competition any more. She did not want to have to watch Moshe and Anjali. Nana had had it with humiliation.

And there was one altruistic reason. She wanted to look after Papa.

It was also a gesture of love.

2

In 1995, the Nobel Peace Laureate, Sir Joseph Rotblat, called for a treaty among nuclear-weapons states. Each state would agree not to be the first to use nuclear weapons in any conflict. On 5 April 1995, a No First Use Policy of

227

the Declared Nuclear Weapons States was duly signed.

I know that Nana and Moshe and Anjali were not nuclear-weapons states. They were obviously not states at all. So this might seem a little melodramatic and irrelevant. But it is not melodramatic and irrelevant.

The No First Use Policy is based on mutually assured destruction. The acronym for this is MAD. And that is a very good basis for an agreement. It is the basis for lots of agreements. But it also has a flaw. This type of agreement only works if everyone is feeling threatened. This depends on people feeling that destruction would be, on balance, undesirable. As soon as someone feels that life could get no worse, then they no longer feel threatened at all. You need to enjoy your life a teensy-weensy bit, in order to feel threatened. If you do not like your life at all, then you do not care about being nuked in return. And you may well break your promise not to be the first to use nuclear weapons. At this point, the agreement no longer has any binding force.

Perhaps this does not parallel Nana's decision to leave the *ménage*. She was not leaving because she thought that her life was hopeless. She was leaving to nurse her Papa. It was noble.

But Nana was not just noble. There was another reason. This was the egotistic reason.

This is where I can see a similarity. And I am specially keen to point this out, because the egotistic reason was a hidden reason. It was not obvious. So I think it is important to emphasise it here. In her more maudlin moments, as she brooded on sexual inequality, Nana thought that she had nothing left to lose. Their tacit agreement to stay together no longer had any binding force. It would be no worse for Nana to leave than to stay.

In Foreign Office circles, there is a nickname for the No First Use policy. They call it No FUN. MAD is No FUN.

Unfortunately, you see, Nana was about to have fun.

3

Nana woke up. She wanted out. She wanted to leave Moshe. She wanted to leave Anjali. She wanted to leave the two of them together. It was what was best for everyone.

The three of them were arranged, this morning, as follows:

Nana, Anjali, Moshe.

Maybe this does not quite express the arrangement. Moshe was lying wrapped round Anjali. He was clinging to her.

As she looked at the two of them, Nana felt very sad. She felt very sad and happy. The sadness, presumably, was obvious. It was sad watching Moshe cuddle Anjali. It was sad watching him be happy with another girl. And it was sad for Nana, thinking that she was going to leave. But if she tried, she could also feel happy. She could imagine herself as the noble wife, abandoning her husband to his mistress.

If she tried, Nana could imagine a different ending to *Casablanca*.

In this ending, Nana plays the part of Victor Laszlo, the Jewish husband and anti-Nazi intellectual. In Nana's version, it is Victor, not Rick, who is noble. It is Victor who is self-sacrificing. He climbs into his small plane with its twin propellers, *and leaves the lovers to it*, in Morocco.

Bergman stays with Bogey. In this ending, Victor is not selfish. He is not so obsessed with his personal happiness.

Moshe rolled awake. He looked up and across at Nana. Nana was looking at him. He asked her what the time was. Nana told him. She leaned over Anjali and kissed Moshe.

Nana, about to leave for ever, said she would make Moshe some coffee.

4

It is not easy – breaking up. There is very rarely a right time. In fact, I do not know when the right time would ever be. This particular break-up took place at eight in the morning. That is not a great time. And Nana was naked. She was in the kitchen, filling the kettle. Moshe followed her. He was naked too.

The only good thing, thought Nana, was that Anjali was not there. At least Anjali was still asleep. Because it is hard enough breaking up with one person, let alone having another person interjecting and explaining.

She said, 'Moshe.' And she paused. Moshe was silent, yawning. So Nana said, 'I, umean I'm not sure this is right.' And Moshe said, 'Wha?' He said, 'Wha?' and then yawned again.

She walked into the bedroom and scooped up a bundle of her clothes. She walked back into the kitchen. She chucked them on to the worktop.

She said, 'Mosh look I do love you. This isn't me rejecting you but. You musn't think this is a rejection. I've just been thinking more and more that I want to be with Papa. And you and Anj. You and Anjli should be together.'

Moshe said, 'Wha?' He was sleepy, Moshe. He had only just got up. Moshe was not at his intellectual best, at eight in the morning.

Nana said, 'I'm sorry I jus it's just I think we need to be apart fra bit. Or I do. Jus for now. An maybe. Maybe we can. I jus don't want you to be hurt.' She paused. She said, 'I'm sorry I'm being like this.'

And Moshe said, 'I don see why. I. I don see why. I don see why we need to give this up.'

It is particularly difficult – breaking up – when you do not entirely want to. And Nana wanted to break up, she really did. She wanted to be with her Papa. But she was still in love with Moshe. She still thought that Moshe was lovely. It was just that now Nana thought that he was happier with Anjali.

So Moshe was not helping her – making it a delicate conversation. Making it a conversation at all was a problem for Nana. He was not meant to be weighing up *the pros and cons*. He was not meant to be reasonable. She wanted out. She wanted to leave for ever. She did not want a conversation. In a conversation, you have to explain things. You have to say that you want to leave for ever. And Nana did not want to say this. That was partly because Nana was kind. She did not want to be hurtful. It was also because it was not entirely true.

The problem with breaking up with someone, if you are a little unsure – and so often, people are unsure – is that breaking up involves persuasion. You have to persuade your ex that it is better this way for everyone. And this is difficult if you have not entirely persuaded yourself. It is especially tricky to do this if you are also naked, and making two cups of coffee.

Nana handed Moshe a coffee. He wandered off with it

into the living room. And Nana followed. She gathered her clothes and she followed.

'But I love you,' said Moshe.

Personally, I think this was a very good argument. It might sound a bit clichéd of Moshe, but I think he has got to the bottom of this. It was true. He loved her. It is a good reason for not breaking up with someone.

He was sitting on the futon. He was not feeling very happy. He was not happy being naked, in this way, while a six-foot and beautiful girl broke up with him. So Moshe artfully and casually draped Nana's shirt over his body. This concealed the fatty folds and creases that nipped and tucked as he sat down.

Nana pulled on some black trousers. Then she stopped. It felt wrong, getting dressed, in this crisis. It felt a bit heartless. So she stopped.

For the rest of this section, therefore, Nana was topless and her flies were undone. This meant that Moshe could see the turquoise lace of her knickers. Her knickers were from the ritzy end of the M&S range.

There was a mini mirror on the table and Nana prised it up with her thumbnail. The mirror had a stainless-steel case. On the case, the word 'Mirror' was printed. She pushed it back down. She said, 'Moshe.' He put his hand round his baggy testicles, coyly, feeling naked. He felt very very naked. Nana picked up a new lipstick she had bought yesterday called Moxie. Moxie was red like Ruby Woo but lighter. It did not seem so interesting now. It did not seem interesting at all. And Moshe looked at the portable clock, standing on a wicker place mat on the living room's drop-leaf table. The clock had fluorescent yellow hands. It was eight thirty. Moshe said, 'You're late.'

She said, 'It doesn't matter.' He said, 'No it's important, you should go. We can. We can talk later.' She said, 'It's only a dentist Mosh.' He said, 'I know, simportant.'

I am not being silly here. He was suddenly obsessed with her teeth. It seemed suddenly so melancholy and important. It seemed essential to be considerate. If he seemed considerate, thought Moshe, then maybe Nana might reconsider. She might realise how nice he was, if he was nice.

Moshe said, 'Look therz something you're sad about. So tell me.' She said, 'No look really there's nothing. It's nothing else. I just wan. I don't know.' He said, 'No, tell me.'

This was not the most articulate exchange, but there it is. It is what happens in these situations. They are very rarely scripted.

Moshe stood up and went to the window. He was not enjoying this early-morning scene. What it needed, he thought, was elegance. It needed to be elegant and subtle. It especially needed Moshe to be elegant and subtle. He needed to *save the situation*. But he could not see how he would do this. He was naked. He stood at the window and watched. Outside, a boy was walking along, holding a tennis racket over his head. It was a Wilson tennis racket. The plastic leather-look cover was his improvised raincoat.

Moshe felt very sorry for this rained-on boy.

Oh, poor Moshe. Soon, very soon, he will have to realise that breaking up is not elegant. It is never elegant and fun. It is lots of lies and evasions. Of course this scene did not have the elegant 1930s class he might have hoped for. No, instead, naked Moshe was just confused. He stood there – mooching, moody, devastated.

And Nana was mooching too. She was thinking about

Anjali again, abandoned in the bedroom next door. The last thing Nana wanted was Anjali to come into the living room, to hear Moshe and Nana discussing a break-up. But on the other hand, she thought, Moshe and Nana still needed to talk this through. It had been *too one-sided*. Moshe had not had his say.

Oh, poor Nana. She did not know what to do. She said, 'Do you want to come to the dentist with me?'

Moshe looked at her. It was not the break-up he was expecting. Well, obviously he was not expecting any break-up really. But if he were asked what a break-up was, it did not involve a visit to the dentist.

He said, 'The dentist?' She said, 'Well if you don wantto, you could just walk me to the tube. It's just. I don wan Anjali to hear. I don think that'd be fair.'

It was not a bad idea, Moshe could see that. It was reasonable.

There was an interlude of comical slow-motion real-time dressing. Then Nana and Moshe left. Without an umbrella, they went out into the rain.

5

In 1920, when the Civil War was taking place in Communist Russia, Nikolai Bukharin wrote a small book called *Economics of the Transition Period*. Nikolai was a Bolshevik. So he was quite in favour of the recent revolution. In his book, he tried to explain why everything was going smoothly. He tried to explain that, while it might look like the country was falling apart, in fact everything was fine. The revolution was fine. Some people might be dying, the proletariat might be dying, but that was all part of the plan.

'From a broader point of view', wrote Nikolai, '– that is, from the point of view of an historical scale of greater scope – proletarian compulsion in all its forms, from executions to compulsory labour, constitutes, paradoxical as it may sound, a method of formation of a new Communist humanity from the human material of the capitalist epoch.'

In the margin, in his copy of this book, Lenin wrote 'exactly!'

But I am not so sure how exact Nikolai is really being. I think that it is possible to be more precise.

Nikolai was saying that, yes yes, lots of people were being shot or forced to work twenty-hour days. But this was not a bad thing. This was communism. If only people took *the long view*, thought Nikolai, if only they stopped being selfish, then they might see how wonderful life was.

I am not sure Nikolai picked the right title for his book. *Economics of the Transition Period* was not quite right. It should have been called *Psychology of the Transition Period*. The psychology of the transition period is this. It is blind optimism. You tell yourself that things are changing for the better when really they are just fucked.

Here are some figures for the heroic period of the Great Russian Revolution.

In 1917, Petrograd had 2.5 million people. In 1920, it had 700,000. In 1913 there were 2.6 million factory workers. In 1920 there were 1.6 million. In 1920, food consumption was at 40 per cent of pre-war levels. Between January 1918 and July 1920, 7 million people died of malnutrition and epidemics. The death rate doubled. Between 1921 and 1928, in the Ukraine, 200,000 Jews were killed, 300,000 orphaned, and over 700,000 made homeless.

Now, obviously Moshe was not a homeless and butchered Ukrainian Jew. I'm not drawing that parallel. No, I am drawing another parallel.

Moshe was thinking like Nikolai Bukharin. In the middle of a revolution, outside the Americana Cosmetics Store on the Pentonville Road, Moshe was being blindly optimistic.

6

'I really don think I understand this,' said Moshe. 'I love you.' He had said it once already, it was true, but Moshe did not think that saying it twice was a problem. It was his central point. It was his central incontestable point. So Moshe paused. He paused for effect. While he paused, Moshe faintly chewed on his lower lip.

Nana said, 'I love you too.' 'So why do we need to break up?' said Moshe.

Moshe faintly chewed on his lower lip.

Then Nana's phone rang. Moshe looked at it. Nana looked at it. She answered. She said, 'Hi no I'm. No tomorro. It's for. Yeah defnitly. Okay cool see you later.'

Moshe looked at the Americana Cosmetics Store's window display. It was the display of a manic pharmacy. And, even at this moment of crisis, Moshe got distracted by the Store's offer of

A1 Unisex
Hairdressing
Afro
&
European

Moshe examined the wigs slumped on polystyrene busts. There was Sindy and Edna, and Simone and Rosa. None of them was pretty. Amputated ponytails were organised in coloured sections. There was a plastic packet of Natural Eyelashes, dyed with rainbow stripes. Yes, even at moments of crisis, Moshe had his homely side. He could always be amazed by the things people paid for.

Moshe said, 'But you can't. I mean. If you mean this. You can't love me any more.' And Nana said, 'No issnot that – I do love you I'll always love you.' 'But you can't,' said Moshe.

I feel very sorry for Nana. I feel very sorry for all nice people. It was too difficult for Nana, explaining why she wanted to leave. It was too difficult explaining all the sad unhappy thoughts.

And then the rain stopped.

This made Moshe even sadder. He had been quite liking the effect. Moshe quite liked the *film noir* connotations of melancholy. Rain, thought Moshe, was at least the right weather for sadness.

7

OK. Let me return to Nikolai Bukharin. I am going to fast forward, from 1920 to 1930.

By the 1930s, Stalin was a little concerned about Nikolai. A lot of people seemed to think that Nikolai did not adore Stalin as much as he should. They claimed that Nikolai was a terrorist, a conspirator.

Obviously, this upset Nikolai. So Nikolai phoned Stalin up.

'Hey Nikolai, *Kolya*, don't panic,' said Stalin. 'We'll sort things out. Of course we don't believe you're an enemy.' And Nikolai squeaked, 'But how can you even *think* that I am an accomplice of terrorist groups?' Stalin thought this was really adorable. Unravelling a paperclip, he said, 'Take it easy, Kolya, take it easy. We'll sort it out.'

I have to say, I do like Stalin's phone manner. I've said it before and I'll say it again. The man was a telephone genius.

In 1938, Stalin put Nikolai Bukharin on trial for treason.

This is the point where there is another similarity between the life of the politician Nikolai Bukharin and the life of two of my heroes – Nana and Moshe.

At his 1938 show trial, Nikolai made a false confession. He pleaded guilty to 'the sum total of crimes committed by this counter-revolutionary organisation, irrespective of whether or not I knew of, whether or not I took a direct part in, any particular act'.

Nikolai claimed, of course, that it was not a false confession. That is the essence of any true false confession.

Previously, Nikolai was like Moshe. Now, he is like Nana.

I think that breaking up with someone is rather like participating in a show trial. There is a general pretence of justice and reason. And the person doing the breaking up accepts all responsibility. He or she makes a false confession.

8

Outside the Americana Cosmetics Store, Nana made a false confession.

'Maybe. Well maybe I just don love you any more.

Maybe you're right. You'd be better off with Anjali,' she said. 'Me I want to be with Papa and it's simpler. Maybe you're right.'

I feel sorry for Nana. I do. It was not nice lying like this. But I feel much more sorry for Moshe. It might have been socially tricky and quietly sad for Nana, breaking up with Moshe, but at least it was her decision. It was her anguished and irrational decision. Whereas it was not Moshe's decision at all. Moshe was not happy. He was lonely. He was suddenly very lonely. Moshe was desperate.

All he could think of was Anjali. This thought did not make him feel less lonely.

He said, 'Wha do you mean about Anjali?' Nana said, 'Well what I said.' She said, 'I mean what I said. You'd be better off with Anjali.' He said, 'But I don want Anjali. I want you.'

A minuscule triangle of skin, just below the cuticle on the second finger of her left hand, was catching on a polyester thread from Nana's trouser-pocket lining. She ignored it. She looked at the JAZZY Professional Glue Gun in the window of the Americana Cosmetics Store. She wondered what it was for.

Nana said, 'No I think you should be with Anjali.' And Moshe said, 'Bud I don't want to be with Anjali. I want to be with you. It was you who brought her in. It wasn't my idea. I'm not the one who wanted to.' Moshe was completely hurt and confused. 'You wanted her,' he said. 'I'm the one who had a problem with it. This should be me. I could have left ages ago.'

Naturally, Moshe had considered leaving. But it was never a real possibility. He loved Nana. He wanted to stay with her whatever. But I can understand why he said this.

I can understand why he wanted to make his declaration of independence. He was making himself feel better. He was being a loss adjuster. He was trying not to feel humiliated.

Because it is humiliating, when someone breaks up with you. It is one of the worst ever feelings.

He said, 'Nana I should go, you need to go to. You should get to the dentist.' And although Moshe sounds noble and calm, he was not being noble or calm. Honestly, he was just at a loss. He was very upset. He had no idea what to say next. In his turmoil, he was worried that Nana would miss her dentist's appointment. Because it was still important to him. He was sincere.

He said, 'I love you more than enthing.'

There was a pause.

'You've got to go,' said Moshe. So he went.

9

Nana's dentist was called Mr Gottlieb.

Mr Gottlieb practised on Cavendish Square. This might make him sound like an upper-class dentist. And he was an upper-class dentist. His practice was located next to Harley Street. But Nana did not go to Mr Gottlieb because of his location.

Mr Gottlieb had begun as a small little NHS dentist in Edgware. Then he had become an upper-class central-London private dentist. But he had said he would keep Nana on. He would keep her on because he was a family friend. It was a favour to Nana's Papa.

In Mr Gottlieb's waiting room there was a fish tank and a selection of magazines. Nana picked up a copy of *Take a*

Break from 1998. *Take a Break* was sticky. Nana ignored this. She started to read *Take a Break*. Very quickly, she started to cry.

Nana had begun to read a true story about a woman called Mandy who fell in love with a man called Alan. It turned out that Alan had motor neurone disease. This true story made Nana cry. It made her cry because, in defiance of death, Alan and Mandy had decided that they would have a child. A child would be a way of remembering Alan. And this story culminated with a deathbed scene.

I showed him an envelope. I pulled out a certificate.

'It's a star,' I said. 'It's named after you and James.'

It was called the Alan and James Wilson star.

Alan smiled. 'You'll tell him all about me, won't you?' he asked.

I nodded.

I held his hand as he slipped away.

He was 48. James was 14 weeks old.

Then Mr Gottlieb walked in while Nana was loudly weeping, beside the mute and tropical fish.

Mr Gottlieb said, 'Nina.' He said, 'Nina.' Nana looked up at him and pushed at her face with the back of her wrist. She said, 'No it's. It's.' Mr Gottlieb said, 'Are you okay?' And she said, 'Yeh I'm, I'm fine.' Mr Gottlieb said, 'And your father?' And because Nana was distraught, she did not remember that Mr Gottlieb was unaware of the recent history of Papa's illness. She cried. She wept. She tried to speak. She tried to say something like, 'I'm scared that he'll die.' But weeping is not a good time to speak. It does not help you if you want to speak clearly.

241

Mr Gottlieb was tactful. He did not want to upset Nana any more. He did not want to press her for gory details. If Nana wanted to carry on with life as normal, then she should be allowed to do this. It was natural, he thought, that Nana should be *distraught*.

I do not think you should blame Mr Gottlieb too much for his assumption that Papa had died.

'Why don't you go home?' said Mr Gottlieb. Yes, he sent the bereaved girl home. There was no place for teeth, thought Mr Gottlieb, in the presence of death.

He was not an ideological maniac, Mr Gottlieb. He did not overvalue a sparkling smile.

IO

I am going to interrupt this story for a moment.

In 1975, Andy Warhol wrote *The Philosophy of Andy Warhol (From A to B and Back Again)*. Well, he did not write it. He dictated it. Anyway, one of the things he wrote or dictated was this:

Sex is a nostalgia for when you used to want it, sometimes.

Sex is nostalgia for sex.

And I think that's true. I think that sometimes it is true. For example, after Stacey and Henderson had broken up, Stacey met a boy she liked called Kwame. Kwame was at Middlesex University, doing a degree in Environmental Theory. Kwame was interesting. He chatted to her about fish in the North Sea. The North Sea was very polluted. This caused a lot of problems for North Sea fish. Unfortunately, however, Kwame was a smallish boy who wore silver wire-rimmed glasses. So Stacey, who was a girl with a taste for size and cool, was not particularly attracted by Kwame. But she had sex with Kwame anyway. She liked him. And she thought that sex was what she liked doing with boys she was fond of. It was what she did with Henderson.

Sex, for Stacey, was nostalgia for sex.

II

This was not just a distraction. This was not just meant to cheer you up, at the saddest point in my story. I had a more important reason.

In a very similar way to Andy and Stacey and Kwame, a few days after Nana left, Anjali was in bed with Moshe. They were nearly falling asleep.

Perhaps this surprises you. Perhaps you are surprised that Moshe and Anjali are still together.

Perhaps you think that if someone leaves a *ménage à trois*, the relationship of the two people left behind might become uncomfortable. It would be all too obvious that they were not naturally a couple. They were just the remnants of a three. And this would put a lot of strain on the couple.

This is right in a way, I think. But it ignores one crucial detail. No one wants to admit to being two-thirds of a three. It is embarrassing. Although there is a lot of strain on the couple, neither is going to admit this. Neither is going to admit that this relationship is tricky. They both have their reasons for keeping schtum.

But what are these reasons?

Well, they can be best described in a sex scene. Yes, a sex scene. Perhaps you are getting tired of sex scenes. Let me reassure you. This is the last sex scene in this book. And it is a pleasant sex scene. Unlike many other sex scenes in this book, there is no need for it to be anatomical. It is just a nostalgic sex scene. And anyway, a nostalgic sex scene is not really a sex scene. It is not a great act of coitus.

So. Anjali was in bed with Moshe.

There was a very simple reason why Moshe was keeping schtum. It was this. He was not convinced that Anjali was an out-and-out heterosexual girl. That was why Moshe was keeping schtum. Bewildered and confused by recent developments, he had decided to *wait and see*.

And I am sure that Moshe was right. From a practical point of view, it was the correct course of action. Anjali was not at all sure that she was an out-and-out heterosexual girl. But she was kind. She could not explain to Moshe that Moshe was not her boyfriend. It would have made, worried Anjali, the *ménage* seem so insincere. And Anjali also had another reason. She was lonely. She missed Nana a lot. And if you are lonely, it is much more relaxing having a person to sleep with than having no one at all.

That was why Moshe and Anjali were still together. Those were the reasons for not discussing the oddness of their relationship.

And I think there was something else too. Although Moshe and Anjali had not been happy in the *ménage*, in fact they had been very disconsolate, that is no reason why they might not be happy as a couple. Feelings can change very quickly in a new situation. For example, I think that it is natural for two people, who have suddenly become a couple, to think that it could work out. It is natural for them to be hopeful.

People have an instinct to normalise. They are naturally optimistic, I think.

And they were both optimistic, Anjali and Moshe. After all, they liked each other. So it was possible, they thought, in secret, that they could be a couple. It was unlikely, but it was possible.

But why was this a sex scene?

Because while I have been explaining what Moshe and Anjali were feeling, they have been touching each other, quietly.

12

A week or two later, Nana and Moshe were walking up Hatton Garden, in the rain. Hatton Garden is the jewellery street in London. It is also a very Jewish street. And this is, obviously, coincidental. I rather hate Snoop Doggy Dogg, who argued once for the philological jew in jewellery. The jew in jewellery is just a phonetic coincidence.

On Jewish Hatton Garden, however, it is true that Moshe was talking about his Jewishness.

While Nana and Moshe walked in the rain, Moshe chatted about the Orthodox Jews, who were sheltering in their wide-brimmed black hats underneath plastic awnings. He just adored these Hasidim, said Moshe. He loved everything about them. He loved their podginess, and the curls dangling round their ears. They had their own sweet style. Moshe appreciated the style with which their trousers flapped above their black ribbed polyester socks. Or the way their kapels were clipped to the one tuft of hair on their heads. Yes he loved this, said Moshe, feeling sad.

I hope you are appreciating how good Moshe is being. He is being very polite. He is being a model ex-boyfriend.

Because although Moshe was feeling sad, he was also being charming. It was a socially difficult moment – spending the day with his ex, while still going out with her other ex. That was finicky enough. And also Nana's father was possibly dying. Therefore, thought Moshe, it was not an ideal day. But Moshe was not a bad person, he was not a selfish person. Because it was socially difficult, Moshe was chatty. He was chatty and very charming.

Moshe said, 'Shall we find somewhere indoors to eat?' And Nana nodded because she was a girl habitually unprepared – in a white Boden shirt in January. So indoors sounded adorable.

Moshe had an idea of somewhere to eat. It was not an innocent question. He was going to take Nana to the Kosher Knosherie.

So they moseyed wetly to the Kosher Knosherie, on Greville Street.

Outside the Kosher Knosherie, the Kosher Knosherie black cab – for deliveries – was parked with one tyre squashed against the kerb. On the driver's door of this cab *Knosh Around the Clock* was stencilled in fat purple italics. This was, Moshe assured her, the best salt beef in the city. Better, he said, than Brick Lane. It was greengrey and fatty, there on the counter, visible twenty-four hours.

They both sat down. Moshe was nervous. Nana was nervous too.

Nana lifted her damp shirt away from her bra's lace foliage. Moshe said that he adored this place.

I do not want you to think that Moshe had suddenly converted. It was not that, in the aftermath of his break-up with Nana, he had found Jehovah. No, he had not become frum in any way. Moshe's relationship to the Jewish race and faith was, as always, purely emotional. The Kosher Knosherie made him feel emotional. Now that he was sad, it made him happy. It made him believe that he liked salt beef. On the occasional moments when he tore strips of salt beef from a bagel in the Kosher Knosherie, Moshe felt a kinship with Jewish City Boy East End Cool.

A man with strawberry-blond fur on his ears was buying a cream-cheese bagel. 'Bu my favrite, always was, was Stanley Matthews,' he said, opening out the door and holding it. 'Yeah,' replied the man behind the counter. The man behind the counter was trying to fit a plastic lid on a cardboard cup of coffee. 'Nonev that hugging,' said the man, closing the door again, pointing with the fist of his scrunched bagel bag. 'He'd just score a goal and shake hands, tap on the shoulders, then he'd run back.'

Moshe looked at the menu. He looked at Nana. He said, 'I've, I've.' He said, 'We've missed you. We've both missed you.' Nana said, 'I've missed you too.' Moshe said, 'I do still love you. You know. I still love you.' And Nana said, 'I know.'

Moshe said, 'Do you remember that time you were helping me learn my lines for what was it, Noël Coward? That was the funniest time we ever had.'

I don't think this was tangential. It might seem that way, but it wasn't. Moshe was in love with Nana. He wanted her to feel nostalgic. He wanted her to miss him too.

Nana said, 'What was it you were doing next?' Moshe said, 'Me? Me, oh. Oh nothing. I've got a bunch of meetings next week. But Anjli's got something on. She's got another advert for someone. I can't remember now. But it was going to pay, it was going to pay pretty well.'

Nana nodded.

Moshe said, 'And how's, how's your father?' Nana said, 'Oh. Oh he's okay. Okayish. I mean his taste is weird. He can't taste anything extreme, he can't do curry. But just everything in the mid-range. Although he still can't tell the difference between lemon and lime.' Moshe said, 'Uhhuh.' And this was not an 'uhhuh' of boredom, I don't want you to get that idea. It was an 'uhhuh' of worry. Nana said, 'You know what came back first?' 'What?' he said. 'Squid,' said Nana. 'Squid?' said Moshe. 'He had this really good squid and he tasted that. It came back after a cold,' said Nana. 'He said he'd got a cold and couldn't taste anything and when it went his taste came back better than before. I mean why's that?'

Moshe said, 'Nana. Nana sweetie. I have no idea.'

Moshe picked up the menu. This action was there to distract from or disguise his next lines. He said, 'I think it might be okay, me and Anjli. I mean. It's odd without you. It's sad. But I don know. We might, maybe we'll do it.'

Now, I am a little surprised that Moshe said this. If he wanted to get Nana back, then it was not really sensible, telling Nana that Moshe and Anjali could be happy. But I think I can see Moshe's misguided rationale. It was, after all, true in a way, and it gave him the chance to be polite. He was trying not to make this trip to the Kosher Knosherie difficult for Nana. So Moshe wanted to seem calm.

But also, I reckon, it made Moshe happy – telling Nana that she had not destroyed him. It was a tiny polite moment of revenge.

And it was a revenge. Nana was fond of Moshe. She was

more than fond of him. It was difficult, being this noble. She did not like living apart from Moshe. She was jealous of Moshe and Anjali. She did not want to think that they might end up happy together.

Nana nodded.

She looked round. A man beside her was doodling with ketchup on his chips. On the walls, there were massive jigsaws like murals. To Nana's right, there was Hieronymus Bosch's *Temptation of St Anthony*. This was indicated underneath in three different languages, each written in a *trompe l'œil* parchment scroll. 'Temptation of Saint Anthony – Tentation de Saint Antoine – La Tentazione di Antonio'. Beside the jigsaw, there was a label –

"The Worlds"
LARGEST JIGSAW
OVER 16,000 pieces

– and on her left there was another jigsaw. It was a lake view. Nana wondered if Israel had any lakes. She wondered if this lake was in Israel. She looked at the plastic menu with maroon varnished leather trim. They had paper-clipped on to the menu a photocopy of an *Evening Standard* round-up of the best salt beef. Nana ordered a bagel and a poached egg. Moshe ordered salt beef.

And that is the last you will see of Moshe. The last you will see of him is this moment, after Nana had broken up with him, when he orders a salt-beef bagel in the Kosher Knosherie.

I can understand why Moshe felt emotional there, in the Kosher Knosherie. It was the Jewish 1950s. Printed on the centre of each plate, in pork pink, there was a massive B and then 'uy loom's est eef' vertically arranged to its right. It was an older world. It was bright pink oilcloth, and gilt curved swirls for chairbacks. It was a much safer and happier world.

And I can recognise this feeling. When I am there, I feel emotional too.

13

But I am not going to get emotional. I am not going to get sad. No. I am going to describe happiness instead. Although, at this point in the story, I do not have many options.

I will try to describe Nana's happiness.

Edgware was making Nana happy. She liked living in Edgware. Because Papa lived there and enjoyed it, Nana thought that Edgware was cool.

Perhaps you have never been to Edgware. Perhaps you cannot understand what an odd variety of happiness this was. Edgware is at the end of the Northern line. It is, therefore, not exactly urban. It is definitely suburban. The tube station was designed in 1923 by S. A. Heap, in a restrained neo-Georgian style. Each year, the station forecourt puts up a ten-foot high menorah, in celebration of Chanukkah. If you turn left out the station, you walk past McDonald's and the entrance to the Broadwalk Shopping Centre.

On Saturday nights, when shabbat is over, a collection of Jewish boys and girls congregate with black and Asian boys and girls outside McDonald's. They sell each other drugs. Sometimes, to pass the time, they get on the tube to

Golders Green and stand outside Golders Green station. Then they come back to Edgware station.

Edgware is a multicultural haven.

If you carry on past McDonald's, you also pass a newsagent, which is sponsored by the *Jewish Chronicle*. There is a board outside the newsagent, also sponsored by the *Jewish Chronicle*. The board is part of the deal. It is where they advertise their headline stories. When Nana returned home, to look after Papa, the *Jewish Chronicle*'s main story was this.

'Win a Pesach holiday for Four in Majorca!'

I am afraid that this, combined with the ten-foot high menorah, made Nana feel sad. It made her nostalgic. Well, perhaps not nostalgic exactly. She was not Jewish at all. Israel was not her personal homeland. She was just thinking sad upset and tragic thoughts about one adorable Jew in particular.

You have to remember. She loved Papa. But she loved Moshe too.

Past this newsagent, on your right, is where the Belle Vue cinema used to be. If you carry on walking, however, you soon come to the architectural extravaganza of the Railway Hotel. The Railway Hotel was built in 1931 by A. E. Sewell in an unrestrained mock-Tudor style, complete with its own fake gallows. And that is the end of Edgware High Street.

Edgware is suburban. It is dismal, quiet, lovable and kitsch.

But no, actually there was another person in this story who was happy. In a way, at this point, she was even more happy than Nana.

Anjali was sitting in Moshe's flat, sleepily dozing. She was sitting in Moshe's flat and thinking about Nana. She was also thinking about Moshe.

Anjali was thinking about love.

I want you to remember Anjali. You must not read this carelessly.

Anjali was remembering her Bollywood films. The loveliest Bollywood film she had seen was *Devdas*. This film was very moving. In its closing scenes, as Shah Rukh Khan dies outside the gates of Aishwarya Rai's house, it shows how wonderful and powerful love is. It shows, thought Anjali, that love is stronger than anything.

And I think that Anjali was right. I like her, I really do. But I especially like her, I think, because although she was drifting off, thinking about the wonder and power of love, she was still practical.

Because Anjali was practical, she was nonplussed. She could not quite understand what she was feeling. It was not love. She knew that. It was just that she was happy. She was suddenly and surprisingly happy.

III

II

The finale

I

AS PAPA SAT on his duvet, with its innovative design of small white lions and falcons and fruit trees on a magenta background, he chatted to Nana about her sweet boyfriend Moshe.

Papa liked Moshe. He liked Moshe very much.

Anjali is not the ending. Surely you must have known that. I was not going to end with Anjali on her own, being happy. No. I started with a bedroom scene and I'll end with a bedroom scene.

'Anyway. How is Moshe?' said Papa. 'When are you going back?'

Before we go any further, I am going to describe Papa's get-up. His get-up was unusual. It was one red Tote sock, one navy Tote sock, a pair of black suit trousers – whose zip was done up but whose button was not – and a white T-shirt printed with a picture of a curlybearded satyr that Papa had bought in Rhodes in 1987.

So, now I can start again. I just wanted you to get his day wear right.

'Anyway. How is Moshe?' said Papa. 'When are you going back?'

You see, Papa did not know that Nana had left Moshe, for ever. Nana had not told him. This was because she did not want to embroil him in her love life. She wanted Papa to feel entirely loved by Nana. And this meant that she could not tell him that Moshe and Nana were no longer together. It would complicate her gesture of pure love. It would make it seem less sincere.

Because Nana was making a gesture of pure love. It was true.

2

I think you should not judge Nana's secrecy here, about her split with Moshe, as entirely crazy. It is very difficult, being moral. It is, I reckon, almost impossible. You have to rely on all kinds of generalisations and theories.

One generalisation is this. People often think that a noble gesture is inherently better than a pragmatic gesture. Even if it is ineffectual and potentially harmful to oneself, a noble act is still noble, it is still moral.

In the vocabulary of this novel, then, staying with Papa is better than staying with Moshe. It may be self-destructive, and potentially harmful to Nana's eventual happiness, but it is more virtuous.

Nana would find a supporter for her theory in the Czech dissident and ex-president, Václav Havel. On 9 August 1969, when he was a dissident, Václav wrote a letter to the former Czech president, Alexander Dubček. This was a year after the Russian invasion of Czechoslovakia. The Russians had invaded because of Dubček's softer, nicer version of communism. They had made Dubček resign as president, but had allowed him to stay in parliament. However, they did not leave him alone. They wanted him to publicly repudiate his nicer version of communism.

Václav did not want Dubček to do this. Václav wanted him to affirm his belief in his nicer version of communism, even if this was dangerous for Dubček and would have no effect whatsoever. That was why he wrote his letter to Dubček, imploring him to be noble.

Because, wrote Václav, 'even a purely moral act that has no hope of any immediate and visible political effect can gradually and indirectly, over time, gain in political significance'.

Václav means that we should not laugh at useless and self-harmful moral gestures. They are not necessarily just for show. They are not necessarily gestures. Some good might eventually come of them.

Unfortunately, Václav's theory never got a chance to be tested. In September 1969, the Russians removed Dubček from parliament as well, a month after Václav's letter. Václav never got a reply.

3

Nana did not immediately answer Papa's question. She did not immediately tell him when she would go back to Moshe. Instead, sitting with Papa on Papa's bed, she opened the post. The post, this morning, was one card. It was a card of condolence from their family friend and dentist, Mr Gottlieb.

Dear Nina,
What a great loss your father is.
With best wishes from
Luke Gottlieb.

She giggled. She read it out. They both giggled.

'What a bastard!' said Papa. 'That's what he sends when I'm dead? One sentence? Give it me.' Papa read it. He read it again. 'What a bastard!' said Papa. Nana put the card on the window sill. It did not balance. She flexed the card out. It balanced. Papa said, 'And what were you doing, telling him I was dead? Why was he sending the card at all, that's what I want to know.' 'I can't remember,' said Nana. 'I dint say a thing. I said, no I dint say a thing.'

Of course, this was not true. She had wept and told Mr Gottlieb that she was terrified of Papa dying. Mr Gottlieb must have misheard. But Nana could not tell Papa that she was scared he might die. No. Nana was too careful for that. She was too kind.

Papa said, 'So. How's Moshe? You haven't said. When are you going back?' And Nana said, 'Mnot going back.' This surprised Papa. He said, 'What?' Nana said, well she sighed and said, 'I broke up with Moshe.'

This surprised Papa much more. It upset him. He tried to say something calm. He said, 'You?'

Nana said, 'We broke up.' Papa said, 'But why? He was a sweet boy. Why did you break up with him?' 'I wanted to,' said Nana. 'But why?' said Papa.

'I wanted to be with you,' said Nana.

She was making a gesture of pure love, she thought.

But Papa did not want her to make gestures of pure love. And nor do I. He was feeling horrified and amazed. Papa was not a selfish person. He was not an egotistical patient. He was thinking that he could not let Nana do this. 'With me?' said Papa. 'But you need to be with Moshe.' He could not let her nurse him, thought Papa. She had a boy, she had a life. He could not let Nana waste time on her Papa.

'No I wanna be with you,' said Nana. 'You go back to Moshe,' said Papa. 'You go back and say that you are sorry. You tell him you've changed your mind. You can't break up with Moshe because of me. It's crazy,' said Papa. 'I mean, how long were you thinking? How long were you thinking of staying with me?'

Suddenly, Papa felt tired. He felt very tired and sad.

I am living too long, Papa thought.

You see, Papa's stroke or possible tumour had caused a particular conundrum. The prognosis was only approximate. Even if it were a tumour, they told him, Papa could still live for another twenty years. He could also die the next day. This lack of predictive accuracy distressed Papa. If Nana had to nurse him for only a week, then he might not have minded. But nursing could mean anything. It could mean years.

He was confused. He thought he was living too long. His life was wasting Nana's life. He was wasting everything. Even the money was wasted. His nursing was expensive. And Papa did not want to use up money for the next twenty years that could have gone to his darling girl.

Papa is the benevolent angel of this story. You need to remember this.

He said, 'Look this is crazy. I don't need a minder.

There's the nurse comes in every day. I don't even need the nurse. I'm fine. You don't need to stay with me.'

This was both generous and mean. That might sound like a contradiction, but it was true. It was generous of Papa. It was mean to Nana.

4

Václav Havel's letter to Dubček had a hidden agenda, I think. Václav was responding to another, rival theory of nobility. According to this theory, making possibly useless noble gestures is not noble at all. No, it is just a form of exhibitionism. An act that might seem noble is therefore just egotistic.

Of course, Václav would not imagine that the motives of noble acts could ever be doubted. Well, he might concede the possibility. But he would not see the point. He believes in transcendent morality, does Václav. In an interview, *Disturbing the Peace*, he states: 'I believe that nothing disappears for ever, and less so our deeds . . .' He will have no truck with people who are sceptical. He will not kowtow to more complicated Czech dissidents, like Milan Kundera.

In 1968, you see, a year before Václav's letter to Dubček, Milan and Václav had fallen out. I am going to give you a quick sketch of this argument.

In December 1968, Milan wrote an article called 'Český úděl'. This means 'The Czech Destiny'. In it, Milan was not defeatist. He was not going to get downcast by the Russian invasion. Milan pointed out that, so far, Dubček's reform policies had not been abandoned. There was no police state. There was freedom of speech. There was the possibility – for the first time, thought Milan, in 'world history' – of creating a new democratic socialism. So the people who were publicly concerned about the Soviet future, concluded Milan, were 'simply weak people, who can live only in illusions of certainty'. They were not moral at all.

But Václav did not like this essay. In February 1969, he wrote an essay called 'Český úděl?' This means 'The Czech destiny?' He did not agree that publicly asking for guarantees was so bad. He thought it was important to allay people's quite reasonable concerns. Milan's vision of Czechoslovakia at the centre of world history was, thought Václav, sentimental.

In reply, Milan wrote another article. This one was called 'Radikalismus a Exhibicionismus'. This means 'Radicalism and Exhibitionism'. In it, Milan tried to explain what he had meant. He thought that all these worries about the Russians and police states just displayed 'moral exhibitionism'. That was what he disliked. And Václav, thought Milan, was also suffering from this 'illness of people anxious to prove their integrity'.

Although Václav seemed noble, therefore, he was just an exhibitionist.

I am not interested in who turned out to be right here. In retrospect, some people might think that Milan was wrong. It does not seem to be the perfect moment, when the Soviet tanks are trundling round the streets of Prague, to be quibbling over ethics. But actually, I do not think he was wrong. Milan was not morally naive. He was making a very true and important point. It is possible, after all, for an act to seem altruistic, but really just be self-serving.

That is a complication.

In the vocabulary of this novel, for instance, staying with Papa would seem noble but really it would be self-serving. The apparent nobility of Nana's sacrifice would simply be motivated by her desire not to watch Moshe make Anjali come. I am not saying this is entirely true. I am just saying that's how it would be.

But Václav would not admit this. And that is why I do not love Václav. But I do love Milan Kundera. I love him very much.

5

'Don't you want me to stay with you?' asked Nana. She was distressed. And Papa said, 'Sweetness, of course I want you to stay with me. Well no I don't want you to stay. But it's not because I wouldn't like it. I want you to go back to Moshe. It's crazy. This is crazy.'

This is the ending. It is where everything gets turned upside down.

Nana said, 'But I can't go back.' 'You can't go back,' said Papa. 'You can't go back to Moshe.' 'Because he's going out with someone else,' said Nana. 'With someone else? Already?' said Papa. 'He's, he's going out with Anjali,' said Nana.

'Oh darling,' said Papa. 'Oh I'm sorry.' 'Sokay,' said Nana. 'Sokay. So I can be with you.' 'So he broke up with you,' said Papa. 'No,' said Nana. 'No, I broke up with him.' 'Well it certainly seems like Moshe did better out of this,' said Papa. 'He certainly seems to be doing quite well to me.'

6

Look, I could end the ending right here. And if I ended this here, it would be a very sad story. It would be the story of Nana's loneliness. If I were nasty, then I would probably do that. But I am not nasty. I am nice. This whole book is nice. Niceness, I reckon, is what you have come to expect from me.

So I will carry on.

7

'No, no,' said Nana. 'Scomplicated. Zcomplicated. We. We.' She paused and paused and paused. 'We were kind of all living together, pretty much,' she said. She paused.

OK, before I go any further, I should explain about Nana and Papa and sex. They were not a prudish couple, they were friendly about sex. It might not have been a usual topic of conversation, but when it was, it was carefree and unfussed. Sex was smilingly neutral. But this does not mean it was easy for Nana, explaining all this. It was still a little tricky, telling Papa about her experience in a *ménage à trois*.

She said, 'We were kind of a threesome.' 'You were a threesome?' said Papa. 'I, yeah,' said Nana. There was another pause. There were a lot of pauses in this conversation. I think you will have to imagine them for yourself. I can't write in all of the pauses. 'Why did you never tell me?' said Papa. 'I dohno,' said Nana. 'I just, I just. I didn't need to, I spose.' 'So how long were you a three?' said Papa.

Because sex was a neutral topic, it was a shock for Papa – discovering that Nana had been part of a *ménage à trois* – but it was not a moral one. It was not disapproving. Papa was not that kind of parent. It was absolute surprise.

He did not quite know why he was chatting to her like this. He was talking to her in the same way he used to chat to her about school. But Papa was not sure what tone to take. After all, it is not the most usual situation – convalescing from a stroke or tumour, while chatting to one's daughter about her extraordinary sex life.

'Oh a few months,' said Nana. 'Since we got back from Venice.' 'A few months. Okay,' said Papa.

Papa felt very tired. He felt utterly amazed and tired.

8

This is another moment in my novel where you must not let your own private theories affect how you read. In this case, you must not let your theories about parents influence you. There are lots of parents in the world. They all have their quirks. So I do not think there is one predictable way for a parent to respond in this situation. When your child tells you that they have just left a *ménage à trois*, there are a lot of options available.

I am just going to describe the way that Papa responded. I am not laying down any general rules here.

'I'm not. I'm not going to pry,' said Papa.
  'No, zfine,' said Nana.
  'I'm, I'm obviously surprised.'
  'Uhhuh.'
  'It's. So this thing, this is over?'
  'Yup.'

So far, Papa was not really responding at all. He was just trying to understand. He was trying to get some definitions.

'No what do you mean?' said Papa. 'You were in a *ménage à trois*? In a, in a proper *ménage à trois*?'

'Yup,' said Nana.

'So all that, all that moving in with Moshe. That was moving in with Anjali as well?'

'Well kind of. Not exactly. She had a key.'

'Oh so.'

'She was there most of the time.'

'Jesus,' said Papa.

It was not that he was a patriarch, Papa. So this was not an angry 'Jesus'. It was an amazed and astounded 'Jesus'. It was a 'Jesus' out of its depth.

'So. So. You haven't broken up with Moshe?' said Papa.

'No I have,' said Nana.

'I mean, but you've broken up with Anjali as well?'

'Well okay with her as well yeah.'

9

So Papa had a mental sketch. This sounded like a classic *ménage*, he thought. It was a filmic *ménage*. It was just like *Jules et Jim*. (Apart from me, you will remember, in this novel only Papa has seen *Jules et Jim*.)

He was *out of his depth*, but Papa was also fascinated.

'What was it like? No I'm sorry. I shouldn't have asked that,' said Papa.

'Sokay,' said Nana.

'But what was it like?' said Papa.

Maybe, just maybe, this shocks you. According to you, a father should not ask his daughter about the details of her sex life. Asking might seem prurient. Well, I disagree. There was a naughty side to Papa. He was finding it very funny, Nana's French and farcical love life. And Papa's naughtiness was making him curious. This may be similar to prurience, but I do not think that matters. It just shows how intimate Nana and Papa were. Prurience, I think, is OK. A *ménage* is fascinating. Surely you know that by now. I do not think I would like a person who was stolid and unfascinated by a *ménage à trois*.

'Well it was weird,' said Nana. 'It was. It was difficult sleeping.'

This was not an answer, really. It was not the kind of answer Papa wanted. It was much too sociological.

'So you slept together?' said Papa. 'I mean, it was always three to a bed?'

'Um,' said Nana. 'Yes.'

'It was difficult sleeping?'

'Anjali gets nightmares. She gets. She gets nightmares.'

'Uhhuh.'

'She was in the middle.'
'Okay.'

'We don't have to talk about this,' said Papa.
'No it's fine,' said Nana. 'I said that.'

The thing was, Papa assumed that Nana was a sexual expert. He thought that she must be a sack artist. Anyone who had been one-third of a *ménage*, he thought, must be a sack artist. It was logical. Repression would not come into it. Asking questions was not a problem.

But Nana was not a sack artist. I assume that you also know that by now.

'I just don't quite understand,' said Papa.
'Don't understand what?' said Nana.
'Well I'm just intrigued by the. I'm just.'
'You're what?'
'Well. Was it. Did Moshe watch while you and Anjali? Or.'
'Yeah sometimes.'
'Right. But not together?'
'Not together?'
'Not all three of you together. At once.'
'Well sometimes.'
'Uhhuh.'
'But it's tricky.'
'Oh the. The positions.'
'Yeah kind of. Yes. You have to be careful.'
'Yes of course. I see. Yes. The positions.'

'Did it just come naturally?' said Papa.

'What the sex?' said Nana.

'Well yes. The, um, the positions. Did it? Did you know where to put yourself naturally?'

'It was. Well it wasn't too difficult.'

'No?'

'It was. It seemed easy enough.'

'But how did you decide?' said Papa.

'We,' said Nana.

'I mean did you discuss what would happen beforehand?'

'We.'

'I don't know. I. It just seems so complicated.'

'And Moshe. He had sex with Anjali as well,' said Papa.

'Yes. Yes,' said Nana.

'In front of you?'

'Well yeah. Or when I wasn't there as well.'

'And this didn't? You weren't upset?'

'Why would I be?'

Nana was trying to be a sack artist. She was trying to sound like a sack artist. And she was doing very well. But quite frankly, Papa was more cool about sex than Nana was, I think.

'Was it embarrassing, like that?' said Papa.

'Like what?' said Nana.

'Together.'

'Oh no no no no no.'

'Really not?'

'Oh no.'

'I just would imagine it would be so complicated.'

'Not. No not really.'

'I mean. It's tricky enough with two of you.'

Sitting together on Papa's bed, whose duvet cover had an innovative design of small white lions and falcons and fruit trees on a magenta background, Nana and Papa giggled. They got the giggles.

'I mean. Had you, had you had sex with girls before? Or did you?' said Papa.

'Me, um, no,' said Nana. 'No.'

'And was that? Was that odd then?'

'What? With Anjali?'

'Well yes.'

'It was. It was fun. It was different.'

'So you enjoyed it?'

'I?'

'You liked it, with Anjali?'

Nana wriggled. She pushed her palm down flat on the duvet, over a white proud lion.

'I'm not going to answer that,' she said.

'So. This must have been Moshe's idea, I suppose?' asked Papa.

'No,' said Nana. 'Was mine.'

'It was yours?'

'Look it wasn't anyone's idea.'

'The, the, what do you call it, the *ménage*?'

'Yeah the *ménage*.'

'But, how do you start it? How did it start?'

'Look Papa.'
'Okay, okay.'

'Were you all drunk?' said Papa.
　'Do you have to ask these questions?' said Nana.
　'I'm just. I'm. No.'
　'I mean it's fine.'

'I have to say,' said Papa. 'I always liked that boy.'
　'Papa!' said Nana.
　'Well it's true. He made me laugh.'

'But. Jesus,' said Papa.

This was a different 'Jesus'. This was a more secure, more comprehending 'Jesus'. It was a fascinated 'Jesus'.

10

Papa was naughty and fascinated. But he also had his more caring side. It made him protective. It made him protective and serious.

'But. I'm not entirely happy with this,' said Papa. 'I have to say.'
　'You're what?' said Nana.
　'I'm not entirely, I can't entirely approve of this.'
　'What, leaving?'
　'No not the leaving. Well. I don't approve of the leaving. But this whole arrangement.'
　'It's not narrayngement. It's over.'

'Well it was an arrangement.'

'Well it's not any more.'

'Was it?' said Papa.

'Was it what?' said Nana.

'Was it ideal?'

'No of course not.'

'I thought it would be a good thing,' said Nana.

'A good thing?' said Papa.

'I thought it would make him happy. I thought it'd make her happy.'

'But what about you?'

'I thought I. I. I don't know.'

'It's difficult to talk about,' said Nana.

'Uhhuh,' said Papa.

'It's, well, was nice for a while. It sounds odd but it was nice.'

'No I can believe that.'

I think we can trace a progression for Papa's emotions in this scene. It is quite an understandable progression. First Papa was shocked. Then shock turned into slight amazement. Then this amazement lurched into amused curiosity. Then this became protectiveness and worry. Worry was now giving way to simple logical thought.

'But then Moshe's not really going out with Anjali,' said Papa. 'He's been left with her.'

'No no,' said Nana, 'he likes her. They're going out.'

'But does he love her? Are they in love?'

'I don know.'

'Are they in love?'

'I don know. Maybe.'

'I mean how long have they? I mean. It's only a couple of weeks.'

'Months.'

'Alright months. Christ. Months.'

'But still,' said Papa. 'Sweetheart, what were you thinking?'

No, Papa was intelligent, no question.

'And what about you and him?' said Papa. 'Does Moshe still love you?'

'I don know,' said Nana.

'You don't know?'

'Well possibly. Well yeah.'

'So okay. This is the thing,' said Papa. 'You have left Moshe with another girl, who he feels sorry for, while he is still in love with you. And you've done this so that you can be with me.'

This was not exactly correct, remember. It was a little more noble than the truth. It was correct as far as Papa knew, but Papa did not know about Nana's worries about sex. He did not know that there was a selfish reason for leaving Moshe as well as a sweet one.

'Well if you put it like that,' said Nana.

When Nana was young, she went upstairs to bed and then would lie there, in the foetal position. She did this because someone at school had told her that it made you feel safe. So Nana curled up. She went to bed early, at twilight. And then she would lie there and wait for her goodnight kiss. She'd listen to the creaks of the landing as Papa came upstairs. And then she would pretend to be asleep as the door was pushed gently ajar. Then his face was close to her and she kept her eyes extraspecially tight. He kissed her, then he left. She went to bed early, at twilight, and the curtains turned the white room blue so that if you woke up from your quickest dream you couldn't tell if it was really a white room in blue light or a blue room resplendent in white light.

When Nana woke up, she would pad off across the landing and find Papa in his bigger bed. And if he was on the side close to the door she'd crawl up next to him, perched on the edge. She looked after him. She did this by dozing with him. And when he got up to go to work then Nana would let herself tumble and end up where Papa had been. And she would watch his crouched breasts and the tuft of his shaving brush and his odd hooked penis through the half-closed bathroom door.

Twice a week the office let Papa go home early to Nana, so that he could watch her while she did her homework at the kitchen table. He squeezed his cufflinks out of his cuffs and made her tea.

Whenever Nana imagined happiness it was in the kitchen with her Papa.

This was her favourite house. There was a rosehip bush

on the corner of the road. There were sleeping policemen, made of red brick with yellow edging. There was a green lounge and a yellow kitchen with dandelion wallpaper. And upstairs there was a white landing with a rucked oatmeal carpet. At the end of the landing there was a window with a stained-glass tulip. On this tulip, Nana had Blu-Tacked a bird she had made, cut out of cardboard – its black felt-tip outline smothered in gluey feathers.

She loved the house. She loved her Papa. I don't want you to underestimate this, now that Papa, sweet practical generous Papa, was making her change her mind.

12

Papa said, 'You are obviously going to have to go back to Moshe.'

Nana said, 'I can't.'

'No. You are going back to Moshe.'

'But I really can't.'

'Why not?'

'I can't go back because there's Anjali,' said Nana.

'Darling I don't see this problem with Anjali,' said Papa. 'Do you love Anjali?'

'No.'

'And do you love Moshe?'

'Yes.'

'Then what?'

'I can't hurt Anjali.'

'Nana. Nana. Anjali is not the problem.'

Of course this is what Nana wanted to hear. It is what she really wanted. She wanted Moshe back and on his own. But it was difficult for Nana, doing what she wanted. It was especially difficult if what she wanted would also hurt someone else.

But this is the ending. It is where everything turns upside down. And Nana would be selfish. That is why it is the ending.

Perhaps you do not agree that this is selfish. Perhaps you think that if Papa wanted Nana to leave, then there is hardly a vexed moral issue. But the issue is not with Papa. Well, it is not just Papa. The issue is Anjali.

I told you to remember Anjali. Anjali was, in an odd way, happy. And Nana knew that. Moshe had told her. She also knew that, if she went back, she would be taking Moshe away from Anjali. Moshe had told her that too. So what I am saying is this. Nana knew all of this, and she would still go back. She would do everything she needed to do.

'You know I love you very much,' said Papa.

And Moshe would come back to her. Of course he would. I know everything. I know Moshe very well.

13

My mother's Czech friend, Petra, disliked Milan Kundera. She thought he should not have left his country. She thought that he was selfish.

I own a weird French edition of Milan Kundera's second novel *Farewell Waltz*. This edition was published in 1979. It has a fake red leather cover, with a fake gold embossed pattern printed on it. As an introduction, there is an interview with

Milan Kundera. I am going to quote you one sentence from this interview. 'No one can suspect what it cost me to leave my country: my hair turned grey,' said Milan.

I think we should remember some dates here. Kundera was born in 1929. When he left Czechoslovakia in 1975 he was, therefore, forty-six. That is quite an old age to leave your country. And he left only after seven years of living, under surveillance, in the forest near Brno, unpublished and isolated. Seven years is a long time to stay somewhere in isolation.

I do not think people are very intelligent about selfishness. I do not think they see how moral it can be. Because it is moral, refusing to be self-destructive. It is a perfectly moral position.

14

Papa was the benevolent angel of this story.

All along, I have been telling you this. It was not just a friendly image. It was true. It was benevolent, telling Nana to be selfish. It was benevolent, telling her to leave. Sometimes you cannot be altruistic. Sometimes, I think, it is too self-destructive. Maybe this seems blasphemous, maybe this offends your own personal morality. But I am right.

This book is universal. I said that at the start. Because it is universal, it is ambiguous. It has something for everyone. And the final ambiguity is this.

I am obviously on Papa's side. I obviously admire his generosity and love. Me, I believe in generosity. But I am not only on Papa's side. I am on Nana's side too. Because

I can see the point of niceness. It is a very wonderful thing.

But what is really wrong with selfishness? Selfishness is sometimes moral too.

Acknowledgements

The author and publishers wish to thank the following for permission to reprint copyright material:

Verso Books for permission to reprint material from *Investigating Sex: Surrealist Research 1928–1932*, edited by José Pierre, translated by Malcolm Imrie; The Random House Group Ltd for permission to reprint material from *The KGB's Literary Archive* by Vitaly Shentalinsky and *Hope Abandoned* by Nadezhda Mandelstam, both published by The Harvill Press; and material from *The Private Life of Chairman Mao: The Memoirs of Mao's Personal Physician Dr Li Zhisui* by Dr Li Zhisui and Professor Hung-Chao Tai, published by Chatto & Windus.

Every effort has been made to trace copyright holders, and the publishers will be happy to correct mistakes or omissions in future editions.